THE BOY WHO RESCUES PIGEONS

Carmen Capuano

Carmen Capuano Productions

ISBN-13: 978-1-9168771-8-4

Cover design by: Ruan Human

This book is dedicated to Mr Gerry McCammick, my dad, who took me in as a six-year-old and made me his daughter.

Love and miss you Dad. xxx

It is also dedicated to my children, for loving me despite my workaholic nature and understanding that our house would often be home to wild animals who needed rescuing.

Love you Ryan, Ross and Sophia with all my heart. xxx

CHAPTER 1

Lucas gazed straight ahead using his peripheral vision to scan the room for something more interesting than Mr Marshall. It wasn't hard to find.

Three rows up and slightly to the right, Emily Matthews, already turned fifteen and more than seven months older than him, was sharpening her pencil with a profound grace and elegance most girls could only dream of, head tilted slightly to one side, so that a smooth curve of neck was visible from where he sat, wrists flicking gently to and fro, fingernails glinting electric blue.

In the stillness of the classroom, Lucas imagined that he could hear the scrape of blade against wood, the particular rasp of steel against lead, the soft crumble of shavings that fell from the pencil, amputated with a careless cruelty. The thought sent a shudder up his spine despite the warmth of the room; stale air imbued with a combination of teenage hormones and desperation.

"Can anyone tell me the value of x?" Mr Marshall exploded into the silence, brown eyes flitting across the classroom like baby sparrows seeking the comfort of the nest, thin chest puffed out as armour against the disinterested glazed expressions which surrounded him.

Lucas wished someone could go one step further and explain the value of *algebra*! What was it with this stuff? Why did it matter if $x=y+3$? So what? What could it change in his life? In anyone's life? He absently rubbed his nose which was itchy with the imagined smell of wood shavings from Emily's pencil.

The action was a big mistake, the slight movement catching the teacher's attention and focusing it on this most unlikely of students. "Lucas Reverential Pertwee, what do *you* think?" Marshall boomed in his deepest voice, letting the sound resonate against the peeling walls and frayed display boards, as if they carried a statement of profound importance, without the voicing of which the world would stop spinning, the solar system implode, and the universe cease to exist. Every word was given such deliberation, such weight of consideration that it lent itself to the ridiculous - like Lucas himself.

Lucas had often wondered why the teacher persisted in using his whole name, rather than just the forename. Maybe Marshall was an android and not a human? It would certainly explain a lot, perhaps even his particular love of mathematical symbolism. Or maybe he just liked the sound of it in all of its full ridiculousness? Well if he did, he was welcome to use it for himself. Lucas was sick of every last syllable of the stupid name and would gladly have traded, even for one as dull as Gary Marshall.

The teacher correctly took Lucas's shake of the head to mean that he had no answer to offer. Eyes bright and slightly fevered, confidence buoyed by the vulnerability of his target, he zoomed in for the kill, fingers of his hands interlaced and held at chest height as if in anticipation; as if only just managing to hold himself back from lashing out. "Use the information I have already given you to work it out," he instructed as if this had never occurred to the boy.

Lucas frowned and tried to focus on the board which seemed to waiver mirage-like in front of his eyes. "Well if x=y+3 then x is obviously 3 more than y," he stated hesitantly.

"Hmm yes, as you so correctly stated, x *is* 3 more than y. It was the *next* bit I wanted..." Marshall's eyes bored into Lucas's skull, seeking knowledge that wasn't there. Scenting fresh kill, the whole class was focused on him now – waiting with bated breath to see what he would say or do, waiting to see what degradation Marshall would heap upon him for his failure.

Had Emily Matthews stopped sharpening her pencil to watch? Lucas didn't need to look to know the answer. Prettier than most of the other girls, he was willing to bet that a cruel smile lit the corners of her beautiful mouth, that her eyes danced in merriment at his shame.

The teacher's words rang in his ears. *The information I have already given you.* The irony didn't escape him. He had information thrust at him daily, everything about trigonometry, geometry, chemistry, history and every other 'ry' that the educational system could provide. But nothing about the one thing that twisted in his head like a fat slug, swallowing everything he threw at it and giving nothing back. Devouring all hope. He knew nothing about *himself.* In fact he knew *less* than nothing. The knowledge of his ignorance threatened to engulf him, a dark tide of swirling sludge that would fill his lungs and compress his heart until every last beat was stifled, muted and subdued to nothing more than a memory.

Terrified by his impending fate, he knew suddenly that it could either paralyse him into inaction or galvanise him into decisiveness. While he still had breath, still had life in his body, he wanted to shout at Marshall, make him realise that there were more important things that he needed to know, than the value of stupid letters.

All around him, the class remained silent.

Tension hovered over Lucas's head like a water balloon, threatening to burst at any moment and suffocate him with the foetid scent of humiliation. It was merely a matter of time. "So x-3=y?" he stuttered, his uncertainty of whether this was what Marshall was getting at, making a question of the statement.

"Yes we know *that* but using the other equation, what does x actually equal?" Marshall rapped an old meter stick onto the whiteboard to illustrate his point. Lucas gazed at the stick. *Is my dad good at maths? Or is he rubbish at it, just like me? Do I take after him in any way at all?*

Bored of waiting for an answer that Lucas was clearly incapable of giving, the teacher resorted to moving the mouse over the other equation, making it jump around on the huge screen and explaining *once again* how to work out the value of *x*. Shoulders rounded over the computer, Marshall ignored the many hands held high in the air, making it obvious the explanation was for Lucas's benefit alone.

No one laughed outright at his stupidity but Lucas could feel them sniggering, stowing their humour away until later when they could pull it out like a magician with a white dove, flourishing it in front of one another as if intelligence was something which could be siphoned off; as if his obvious lack of knowledge made theirs even greater.

What did it matter? What relevance would stupid old simultaneous equations ever have in his life anyway? What relevance did any of it have when the biggest mystery in his life remained unsolvable? Lucas wanted to stand up, scrape his chair out from under his desk and challenge them. What right did any of them have to be judging him?

The seat on which he sat seemed to be burning a hole into the very centre of him, scorching through flesh and bone as if it sought to fuse itself with him. So strong was the sensation, that he was forced to look down, to check that no orange tongue of flame lapped hungrily at him. But the chair looked as it always had, grey and square, much like everything else in the classroom. Beneath him, he could feel the hard plastic which curved around the metal frame, its flat seat and back providing minimum comfort and maximum proficiency. In a way the chair was just like Marshall himself.

Lucas stole a glance towards the teacher and was relieved to see that he had already moved on to his next victim. Lucas didn't care whether the next kid knew the answer or not, it had no relevance to him or anything in his life. But at least he felt the focus of the class shift, he was no longer the pinned bug under the microscope. He spared a small flicker of empathy towards the poor sod whose turn it was now.

"Got this today, just before we left for school." Josh spoke in the style of a ventriloquist, issuing the sounds from one side of his mouth, keeping his head towards the front and his lips as closed as possible. He pushed something under the table and towards Lucas.

Lucas fumbled his right hand towards Josh's hidden left one and felt something like thin card gently scratch the tips of his fingers. He scrambled to take hold of the edge, fearful that the card would slip out of his fingers and fall to the floor.

"Careful you don't bend it!" Josh whispered urgently, still looking straight ahead. Lucas pulled the postcard out from under the table just far enough to read the back. It was addressed to *Mr Joshua Cole* in large rounded letters as if the writer thought it was the best name in the world. Compared to Lucas's own, he wasn't in a position to disagree.

'*Having a few well-earned days on holiday in Hawaii. Got a big part coming up in a Daniel Craig movie next! No rest for the wicked! XXX*,' he read. It was signed '*Dad*' with a big flourish, the D slanted and curled into itself as if it was the most important letter in the alphabet… as if its writer was the most important *dad* in the universe.

Lucas wanted to turn the card over to see the picture on the front but he didn't dare lest he got caught. Instead he looked at the postmark which confirmed it had indeed been sent from Hawaii. He looked again at the words in their smugly looped letters and imagined what it must feel like to receive post from your dad; to have some indication that you were thought about, at least occasionally. Would it be enough? Would it make it okay that everyone else in the world thought you were a jerk, a no-hoper who didn't even have a normal name?

He waited until Marshall was writing something on the board, whiteboard pen poised as some nerd told him the answer he'd been looking for. Lucas flipped the card over. The picture was as he had imagined, only better. Lush pale sand met ocean in a blaze of colour which almost hurt his eyes after the drabness of the classroom, the drabness of his life.

"Doesn't say when he will come see you though." As soon as the whispered words were out of his mouth he regretted them. It was a cheap and nasty dig at Josh, his one friend in the whole world. The one person who was closest to being in his own situation. The only person who could possibly understand how he felt.

Josh visibly smarted. "At least I know who my dad is!" he sniped back, low but harsh, snatching the postcard out of Lucas's hand, uncaring whether or not they got caught. The laminated card made a brief farting noise and Lucas blushed, knowing what those close enough to hear would immediately think. Someone behind him sniggered quietly. He guessed they didn't want to bring Marshall's attention onto themselves. Lucas ignored the noise.

"I'm sorry," he whispered to Josh. "I didn't mean it like that." So how had he meant it then, he wondered to himself. Josh was right, Lucas didn't even know who his father was, let alone receive mail from him. Who was he to turn his nose up at the postcard? Shame bit deep into him and he would have given anything to have left the words unsaid. If only...

The bell signalling the end of the school day interrupted his thoughts and he was relieved that he could turn his face away from everyone, hide himself in the process of getting together all his things and packing them into his rucksack. It wasn't that he was envious of Josh. Well not exactly. But the truth of Josh's words hurt more than anything he could have imagined.

"I'm sorry too. S'not your fault you don't know your dad," Josh apologised.

Lucas thought about that. If it wasn't his fault then whose fault was it? His mother's? His grandmother's? Or was it his father's himself? Did his dad even know that Lucas existed? Those were questions he could not answer. Perhaps they would never be answered! He shouldered his bag and waited for Josh to be ready. Together they walked towards the doorway.

"Gonna change your name to Peepee," sniggered Harry Davis as they passed close by. Lucas felt a lump rise in his throat. Not because of what Harry had said, or even what Harry thought of him but because it was said in front of Josh.

"Shut up *Harold!*" Josh replied. "Why don't you go and play with one of your sister's dolls?"

Harry tried to take a step forward, blocking their passage through the door but one look at Josh stopped him in his tracks. "She's not my sister. She's my step-sister!" he spat out contemptuously as if the idea deeply offended him.

"Step-sister, half-sister, quarter-sister, I don't care, just get your ugly fat face out of mine!" Josh said with a quiet authority and pushed Harry aside, barging past him and unscathed into the corridor beyond.

Lucas stepped past Harry too, almost expecting a blow to the back of his head in passing, but it never came. He turned round to find that Harry wasn't even looking at him. The other boy's gaze was fixed firmly on Josh, a nasty sneer pulling down the corners of his mouth and tightening his eyes into dangerous slits.

"I can't believe he always backs down with you," Lucas said, matching his pace to Josh's as they neared the school exit. "Have you seen what he's done to some of the other kids?"

"Bullies like him just need to know their

place. And he's scared 'cos my dad is a stunt-man."

Lucas tried to be diplomatic this time. "Yes but it's not like your dad is around is he? I mean…"

"I know what you meant," Josh cut him off. "But it's the idea of it that worries Harry." He elaborated, "I mean if my dad thinks nothing of leaping off tall buildings into raging fires, then he's not going to think twice about landing a punch on Harry, is he?"

"Well I don't think he'd actually hit a kid would he?" Lucas asked doubtfully.

Josh sighed. "Well Harry's dad then!" he countered.

"But your dad is in Hollywood most of the time!" Lucas argued, wondering why he felt the need to push the point, why he couldn't just let it go.

"Yes, so he has the cash to jump on a plane whenever he wants to come over," Josh answered. Lucas accepted there was a logic to the statement but it made the fact that Josh's father hadn't jumped on a plane to visit, for as long as Lucas had known Josh, even more pathetic. He decided to change the focus of the conversation.

"What do you really remember about him?" Together they passed through the school gates, heading home to the same street, albeit opposite sides and ends. "I mean remember, from proper memories… not just from old photos."

Josh almost paused his steps, seemed to

falter and take a misstep before catching himself and walking on normally. Lucas had asked this same question before but never had his friend taken so long to answer, nor behaved in so strange a manner. "I remember him talking to Joanne." Josh's voice was quiet and for a moment Lucas thought he had misheard. "I was five and off school with a virus and mum had to go to work, so my dad was supposed to look after me. It was just before me and Mum moved here, before I knew you. Before everything... happened."

Children surged past them in every direction, heading home after a long day at school, heels clipping the pavement in a weird staccato beat which sounded to Lucas like an invading army. He tuned them out; the footsteps, the cheery calls and challenging taunts they threw at one another, no longer important. This was a part of Josh's story he had never heard before. Something about the memory of a time nine years ago clearly had some new significance and bearing in his friend's life. Lucas strove with all of his being to pay attention.

"Joanne was our next-door neighbour at the old house," Josh clarified, in case Lucas had forgotten the woman's name, let alone her significance to his friend. "She was also my mum's best friend. And she was the woman my dad was having an affair with." Lucas nodded, he already knew that part. "Even though I was only five,

I knew there was something wrong about how they were together… what they were saying, how they looked at each other," Josh's steps slowed once more as if he was reluctant to arrive home or perhaps as if he couldn't walk and replay the memory at the same time.

"He ran off with her didn't he?" Lucas prompted tactlessly, eager for Josh to get to the point.

"Yes." Josh was quiet for a moment, reflecting on what he was about to share. "But I remember them together, whispering and laughing. And I remember how alone I felt." Lucas knew that feeling very well but he said nothing, waiting for Josh to continue. "Then it was just Mum and me. And I *liked* it that way."

Was that it? Was that the big revelation that he had thought Josh was about to share? Lucas let out his breath. There was nothing new after all, no secrets Josh had been keeping, either intentionally or unintentionally. "Yes, I know what you mean. It's like it's true what they say, about three being a crowd and everything," Lucas said. "Well maybe it's not if it is three adults or three children but when two of the three are adults and one isn't…" At least that's how it felt when his mother, grandmother and himself were all at home.

"Yeah." Josh still seemed reluctant to meet Lucas's eyes. He walked with his head lowered, face bent towards the pavement and his scuffed, black school shoes. He walked several steps without raising his gaze. "My mum's got a boyfriend," he blurted out on a breath that was forced between clenched teeth.

"Yeah I know. She's had a few, on and off," Lucas agreed. "They never stick around long." He hoped Josh would take his words as they were intended, as a reassurance that nothing would change really, and not as a slur on his mother. His mouth had gotten him into enough trouble for one day!

"But this one's different. Mum says we're moving. Because of him," Josh shot Lucas a desperate glance. "We're going to live with him and they're gonna get married. I even heard her tell her friends that he wants to have a baby *of their own*." Josh couldn't keep the quiver from his voice.

Lucas felt the foundations of his whole world shake as if Atlas had lifted the Earth up onto his shoulders once more. He remembered the tale from history class and thought that for the very first time he could understand the point of it, the specific and eternal punishment that it had been. "You are moving *away*? To where? When?" his voice seemed to have spontaneously gone up an octave.

"The other side of town," Josh replied despondently, refusing to look at him, focusing once more on his shoes.

"Oh!" It could have been worse, at least they would still be able to see each other every day at school. But perhaps he was being premature… "You'll still go to our school, right?" he asked, a quiet dread trying to lodge itself in his soul.

Josh shook his head, his steps slowing so that they barely made any progress down the road towards home. They were alone on the street, the other children already at their destination and it seemed somehow apt that the road was otherwise deserted. It made Lucas think of a post-apocalyptic scenario where he and Josh were the only survivors of a nuclear holocaust. Bizarrely, he almost wished that was the reality instead of what it was actually turning out to be.

"Mum says it's too far to walk and she can't take me and pick me up because of her work. She got a place for me in North High Comprehensive. I start on Monday."

Lucas couldn't take it all in. "On Monday? But this is Friday! Do you mean that was your last day at our school? That now it's just *my* school?" he asked pointedly, feeling utterly betrayed. Josh nodded his head sadly.

"And you didn't tell me?" Lucas was distraught and angry at the same time. How could Josh have let him go through the whole day without knowing? The whole week? In fact how long exactly had Josh known about this? And how could he have betrayed their friendship like that? Life was just so unfair. "When are you moving?" he asked more harshly than he had intended.

"I didn't know until a few days ago," Josh said quietly, as if he had read Lucas's mind, "about the school I mean." He carried on quickly. "And I didn't say anything to you 'cos I just kept hoping that she would change her mind. That maybe they would split up or something... but that didn't happen," he sounded bitterly disappointed but still not as disappointed as Lucas felt. "And then I didn't know *how* to tell you."

"When?" Lucas repeated, feeling as if he stood at the top of a high platform with no visible way down, other than to jump into the abyss. "When are you moving?"

Josh's answer was so short and so quiet that Lucas almost didn't hear. "Tomorrow."

Lucas felt the spit in his mouth turn to dust. There were no words which could adequately convey how miserable he felt. How lost and alone. And how much more lost and alone he would feel come Monday.

Together and in silence the two boys made their way along the street that for the very last time they could both call home. Unable to utter a single word, all Lucas could do when they reached Josh's house was to pat his friend sadly on the back and watch as Josh walked away from him, feet dragging on the pavement, school bag low on his back, like a half-lowered flag.

Further up the same road was the little house that Lucas was supposed to think of as home. Four brick walls sat square in the middle of a small garden, neat rows of flowers lining the path from front gate to front door. Despite its prettiness and homeliness it might as well have been a grey concrete prison for the amount of enthusiasm with which he slotted his key into the lock.

In the split-second before the door swung open he imagined a different scenario, one where he was met by the sight of his father's coat or his father's slippers. Something, anything - to suggest that the man himself was not forever gone, not unknown, not a forbidden topic. But as ever, all that adorned the hallway was an old battered copper umbrella stand and a worn mat that might once have said WELCOME but that now was virtually illegible.

He stepped into the hallway, taking care not to catch his coat on the spokes of the stand and topple it over as he had done so often in the past. He didn't look behind him as he closed the door, didn't want to look at the world he was shutting out or to bear witness to the disappointment of the one he had entered.

The air in the house smelled different to that outside. It was neither good nor bad. Like so many other things in his life it just was. And maybe most days that was good enough. But not today. Not this day. He stepped out of his shoes, leaving them where they fell on the faded mat and went in search of his mother.

CHAPTER 2

"We have been over this a million times, Lucas." Anna Pertwee continued to peel potatoes into the sink as she talked, her movements more jerky than normal, testament to her annoyance that the subject had been raised once more. Behind her glasses, there was a strange flicker in her normally clear eyes.

"And a million times you have refused to tell me his name, or anything about him." Lucas could feel himself getting angry and he tried to contain it. If he let his anger get the better of him, all discussion would end and his mother would send him to his bedroom. Again.

"Because none of it will do you any good!" Anna raised a muddied hand to her brow and pushed her glasses higher up the bridge of her nose, leaving a dirty streak across one cheek. She didn't wipe it away.

"But Mum!" Lucas stepped closer to his mother, trying to force her attention onto him. It didn't work. Frustration bled from his every pore, coating him in a blanket of temper.

"What's going on?" the clipped voice of Valerie Pertwee indicated his grandmother's arrival into the kitchen. Standing as wide as she did tall, with ghost-white hair clouding around her face, she personified the traditional image of a gentle old lady. Shrugging off a bright red plastic raincoat, she struggled to hang it on the hook behind the kitchen door, standing on tiptoe and lurching at the peg, forcing Lucas to come to her aid and lose eye contact with his mother.

"Well?" Coat safely hung up, Valerie waited for an answer, looking from her daughter to her grandson and back again without moving an inch, deliberately barricading the exit from the kitchen until her curiosity was satisfied. There was a silence which both mother and son were reluctant to fill. The room seemed to shrink under the old lady's gaze as if all the air had been drawn out of it until it was on the very brink of collapsing.

Lucas sucked at the thin air, hoping it was enough to give him the strength he would need. It felt too reedy to offer sustenance. "I want to know about my father," he said in what he hoped was a mature, considered request.

"Stuff and nonsense!" his grandmother declared, dismissing the idea instantly and moving to peer into the bowl of peeled potatoes as if to examine them for their aesthetic quality. She pointed to one. "Mind you get that bit of peel off, Anna!" Anna Pertwee picked up the indicated potato and re-peeled it before placing it back into the bowl. Lucas watched his mother's actions incredulously and was shamed out of his enforced silence.

"No Gran it's not!" He had never stated anything so forcibly before and knew that from that moment on, they were in uncharted territory. He held his grandmother's gaze but the old woman refused to look away, refused to be beaten and after only a moment he wondered who was holding whose stare exactly. He worried whether he had the inner strength to continue to stand up to her. There was no good in hoping his mother would come to his aid; any spirit Anna Pertwee might have shown her mother had been quashed out of her years ago.

"No good can come of it!" his gran declared as if that ended the subject.

"I already told him that!" Anna exclaimed, exonerating herself in the old woman's eyes; but Lucas noticed how she refused to look at her mother *or* her son. For the first time he wondered if his gran actually knew his dad's identity. Or had his mother kept that secret to herself? Was it possible that the old lady hadn't managed to brow-beat it out of her daughter? In all these years?

"I should think so too! Now what are we having for dinner?" Valerie's azure blue eyes lit up in expectation of a treat. Apparently the matter was closed.

"Cottage pie, Mum. Your favourite," Anna soothed, her own face softening into her normal pretty expression.

Lucas refused to be dismissed so easily. Not this time. "I have a right to know. He is my father!" He felt his voice rise unintentionally high. His mouth drew tight over the next words, fear and anger biting into him. "Does he even know I exist? Did you even tell him about me?" he shrieked, half-question half-accusation. Why couldn't they see his point of view? Why would they never give him even the smallest bit of information? What was so terrible about the whole thing that it had to be kept shrouded in mystery forever?

Neither of the women deigned to answer but he saw the look which passed between them – a knowing glance that said everything and nothing all at once. Suddenly Lucas was filled with a hatred so intensely devastating that he could not contain it. It bubbled up and out of him, pounding through the top of his head in an explosion of disgust and despair.

"I have a right to know!" he screamed, bringing his fist down on the ceramic bowl that lay waiting for the pie filling. A shaft of pain radiated along the edge of his palm and up to his wrist as the bowl splintered and shattered. The broken pieces lay accusingly on top of the work surface, pristine whiteness glinting in the beam of the overhead lights. Innocent of any wrongdoing but broken nonetheless, its promise unfulfilled, fragments of the bowl, sharp and uneven, sat side by side - once a part of something bigger, something whole and complete but now broken beyond repair. Just like him.

"Go to your room Lucas." His grandmother's voice betrayed no emotion but her face was less controlled. Worry knitted her brows together and the fine lines at the edges of her eyes seemed steeped in concern. But before he could move an inch she had firmly grasped his hand and turned it over, looking for cuts or punctures in the skin. Finding nothing she let go and he let his arm drop limply to his side. He didn't care if his hand was bleeding. His heart was a raw wound, torn and ripped. What little concern could he have for his hand?

He turned on his heel and moved towards the doorway. His mother continued to work at the potatoes, slicing and dicing them and refusing to meet his eyes. "Mum?" part-question, part-entreaty, he was disappointed but not surprised when she refused to meet his gaze.

"Dinner will be ready in about forty minutes. I'll call you down then," she said, eyes fixed firmly on the shiny blade of the chopping knife. Lucas said nothing in response; head down he went through the door and up the stairs to his room.

His bedroom was the smallest in the house. A bed, wardrobe and bedside table took up most of the space but at least it was his to call his own. His mother and gran had the other two bigger bedrooms at the front of the house, but Lucas was happy with his and would not have swapped with them for anything. His bedroom was the one with the view. He closed the bedroom door behind him and walked over to the window which looked out over the back garden and the fields beyond.

Rolling meadows topped with lush green grassy knolls soothed his disquiet. Beyond these, the earth was stripped of its crops at the moment, bare and empty. The barren fields reminded him a little of himself - devoid of purpose, waiting for someone to come plant a seed that would germinate and flourish until he and they were ripe with purpose and had fulfilled their promise.

The only difference was that the farmer *would* come, he *would* plant those seeds, but Lucas's mother and gran would forever hold back, forever refuse to give him what he wanted, what he *needed*.

On the windowsill, his phone sat fully charged. He reached for it without being consciously aware of doing so. His fingers hesitated over the button for video calls. Did he want Josh to see the strain on his face? Could he bear to see Josh's expression? He ignored the video call button.

The phone was answered on the first ring. There was no need to tell Josh who was calling; there was also no need for small talk. They were friends and always would be, but they were also victims of their own circumstances. "How will your dad know where to send the postcards when you move?" he asked.

"Mum says she gave him the new address and just in case he's lost it, she's having the mail redirected for a few months."

"Oh." Lucas tried to figure out how to put what he wanted to say into words. "You could have phoned him and told him yourself."

"He phones me sometimes but mostly the time difference means that when he's free to talk, I'm asleep in bed or the other way round, I can never quite remember. He works really long hours and America and all the different countries he works in are in different time zones to us," Josh explained.

Lucas nodded, "I guess." He paused. "But you could have texted him though."

"It uses up tons of credit to text him and then I'm never really sure if he gets the texts or if they just go... wherever it is that undelivered texts go to."

"Text heaven," Lucas joked. "Yes, I suppose so..." He brought the conversation around to his own dilemma. "I tried again to get my mum to tell me what my dad's name was…" he corrected himself, "I mean is. But she won't say."

"Your mum must have a reason." Josh's voice sounded pensive and distant through the small device but when Lucas closed his eyes on the brown fields and green, rolling hills, he could almost imagine his friend standing there beside him. And straight away the blatantly obvious truth was there for him to see. He had been blinded by the idea that she didn't want him to know because it might hurt him. But now the truth was laid bare. It wasn't him she was protecting! She was protecting his father!

And if she was protecting him then she must have had a good reason. Perhaps he was famous! Or important in some way! A politician? No, he could not imagine someone who made the laws of the country being in love with his mother, she was too unopinionated for that. A businessman? Perhaps, but again he thought that such a man and his mother would have so little in common that they would be unable to even hold a conversation. All his mother ever did was go out to work as a part-time cashier at the local supermarket, tend to the house, and watch DVDs of stupid rom-com movies. In fact she was almost obsessed with movies. In particular…

The tiniest seed of something took root in his head, curled itself around the sparse information there and drank greedily from his imagination, flourishing instantly into full bloom. *Oh my God*, he thought. *My father is an actor! An actor from the movies! From Hollywood!*

But surely that was insane? Where could his mother have possibly met a famous Hollywood actor? She had never even been to America. The furthest she had been was London and that was only for a few weekends before he had even been born. London. A famous actor. The facts coalesced in his head. Not just a famous English actor who had made it big in films and therefore Hollywood, but THE famous English actor! None other than the king of rom-com himself! The man whose face adorned many of the plastic covers of the DVDs stacked high on the shelf under the TV! The films his mother watched over and over again, never seeming to tire of them!

The enormity of the situation made him stagger backwards. The back of his knees hit the side of his bed and he flopped onto it, the phone still held close to his ear. "I know who he is!" he breathed into the mouthpiece, almost forgetting that Josh was on the other end of the line.

"You know who he is? Your father?" Josh asked stupidly, as if he had not been following the conversation. "So who is he?"

Lucas took a huge breath before he let loose this momentous piece of information. "Hugh Grant!"

"What?" Josh snorted as if the idea was

completely preposterous.

Lucas shook his head as if Josh was actually there in the room. "She went to London for a few weekends before I was born. She's never talked much about what she did and where she went and when I ask she goes quiet, just like she does when I ask about my dad." It was all so logical, why hadn't he worked it out before? "She loves movies, especially ones with Hugh Grant in them. It all makes sense!" Lucas stopped talking long enough to examine himself in the long mirror attached to the wardrobe door.

Did he look like Hugh Grant? He had the same dark hair and general build but his face was rounder than the actor's and had none of his father's fine bone structure. Then again everyone said he looked like his mum so that was no indication one way or another.

"None of that means anything…" Josh began.

Lucas interrupted. Josh was merely jealous because up until now he had had the upper hand because his father was a famous stunt man in Hollywood. But Hugh Grant had topped that. Hugh Grant could top anything. He was the scissors that cut the paper in Scissors, Paper, Rock and the paper that covered the rock in the same game. Hugh Grant was everything. And he was his father! "You're just jealous because your dad will never be as great as mine is! Hugh Grant - my dad!"

The line went abruptly dead and Lucas knew that he had won the argument, although why it had become an argument in the first place confounded him. Why was his friend not as pleased for him as he always was for Josh? The inequality in their relationship startled him. Surely their friendship didn't hinge on the fact that Josh could show off and feel superior to him, with his absent stunt-man dad? Surely there was a firmer footing for their bond than that?

Lucas pulled the phone away from his ear and stared at the display with dismay. Josh had hung up! Two competing sensations fought for his attention. The first was an intense throbbing in his head, just above his eyes and which curved round to the side of his head. The other was a cold, empty feeling in the pit of his stomach. He had found his dad but lost his friend. How was that fair? He tossed the phone onto the floor, not caring where it landed. The only person he ever called was Josh and it wasn't as if he would be doing that anytime soon.

He lay on the bed and crossed his arms over his stomach, trying to hold some warmth and comfort in. Why was it that whenever he tried to pull things or people to him, to hold them tight and keep them safe, to build a perimeter fence around them and protect them, it always turned to dust? All he had ever wanted was a family that he could feel part of. A mum and a dad to call his own.

Perhaps it wasn't the perfect situation, living with his mum and gran in this little house whilst his dad lived elsewhere, living the life of the Superstar that he was. But surely it wouldn't be forever. Not once his dad found out that he had a son! Not once his mum and dad realised they still loved each other, even after all these years! Not once they realised they couldn't possibly bear to spend another minute apart!

"Lucas! Dinner's ready!" The comforting aroma of his mum's special cottage pie filled his nostrils as he made his way down the stairs. Did his dad know his mum could cook, he wondered. Of course superstars probably didn't eat things like cottage pie. He wondered what his dad would be having for dinner. Probably lobster and caviar, washed down with glasses of expensive champagne.

Will you open a new bottle when you find me, Dad? Even in his thoughts the word 'dad' had a tantalising appeal, an alluring ring. He conjured an image of Hugh Grant and his mother standing with champagne flutes, toasting their everlasting love, with himself standing between them. Now he knew who his father was, things could only get better. He bounded down the last of the steps and into the kitchen.

CHAPTER 3

The removal van was bigger than Lucas had imagined. He wondered how a smallish three bedroomed house could fill a van of that size. And yet at the same time he couldn't understand how a whole life could be packed up so easily, could be boxed and carted away to somewhere new. Like uprooting a tree, tearing it from its earthen anchorage so that its roots emerged into the harsh daylight, ripped and frayed and splintered beyond repair, Josh was being broken off and forcibly removed from his home, his friend, his life. Shouldn't there be some permanent scars upon the earth to forever show what damage had been wreaked? To indicate what devastation had been inflicted?

Lucas had spent the previous evening thinking long and hard about going to see Josh before he left the street for good, but when confronted with the reality of the removal van he almost wanted to turn around and go home, burrow his head under the bedcovers and pretend none of it was real.

He had taken most of the morning and the previous night to decide that he was big enough to put Josh's behaviour aside. They had been friends ever since Josh had moved into the row of council houses and for all of that time Josh had had the upper hand, so Lucas couldn't really blame him for being put out by this turn of events.

He found Josh standing watching the removal men load the van, pale–faced, freckles standing out in stark contrast to the rest of his skin, eyes dark and troubled. The gaze that he turned on Lucas seemed somehow wrong, as if it was unfocused, turned inwards rather than out.

"Will you have your own room in your mum's boyfriend's house?" Lucas asked, biting his lip at the stiltedness of the question. He didn't want to mention his dad Hugh Grant again, partly because Josh would try to douse his bonfire with his disbelief and sarcastic comments but also partly because the revelation was a thing of wonder, something to be savoured, to take out in the darkest hours of the night and be examined as a thing of wondrous potential, of great and unique beauty. No disrespect to his friend, but Lucas didn't think that Josh had the mental wherewithal to appreciate how exceptionally favoured by the Gods Lucas had been.

Josh nodded. "Well unless they have a baby together and it's a boy."

For a moment, lost in his own reverie, Lucas forgot that he had asked a question. He refocused his mind. "What about The Bat? You won't have to share with her will you?" The thought of Josh having to share with Catherine the Goth filled Lucas with horror. He had seen her a few times when her father had brought her with him to stay at Josh's house, but she was too weird to hang around with.

"The Bat only stays one night a week, so Mum says I will have my own room. But if they have a baby…" he trailed off worriedly.

"Well maybe they won't have a baby. Or it will be a girl and then it will have to share with The Bat," Lucas said, genuinely hoping things went well for his friend. He wondered if his dad had other children and how they would cope once it became known that Lucas was also a Grant, the *original* Grant. The first born son!

Josh shivered as if someone had stepped on his grave. "Mum says I will like The Bat when I get to know her properly."

"She actually said that? I mean called her The Bat?" Lucas asked in surprise.

Josh looked at him as if he had lost all credibility. "No of course not! She calls her 'Cath'," he put on a sugary tone and sickly expression. "Mum says it's 'a phase' and that The Bat will 'grow out of it'."

Lucas laughed. "Well if I was a baby I

wouldn't want to share with someone who dresses like they are going to their own funeral and looks less lively than the average corpse!" His mind licked over the image of a vast bedroom like the ones he was sure his dad's house in London must have, with cool marble floors and wide patio doors which led onto balconies from every room.

The image in his head morphed suddenly as the imagined landscape beyond the bedroom windows changed. Where there had been oak and birch trees standing sentinel in the well-tended garden, their branches swaying gently under the pale English sun, there were now American trees, taller and somehow more fearsome than their British counterparts; vast expanses of trees which led out from the wooden porch towards the wide tree-lined boulevard at the front of the clapboard house and the corrals at the back where horses snickered and neighed under the buttery American sun.

It was more than likely that his dad spent some time in both America and England. A sheen of panic salted Lucas's upper lip in fine beads of sweat. What if he couldn't contact him? What if he wrote to his dad in London when he was in America and vice versa? What if he was just never in the right place at the right time?

"We will stay in contact, right?" Josh asked, unwittingly almost echoing Lucas's thoughts. It was so close to his own worries, that somewhere in the deepest part of Lucas's imagination it was himself who asked the question and his absent father who answered.

"Course we will. We will always be in each other's lives!" Lucas said absently. He didn't even notice the bright gleam which came over the other boy's eyes, he was too busy thinking about how his father would ruffle his hair as he said the words, cheeks cleaving into dimpled furrows as he grinned widely, blue eyes piercing his son with genuine love.

"Josh! I need you to start moving the boxes in your room. Bring them downstairs for the removal men, please." Josh's mother appeared, dumping a large box into the arms of one of the overalled men. "Oh hi Lucas, I didn't see you there," she said too brightly.

"Hi," Lucas responded sadly. *If I tell her who my father is, will she change her mind about moving?* But it was a stupid idea. She would not see how it would benefit Josh to be the best friend of Hugh Grant's son, the advantages and privileges that would be granted him. She would probably realise that Lucas would be moving anyway, as soon as his dad knew of his existence.

"I know you two will miss each other but we are not moving far away," Sandra Cole said a little too dismissively, as if she hadn't really given a second thought to the situation. She turned back to her son. "C'mon Josh scoot already! I need you to help!" And with those last words she was gone, bustling away to oversee some other part of the move.

Josh started forward in her wake, one foot thrust outward, the other still where it had been a moment ago. Lucas thought he looked like someone caught between two worlds and perhaps that was the actual crux of the matter. Josh's old life was about to be over – the life that he had lived in this street with his best friend only doors away. By this evening he would be part of a new family, living in a new house, going to a new school and undoubtedly making new friends.

"I have to go," Josh said and in those four words Lucas heard a soliloquy, a monologue that confirmed all his worst fears.

"I know," Lucas said sadly and turned away. Despite their best intentions, Josh already seemed distant and gone; their friendship something that had once shone with promise, now dulled and tarnished. Without looking back or turning his head for one last glimpse of his friend, Lucas shuffled back the way he had come, seeking the refuge and comfort of home. Shoulders slumped, he didn't even glance at the homes which were occupied by other members of his class or school. None of them were friends of his. None of them meant anything to him.

In number 15 the Gilmore twins lived with their mum, dad and little sister. Faces like pigs they were an ugly and argumentative family and he had had no wish to associate with them in the past, nor would he do in the future. Opposite them in number 16 lived Hattie Minnow from the year below him. She lived with her step-mum and her dad and her three step-brothers. He wondered how they all fitted in. Hattie was a spiteful girl. Considered pretty, Lucas thought that her eyes were too big for her face and her head too large in general for her skinny frame. She looked like nothing more than a human lollipop.

Further up the street lived Tom Spencer with his mother and her boyfriend. Lucas couldn't stand Tom ever since the boy had suggested that it was weird that Lucas lived with his gran and that his mum never had a man around the house.

Not that he did live with his gran, she lived with them – him and his mother. It wasn't the same thing at all, was it? Although the rent book was in his gran's name, it was his mother who did all the shopping, cooking and cleaning and who went out to work to pay the rent, so if anyone lived with anyone else, it was his gran who lived with them.

And of course now that he knew his father was Hugh Grant it was obvious why his mother had never got with another man. Who could possibly compare to Hugh Grant? What other man could have been half as charming or witty, a fraction as charismatic or even nearly as attractive as his celebrated father?

Lucas slouched past the other houses on the street, as familiar to the occupants who resided there as the image of their own faces would be, yet as reviled and despised as a flesh-eating, fang-gnashing, bone-crushing alien with two heads and a mandible for a mouth.

The front door to his house was closed but not locked. He pushed the handle down and stumbled into the hallway, slamming the door closed behind him, relieved to be home safe and secure where no one could taunt or tease him. The living room was empty but he could hear his gran thumping about upstairs. He hoped she hadn't got her hearing aid in, perhaps then she wouldn't realise he was home. He switched on the laptop which sat in the corner of the room and waited for the screen to light up.

Dark thoughts lit his mind and his heart pounded a staccato drumbeat in either fear or excitement. He couldn't tell which. Long seconds ticked past until he had the Google search bar in front of him, cursor blinking in the rectangle, waiting for his fingers to tap in their request. He laid his fingertips over the black keys, feeling the warmth of the machine translated to his palms, savouring the moment, the very last moment in life where he did not properly belong to anyone other than two women who kept secrets.

The cursor blinked once more and tentatively he typed in the two words which would forever change his life: Hugh Grant. Without even hitting return, the screen was filled with a multitude of images for the actor. Head shots, publicity images… all of them showing a tall, dark and handsome man who anyone would be proud to call dad. Lucas grinned from ear to ear.

To the left of the screen, various websites were listed which had made reference to Mr Grant but it was one in particular which grabbed his attention. *"Hugh Grant's Instant Family Shocker,"* one of the headlines proclaimed. But before he could click onto the site, he heard the thump, thump, thump of his gran's heavy treads on the stairs.

Heart racing in case she walked in and found him with his father's name and picture all over the screen, Lucas pressed the close button repeatedly until the screen went blank and dark. There was no point in letting either his mother or gran suspect that he knew their secret. What they didn't know about, they couldn't prevent.

Without testing his theory, he knew that if they even suspected he knew, they would ban him from contacting his father. He didn't know what he would do if he was put in that situation. Would he ignore outright their threats or would he acquiesce, put any idea of contacting the man on hold, for the time being at least? Certainly in this instance prevention was better than cure. If they didn't know he knew, then he was free to do whatever he liked with the information, he decided. If only his gran wasn't around to interfere!

She was almost at the bottom of the stairs now, her steps closer and closer, the thuds rhythmical and evenly spaced… and then a hiatus… an interruption or gap where there should have been a footstep. The second hung moth-like in the air, an impossibility, a gossamer-spun moment which clutched at infinity like a larch at a twig.

Had she paused on the stairs a moment for some reason? And then the terrifying sound of a body falling, crashing and ricocheting from one side wall to another, one higher step to another, lower one. Was there a high but short-lived scream or did that sound exist only in his imagination? In a single bound he was up, away from the computer and flinging open the door which connected the room to the hallway and the stairs beyond.

A crumpled body lay at the foot of the stairs. Twisted and broken it was the most horrifying sight he had ever seen. The logical part of his brain told him that it was his gran who lay there so silent and still. But somewhere else in his head, his mind insisted that it was nothing more than a giant ragdoll. A doll which just happened to be wearing his grandmother's clothes, the low heel of one shoe still caught in the hem of the dark navy trousers it wore.

His attention was riveted on that one detail – how the stitching had pulled and frayed and how the heel was firmly embedded in the material... Lucas swallowed hard. The foot which was strapped into the shoe was so small, seemed so innocuous, it was impossible that it had been the cause of the accident. But the facts were undeniable.

"Gran?" his voice came out weedy and too, too quiet. There was no response. Because of the strange way she had landed he couldn't see her face. Instead it seemed pressed into the unforgiving laminate which decked the ground floor of the house. He pulled air into his lungs which had the viscosity of treacle and tried again.

"Gran? Are you okay?" This time it was louder and more like his usual voice but still there was no response. He reached out a hand and noticed how it shook and trembled. He placed it on his grandmother's back. She was warm to his touch. "Gran I need to turn you over, okay?" There was no answer and she did nothing to resist him but he felt obliged to explain his actions to her, to seek her permission. Carefully he slid an arm under her neck and placed the other hand lightly on her shoulder. It didn't take much effort and yet his breath rasped in his throat, drawn in raggedly and expelled unevenly.

He gave a slight tug on her head, a small pull on her shoulder and then suddenly she was half way round and momentum took over. Gravity pulled her body back down to the ground and she would have slammed into the hard floor again if not for his restraining arms around her.

Her face was slack, empty of expression, devoid of life. In death she was what she had never been in life – quiet and at peace. Her face had a certain wistfulness to it as though she had finally understood the merits of keeping her opinion to herself. He was instantly ashamed of the thought. Shocked at the feelings which tumbled through his head, where agonies of grief and loss spun finely with surprise at how rapidly everything had changed, Lucas's throat constricted. "Gran can you hear me?" he asked, even though he already knew the answer.

His voice was hoarse and it almost hurt to push the sounds out, to form them into words and yet he felt there was an importance to it. Perhaps she was already dead but wasn't it also possible that some vestige of life remained in her which would hear and understand him? Or perhaps her spirit hovered nearby, watching and listening and preparing to depart to wherever souls went when their host bodies died. He didn't know nor was he even sure he cared. All he knew was that he had something to say and that he had to say it before it burned a hole in him, ripped through his core until nothing of him remained.

"Gran I know that in your own way you always loved me and that you were trying to protect me. And I know that you loved Mum too. But I know who my dad is now. And though I wish this had never happened to you, I wish that you were in the kitchen right now, making a cup of tea, I..." a large wet teardrop slalomed down the curve of his cheek and onto the slope of his nose, glimmering there for a moment.

His breath caught in his throat as he saw the droplet quiver in the air; it seemed to be suspended, captured in slow motion as it made its journey from grandson to grandmother, from the living to the dead. It was as if the teardrop was a glass globe in which his whole life was contained. And when it landed on the old woman, splashing onto her skin and running off until nothing could be seen of it but a thin train of diminishing moisture, he knew with a certainty that stemmed from the marrow of his bones, that he had caused this terrible thing to happen.

Because of him, because of his longing to meet his dad, because of his certain knowledge that his gran would never allow it, would always ban him from contacting his dad, he had caused this. He hadn't pushed her down the stairs, hadn't

fed her pills to make her dizzy, or ripped the
hem of her trousers in the hope that she would
trip and fall. But in the longing for his dad, the
compulsion to contact him and be a part of his
life, he had caused his gran's death just as surely
as if he had planned and instigated it.

"Gran I'm so sorry. But I have to meet
him." Lucas closed the dead woman's eyes lest she
be upset at how distraught he was. Mucus and
tears ran unchecked down his face, mingling and
merging to form a thicker stream which soaked
into the collar of his t-shirt. He brought his hands
up to his face, wiping the tears away and pulling
the back of his hand roughly under his nose.

"I loved you Gran and I'll miss you." Slowly
he stood up and reached for the phone. He dialled
without even thinking about the keys he pressed.

"Which service do you require?" the
emergency services operator enquired.

"It's my gran. She's dead," he said in a flat
voice. Vaguely he understood that he was giving
answers to questions he wasn't even aware of
being asked. After what seemed like a very long
time he felt that he had given all the information
he needed to give. Quietly he placed the phone
back on its charger before lifting it up for a second
time.

Once more it rang only briefly before it was
answered. This time it was his mother's voice he
heard. Perhaps she was on a break because if she

had been working she would not have been able to answer the call. He didn't know if it was better that he could speak to her in person or whether it would have been better if he could have left a message for her to come home. It was academic, she had answered the phone and he had to deal with it. "Mum, come home."

"Lucas I'm working, I know you are upset about Josh but- " she said immediately, before the unusualness of his call and the flat sound of his voice startled her into a realisation that something out of the ordinary had occurred.

"It's not about Josh," he stated, waiting for her to ask what it was about then. When she said nothing he was forced to speak into the uncomfortable silence. "It's Gran, Mum. She's dead!" Strangely it wasn't the sight of his dead grandmother at the foot of the stairs, or gazing into her warm but lifeless face that was his undoing. Instead it was the sharply inhaled breath of his mother down the telephone line.

"She's dead! And it's all my fault!" Lucas bent over the phone, cradling the receiver to him as finally his emotions burst through the dam which encircled them. Hot thick tears fell and every one was carved in guilt.

CHAPTER 4

At first there were many people rushing around, moving so fast that their silhouettes seemed almost to blur into one another. Lucas had been obliged to move outside, not just to give them all space but to enable him to breathe. The air inside the house seemed leaden, made of treacle and sponge and he could not force it into his lungs no matter how hard he tried. He heard himself try to draw it in on great big whoops of sound but his lungs lay deflated and near flat inside his chest cavity. He clawed at the neck of his t-shirt, thinking that the material there was too tight, too constricting to allow him to breathe but even with the neckline torn away, the feeling of restriction had not eased.

The paramedics hadn't taken long to arrive; they took even less time to pronounce what Lucas already knew. "I'm sorry, she's already gone," the lady paramedic said, trying to wrap her arms around him for comfort.

Without him knowing when or how they had arrived, there were suddenly policemen everywhere, as if they had sprouted up from the cracks between the paving slabs. They seemed to be multiplying too; every time he looked there was another he hadn't seen before. They were inside the house, outside the house, taking photos, making notes, looking everywhere, except at him. Lucas shrugged the paramedic off. "What do you mean 'gone'?" He hadn't meant to sound aggressive but that was how it came out anyway. "She hasn't gone anywhere!"

The paramedic coughed. "She's dead Lucas. We can't help her now. I'm sorry."

He looked carefully at her face. To be truthful she did look sorry, even though she hadn't known his gran. He wondered too how this could be. When that thought petered out in his head he wondered how she had known his name. "How did you know my name?" he asked, because that was the thing that perplexed him the most.

"You gave it to the emergency operator, remember?"

He shook his head. He didn't remember at all! He couldn't remember one single thing. With a start he realised that he couldn't bring his grandmother's face into his mind. He couldn't remember the slightest little thing about her, as if now that she was 'gone' everything about her, every memory that had been made of her had been erased, wiped away like nothing more than a smear of dirt. The smear of dirt that his mother had left upon her face whilst peeling potatoes.

Who had erased his brain? Who had done this to him? He looked suspiciously at the paramedic. Had it been her? Or her partner? "Did you take my gran's memories from me?" he asked. A strange look crept over the woman's face. Lucas thought that it was guilt, or perhaps worry that she had been caught.

At that precise moment a long black car pulled up to the kerb just behind the ambulance. He wondered if this was the CIA or the FBI, even though he lived in England... But the woman who emerged, ashen-faced and trembling, looking ten years older than she had that morning, was his mother, or if not her, some imposter who bore a striking resemblance to her.

"Oh my God, Lucas!" Anna's eyes swivelled from Lucas to the paramedics. Without even bothering to close the car door she flew to him, wrapping her arms around him and hugging him fiercely. He could almost not breathe again but he didn't complain. Perhaps if she squeezed hard enough, she could take the pain away, make everything all right.

Another woman got out of the car, closing the driver's door behind her before coming around the other side to close the passenger door his mother had abandoned. He recognised her as his mother's boss. She had clearly given his mother a lift home and decided to stick around.

Lucas wondered why she would do that. His mother was home now, everything would be fine, wouldn't it?

"I'll pop the kettle on," the woman said, walking past him and into the house as if she had every right to be there. Lucas wanted to shout out a warning to her. His gran would go mad if some stranger started messing about in her kitchen. He opened his mouth to speak but his mother got there before him so he closed it again and let her take care of the warning.

"Thanks Alison," his mother said wearily. Lucas pulled his head away to examine his mother more carefully. Something was very wrong with all the people here...

"Are you the boy's mother?" the paramedic asked.

He watched his mother nod. "Yes and it's his gran, my mother who has... actually I don't know what's happened. Is she going to be alright?"

The paramedic shook her head. "I'm sorry, she was already gone when we got here. Looks like she tripped coming down the stairs," the paramedic explained. "Lucas is in shock, but he will be okay if you just keep him calm and keep him talking." She put a hand on his mother's shoulder for a moment before turning and disappearing back inside the house.

"Do you understand your gran is dead, Lucas?" his mother asked, lifting his chin so that he was forced to look at her. Huge tears ran unchecked down her face, it reminded him a little of a place in the Peak District they had visited once. A tiny little town, bisected by a small stream, it had the most unlikely waterfall he had ever seen, just two or three trickles of water that had quietly splashed into the pool below. It hadn't been dramatic but he had thought it beautiful nonetheless. "Lucas, do you understand that?" His mother shook him gently.

Unwilling to re-enter the real world, to admit that what was going on here was reality and not some warped fantasy, he tried to hold out, tried to evade her question but a bright pain bloomed near his heart and he knew he had to confess again. Had to purge his guilt. "She's dead because of me!" he gasped, feeling the pain explode from his heart and radiate outwards, enveloping his whole body with a burning ache. He looked up the street towards Josh's house but the removal van was gone, the house already empty. He had never needed his friend more than he did now and Josh was gone!

He felt her body stiffen and her head turn away from his gaze. For a moment he thought it was in reaction to his words, until he followed her line of vision to the blanket shrouded heap that was carried on a stretcher between the two paramedics.

"Mum!" Anna Pertwee cried but it was

neither a call to the living or to the dead. Instead it was a cry to the heavens, an entreaty heartfelt enough to have riven the stars above them into bright fragments, to have cleaved the heavens itself into pieces.

Her arms fell loose around her son and she stumbled over to the body which now lay sedately in the back of the ambulance. Climbing inside, she sank to the floor of the vehicle and gently pulled back the covering sheet. The lady paramedic offered what solace she could. "It looks as if she tripped coming down the stairs, or perhaps going up them. It would have been very quick. We will need a post mortem to confirm it but I suspect that the shock of the fall induced a massive heart attack. It would have been over very quickly."

Anna nodded. The motion caused tears to flick from her cheeks and new tears to form in her eyes. She tried to smile but it was the saddest thing Lucas had ever seen. "Thank you. It helps a little to know that she wasn't in any pain." She took her mother's hand and kissed the back of it before kissing the old lady on the forehead. "Goodbye Mother. Thank you for always being there for me. I will always love you." She tucked the sheet carefully around the body as if tucking the old lady snugly into bed.

Lucas watched from outside. He wanted to say goodbye too but was almost afraid his gran would rise from where she lay and point an accusatory finger at him. "Do you want to come say goodbye to your gran?" his mother asked, not moving from where she knelt. Lucas shook his head. He hoped she would not make him.

"There will be plenty of times for goodbye later," the paramedic said softly before speaking in a quieter voice to his mother. He strained to hear but from his position outside, caught only the odd word. His mother nodded her understanding and slowly unfolded herself to stand upright. Dazedly she climbed out of the ambulance and watched as it drove away, taking away the person she had relied upon her whole life. It seemed to Lucas that everyone he loved was being driven away in some vehicle or another. Like a warped Agatha Christie film now there was only him and his mum left. "What did she say?" he asked. "The ambulance woman I mean."

"Just that you had clearly loved your Gran," his mother replied, inadvertently compounding his guilt. She took Lucas's hand in hers and gently pulled him towards the house. "Time to go in now, honey." He wondered if it was the same hand that she had used to hold onto his dead gran, just a moment ago. He was surprised to find that the thought did not provoke the revulsion he would have thought it would have done. Instead there was only an infinite sadness. Together they re-entered the house.

*****

The next few hours were a blur. There were statements made to the police about the circumstances of the accident. Once or twice Lucas was tempted to have told them it was all his fault. That he had inadvertently wished that his gran was out of the way. But to have explained it would have necessitated him disclosing the fact that he had discovered who his dad was and he wasn't at all sure that was a good idea, under the circumstances.

For one thing he wasn't entirely sure that he hadn't somehow magically caused the accident. How would his mother feel about him once she knew he had been the cause of his gran's death? For another, he wasn't sure that his mum wouldn't still forbid him to contact his dad, for whatever reason she might have. And lastly and perhaps more importantly, it was the wrong way to let his dad know he existed. If the police went to Hugh Grant to explain that not only did he have a son he didn't know about, but that the boy was somehow implicated in his grandmother's death... well everything would be ruined. The news reporters would have a field day!

So he kept it all to himself. But when everyone was finally gone, when her boss had decided she had made enough tea and given enough sympathy, when the police had taken enough photos and enough statements and when the house was finally still and quiet once more, quieter than it had ever been with only the two of them now in it, Anna asked him the question he had been dreading.

"Lucas, when you phoned me... you said it was your fault?" the statement was softened into a question not just by the slight upturn in her voice but by the concern in her eyes and the arm she wrapped round her son.

"She was coming down the stairs... I should have helped her!" he bluffed, hoping that his mother would not see the misery in his eyes.

"Honey, my mother, your gran was the strongest woman I ever knew. And you know what she would have said if you had suggested that she needed any help, don't you?" she tried to smile.

He nodded slowly. Suddenly the image was there clear in his head again. His gran in the kitchen, his gran watching TV and laughing about something stupid as she passed around the biscuit tin and then one of the most recent images. Her in that silly raincoat she wore, struggling on tiptoe to reach the peg it usually hung on. "Stuff and nonsense," he said slowly. "That's what she would have said, isn't it?" he asked, not really needing the answer.

"Yes, that's exactly what she would have

said!" To his surprise the laugh that his mother emitted was genuine and warm. "And believe me, if my mother could have chosen the way she exited this world, that would have exactly been it. She always did love to be the centre of a drama! And she wasn't the sort of woman who would have taken kindly to a long, lingering, debilitating illness. A wasting disease where she had to rely on someone to bring her meals and take her to the toilet."

Lucas knew that every word his mother spoke was the truth. "No, she would have wanted to go out with a bang." She got up from the kitchen table and began to rummage around in the back of one of the cupboards, emerging with a bottle of sherry. "She always had a little tipple at night, your gran." She fetched two small glasses out of the cupboard and set one down in front of him and one down for herself, filling both of them to the rim with a dark red liquid.

Lucas looked at the full glass in front of him. He reached out a hand to it but hesitated to lift it to his lips. "I know you haven't had alcohol before but you are fourteen and this is a special occasion. To Valerie Pertwee!" His mother remained standing and lifted her glass in the air in a toast.

Lucas copied her, scraping his chair back from the table and lifting his glass above his head. "To you Gran! We will never forget you!"

His mother clinked her glass to his and tossed the drink back in one go. Hesitantly Lucas brought his own glass to his mouth. He took a sip of the fiery liquid which burned a path down to his stomach. He could feel its progression through his system in a way that was neither pleasant nor unpleasant but just plain strange. Anna sat down at the table and refilled her glass but she didn't refill Lucas's and he didn't ask her to. "What happens now?" he asked.

She shrugged her shoulders. "I'm a bit new to this too. Your granddad died when I was very little. I don't even remember him and your gran never talked about the funeral."

"Funeral," he echoed, not realising he had said it out loud. It was a horrible word and yet it fitted its meaning very well, conjuring up images of infinite darkness and a heaviness of the soul.

"The Funeral Director will take care of most of it I would imagine but we will need to contact everyone who would want to come to the funeral and we will need to get you a new white shirt and black trousers."

"I could wear my school uniform," he suggested.

"No, most of them are quite worn. You will need new clothes," she said absently.

"Who will come?" he asked.

"What?" she poured a third glass of sherry, seemingly intent on drinking the whole bottle.

"You said that we would need to contact everyone who would want to come to the funeral. Who did you mean?"

She looked at him blankly for a moment, either surprised by the question or thinking about the answer. "Well…" she rubbed a hand over her eyes as if to clarify her thoughts. "She had a brother and a sister. But her sister, my aunt Agnes died years ago…"

Lucas interrupted her. "You had an Aunt Agnes? I had a great aunt? Why did I never meet her?" he was angry that once more another secret had been kept from him.

"It wasn't a big secret honey! She died before you were even born. She got cancer and had never married or had children so there was no one left from her line. I thought you knew about her!" her brow creased into a furrow.

"No, I didn't!" his voice came out surly and he was a little ashamed. Now was not the time to be berating his mother for past misdemeanours.

"Sorry. I guess she just never cropped up in conversation when you were around."

"You mentioned a brother. I think I have heard of him. Is that your uncle Edward in New Zealand?"

Anna nodded. "He is… was… a few years older than your gran. Don't imagine he will be well enough to fly over for the funeral. And his children never even met your gran anyway, even though she was their aunt."

"So what does that leave us with?" he asked.

"Well there will be you and me and I'm sure Josh and his mum will come. And then mum's friends from the social club. They will all want to be there I'm sure." Lucas nodded. He was glad that she thought Josh would come. The thought of it just being him and his mum and a bunch of old folk was just too grim to contemplate. "I will phone Josh's mum in the morning and then you and I will go get you some clothes for the funeral, okay?" she smiled sadly at him.

"But it's Sunday tomorrow. Won't we have to wait until Monday?"

"Tomorrow is going to be the worst day of all Lucas. It's the very first day we will spend without her in our lives. I don't think it will be good for us to sit here and brood. We have to keep active, keep busy the whole day long. We will find somewhere that's open, don't worry."

He nodded, trusting to her wisdom. But an ever-present thought sneaked from the back of his brain to emerge on the tip of his tongue, bypassing all censure. "What about my dad? Shouldn't we tell him too? He might want to come to the funeral?"

The slow turn of his mother's head and the tightening of her lips adequately conveyed her dismay that he had chosen to bring that particular subject up once more and at such a painful time. "Goodnight Lucas. Try to get some sleep and I will see you in the morning."

He looked at the clock. It was only 8 pm but there didn't seem to be any point in arguing. Neither of them had eaten throughout the day since the accident but he wasn't hungry. Perhaps the copious amounts of tea that his mother's boss had almost forced upon him had dampened his appetite, or perhaps it was just the stress of the situation. It didn't matter either way.

"Goodnight mum," he kissed her on the cheek and made his way up the fatal steps to his bedroom, mentally ticking off every step he took. Had this been the one? Or this? Which of these inanimate lumps of wood had claimed his gran's life? He kicked each one as he stepped onto it but the wood was unremorseful and the hands of time did not whizz backwards.

Alone in his room, he lay down on his bed and closed his eyes. It had been an accident. Even if he had not been in the house, it would most probably all have happened the same way. He told himself that over and over but a disquiet had taken firm root in his heart and refused to be so easily budged.

CHAPTER 5

They took the train into Birmingham but rather than exit the station for the shopping centre above, they caught another train directly out, taking them to another unknown city or town. "I thought we were going to a shop in Birmingham!" Lucas said as they boarded another train.

His mother nodded. "I thought about it at first but it wouldn't have used up the whole day. We would have been finished too soon and then what would we do? Return to an empty house to sit and stare at the walls?" She had a point. "Besides I didn't want to one day come back into Birmingham on a day out and have to pass the shop where we bought funeral clothes. Coming into Birmingham a few times a year has always been our treat – I don't want that to change or be tainted." She smiled sadly. "We have a lot of happy memories here, don't we?"

He nodded, unable to say anything over the lump in his throat. "Do you remember your gran's birthday last year, when we took her to that Chinese restaurant and she said," she tried to affect her mother's tone of voice, "'aren't Chinese people tiny!'" Anna couldn't stop herself from laughing at the memory.

Lucas joined in. "Even though most of them were taller than she was!"

Anna wiped a tear away. "Yes she was a funny woman, your gran!"

There was an awkward silence a moment that was as deep as it was long. "So where are we going then?" Lucas asked.

"Wherever the train takes us!" his mother answered cryptically. Lucas wondered if they were heading to London but somehow he thought not. If there was one other place that his mother would not wanted tainted with today's sadness, it was surely there. He turned to look out of the window.

City offices and architecturally designed shopping centres soon made way for crumbling terraces and garish multi-coloured high-rise flats as the train left the city centre for the suburbs. One area bled into another, semis and detached houses seeming to vie with one another for his attention, white windows, brown windows, painted windows flying past in a careless whirl of colour. Green spaces stretched out from one estate to another, bridging the gaps between the well-to-do and the less salubrious. After a while the built up areas became less, the green spaces more frequent and then finally the whole conurbation of Birmingham was left behind.

He had never been this far from home. Okay, he told himself, that wasn't actually true. Every year they went on holiday to a rented caravan at the seaside. But this *felt* further. Even though it probably wasn't.

The train stopped several times before it reached its final destination. Each time it stopped he looked towards his mother and she shook her head. Only when it seemed to settle into its final stop did she stand up from her seat. "Well we are here!" she said a little too brightly. She had been silent most of the journey and he wondered if all of her thoughts were about his gran or whether there were some that wondered just how different her own life might be from this day on.

"But where is here?" he asked.

She shrugged. "Doesn't matter, does it? Let's just get you those clothes."

Some of the shops were closed but many were open, despite the fact that it was a Sunday. They looked through a few of the men's shops but the trousers on display were either too formal or too expensive. Sometimes both. "What we really need is a supermarket," his mother declared finally. She went to ask where the nearest was and returned a moment later. "There is a big one at the top of this road, just as it reaches the corner apparently."

The sun had come out whilst they had been in the last shop. As they walked together in the sun's warm glow Lucas thought once more about his gran. "It's funny to think she won't be there in the morning, hogging the bathroom when I am trying to get ready for school, or sitting at the kitchen table drinking tea when I come home…"

Anna reached out and laid her hand on his arm. "She was an old lady Lucas. She had her time. And it's far less a tragedy that she died, than if *you* had."

Lucas was shocked. "How can you say that Mum? She was your mother!"

Anna nodded, not halting or slowing her stride in any way. "Because it's nature. Because the old should always precede the young, because no mother wants to outlive her own child. Believe me, your gran would have been the first to agree with that."

He thought about that for a long time. The supermarket was busy. Busier than he would have thought it might have been. He wondered where all the people who used it lived. Did they live nearby, or had they too travelled miles just to get there? He wondered what his gran would have had to say about all these people.

The clothing selection would not have been considered high fashion but it was adequate for their purposes. "Find something that fits. I'll go get you some shoes," his mother instructed.

Pulling a white shirt and pair of black trousers off the rails, Lucas made his way towards the changing rooms, following the huge signs that hung overhead. It was then that he spotted him. Shop uniform stretched over taut body-building muscles and skin the colour of aged oak, the male assistant was talking to a customer, perhaps advising her. The woman had a basket instead of a trolley and held it against her in a way that made Lucas think it was affected. Something about the proximity of the couple and the angle of their heads seemed incongruous, as if he wasn't merely advising her on products but was intent on flirting with her.

At first Lucas wondered at himself. What did it matter? The woman was not his mother! But it wasn't the woman who had captured his attention. It was the man. Something about the man rang alarm bells in Lucas's head. And yet he couldn't grasp the tail of the thought which evaded his examination. But there was *something* about the man. Something familiar!

'Stuff and nonsense.' He heard his dead grandmother's voice like she was right there beside him. He almost looked to the side, convinced that she would be there, hands on hips and looking… looking… 'as if butter wouldn't melt', his mind finally supplied, using another of her favourite phrases.

But there was definitely something familiar

about the assistant. Something about his muscled arms and the shortness of his neck... Lucas began to walk slowly towards the couple, eyes riveted on the man, uncaring that the stranger might turn and catch him staring. His hair too reminded Lucas of something – some*one*. Lucas hesitated mid-stride as a memory crashed to the forefront of his brain. Walking home from school with Josh. A few months ago. The photo that Josh had been holding, passed to Lucas to admire. The muscled man sitting on a park bench, grass and trees in the background, his skin darker than you would expect of a native Englishman, hair lightened by the fierce American sun.

Lucas was looking at him again. That same man but not the celluloid rendition, the real flesh and blood one. The closest that skin had got to being changed by the foreign sun was a trip to the local beauty salon and the tanning booths it contained, Lucas was willing to bet.

But perhaps his eyes were deceiving him. Perhaps it wasn't Josh's father, the stunt man who stood before him now, but was instead a lookalike. It was possible, wasn't it? Or maybe he was over here making a film? Perhaps he was stunting for someone who played the role of a supermarket sales assistant? But that was ridiculous! Where were the cameras, the lighting men, the make-up women? The *actors*?

He had to know for certain. *But what do I do?*

What do I say? Inspiration came in a flash. "Excuse me, I'm looking for a belt for these trousers. I can't find any."

The man didn't look too impressed at having his flirtation interrupted and for a moment Lucas was a little scared. The woman fiddled with the goods in her basket as if mentally ticking them off, but didn't move away. The assistant glanced down at the trousers then up to Lucas, a wide, false smile on his face. "Those trousers don't have belt loops," he said.

Lucas was transfixed by the smile. There could be no doubt that this was Josh's dad. He was identical to the man in the photo. He couldn't remember what the man had said, he had been too focused on his own thoughts. He wanted to ask the question outright but when he opened his mouth another stream of words erupted. "I have looked everywhere for the belts," he lied, feeling his face redden with the shame of sounding so dumb.

"You don't need a belt for those trousers." Josh's dad leaned forward and pointed to the waistband of the trousers. "See there are no loops for the belt to go through," he said, speaking slowly and concisely as if to a five-year-old. But as he straightened up his name tag became visible once more. Close enough that he could read it now, the words almost sent Lucas into a paroxysm of hysterical laughter.

'Richard Cole', the tag proclaimed, with the store logo, *Happy To Help*, printed jauntily underneath. Lucas staggered backwards away from the couple. What were the chances that today of all days he would uncover the lies and deceptions of someone else's father, when he still hadn't even had a chance to tell his mother that he had discovered who his dad was and that she could now live the life she should have had?

He wondered how he should break the news to his best friend. Josh would be devastated. For years he had believed that his dad was in Hollywood or some other glamorous location. Now Lucas would have to rip that dream from him and replace it with the lacklustre truth that not only was his dad a lowly shop worker, but that it was entirely possible that the whole stunt man thing had been made up just so he could have an excuse not to visit.

Lucas felt a sickness coil at the pit of his stomach. The deception perpetrated upon his friend was like a slap on the face and he wanted to shout and scream at the pathetic man who stood in front of him. *Don't you know how much your son idolises you? Don't you know how proud of you he is and how this will destroy him? Don't you care?*

It would not have mattered to Josh what his father did for a living, whether he was a pilot or a bin man. What *had* mattered was that his father had kept in contact all these years, even if it was sporadic, pretty much only the odd postcard from a foreign land, because that was all he could manage with his busy filming schedule. But now he would be forced to face the truth that his father just couldn't be bothered to visit.

How did you do that? Lucas wondered. *How did you get those cards to arrive stamped with postmarks from Italy and Hawaii and all those places? How did you organise it?* But in the grand scheme of things that was one of the things which mattered the least.

"Lucas? Did you try them on?" his mother asked, appearing with a pair of black shiny leather shoes in his size. He shook his head no, not trusting himself to speak. He had to tear his eyes away from Richard Cole to look at her. Her pupils widened at the sight of his shocked face. "I shouldn't have left you alone, I'm sorry. But I was only over there," she pointed to the shoe racks a little distance away, misinterpreting his pallor for panic that he had somehow lost her too. He tried to smile but his face would not oblige. "Go and try them on now and take the shoes too, that way we will see how it all fits together," she instructed. "I'll wait outside the changing room. Come and show me how it looks when you have it all on."

He nodded and together they made their way over to the changing room. But every step he took from Richard Cole was an effort. Like trudging through sinking sand he felt his limbs held against his will, rooted to the spot, sucked down by forces beyond his control. He wondered if the man gazed at his retreating back. Had he somehow sensed that Lucas was more than he appeared to be? That Lucas would be the undoing of his lies?

And then more worrying thoughts. Should he confront the man? Was that what Josh would have expected him to do? Had the shoe been on the other foot as it were, would Josh confront *his* dad, make him stand up to and acknowledge his responsibilities? On the brink of deciding that this was what he should actually do, he turned around but the moment was lost, the man and the shopper he had been chatting to were gone. Lucas shuffled into the changing room.

He took a long time folding his own clothes and putting the new ones on. Normally he would have just abandoned his clothes to the changing room floor but today was different. Today everything was different and he needed the time and solitude to try to work out in his head what he should do.

Even redressing slowly, he was done more quickly than he would have liked. He regarded his image in the mirror. The new clothes were pristine and sharp but what of the boy inside them he wondered? Was it possible that Hugh Grant was not his father after all? If Josh's dad had turned out to be a supermarket assistant and not

a stunt man, was it possible that Lucas was just
fooling himself? He looked his reflection directly
in the eyes through the medium of the mirror
but what he saw there was not a liar or a cheat
or a self-deluder. What he saw was a boy who
was so desperate for the truth that he had pieced
together disparate clues into one cohesive whole.
And yet it had to be right. It had to be true.
Because if it wasn't…

His eyes regarded him back with a frankness
that reassured him. His mother had gone to
London before he was born. She and his
grandmother had protected his father all this
time, probably fearing his reaction or perhaps the
intrusion of the national press into their lives…
but now that his grandmother was gone, now
that that time was over… things would surely
change. The clues didn't lie. The huge stack of
Huge Grant DVDs in the lounge was not just a
coincidence. It couldn't be! The fact that Lucas's
hair was brown and had a tendency to flop onto
his forehead, that couldn't be a coincidence either
surely! He made his way out of the changing
room.

His mother was where she had said she
would be. It had been a while since they had
been clothes shopping together. But in the past
she had always remarked on how well something
had fitted or not, whether he needed a larger or
smaller size. This time her eyes filled with tears

when she saw him. The orbs shimmered with droplets that splashed onto her cheeks and ran down her neck. She did not lift a hand to wipe them away. "Your gran would have been so proud of you," she whispered, her voice seeming to lack strength and yet booming around him as if relayed through the shop tannoy system.

Lucas felt his stomach heave and all at once the entire contents of his stomach were ejected in a thick puerile rush. Shame and humiliation stopped him from sinking to his knees and he was only vaguely aware of a chair being positioned under him whilst a first aider took his pulse and his mother fretted at his side. "I'm fine, honestly!" he protested.

The manager of the shop appeared. A huge barrel of a man he was not taking no for an answer. "I think under the circumstances Ms Pertwee," he said, after Anna had explained the reason they were there, "the least we can do is offer you a taxi back to the train station. In fact as general manager I am going to provide Lucas with the outfit for the funeral, at no cost to yourself. The shop can easily afford it and we are privileged that you have come so far to shop with us today." Lucas guessed that was business speak for 'it's a good public relations stunt'.

"Thank you Mr Smith," his mother's smile was frayed at the edges. Someone took Lucas to the staff room to get cleaned up and collected his clothes and shoes from the changing room for him. Then he was presented with a large gift-wrapped parcel, presumably containing clean versions of the shoes, shirt and trousers that he had been wearing. Finally they were hustled into a prepaid taxi and sent on their way. *And isn't that a sign too, of how we will be treated once everyone knows the truth of who I am?* Lucas told himself. Strangely there was little comfort in the thought.

CHAPTER 6

The train journey home was particularly depressing. Neither of them seemed to know what to say to the other. Small talk was pointless, an artificial social nicety that was not in keeping with their close relationship; dredging up memories was too painful, too raw for the moment and the future was clouded with uncertainty.

He sat next to the window again, face averted from the other passengers. "How are you feeling now?" his mother asked. He felt the weight of her gaze on him but he kept his eyes on the ever-changing view from the window.

"Terrible."

Anna nodded. "You should stay off school tomorrow. Maybe even for a few days." The train passed through a dark tunnel and in the brief blackness his face was reflected back to him in the fluctuating of window to mirror. Eyes that didn't seem to be his regarded him, their gaze cool and assessing. His skin stretched too tightly over his cheekbones and there was a greasy sheen to it that made it appear to be a waxwork rather than a real-life face.

The mirrored eyes were pools of lightlessness, dark orbs of infinite depth and momentarily he was drawn in. But without warning the image was gone, replaced by redbrick houses, each one a little different from the one before, as if the occupants strove to distinguish themselves from one another. "Will we have to move?" he asked tremulously, wondering if the memories would cause too much pain to allow them to stay. He couldn't bring himself to look at his mother yet but he felt the shrug of her shoulders.

"I don't know. I don't think so because we have lived there since before you were born ... but I really don't know."

"If we do have to move, will I still go to the same school?"

Again she shrugged. Moving didn't seem as big a deal as it once would have. With Josh no longer just across the road, there was nothing to keep him there. Perhaps if they had to move he could get a place in the same school as Josh. They could pick up on their friendship just like nothing had ever happened. Except that it had! A wave of guilt clenched simultaneously at his stomach and his mind. That was almost like saying his gran's death had had a purpose... that it had happened so that his mother was forced to leave their street, following Josh's mum to the other side of town. And then of course there was his father. But that move was just too huge to contemplate right now.

"If we do - have to move I mean, we might as well move to somewhere closer to the sea…" his mother's voice was wistful.

Without him being consciously aware of it, his face swivelled towards hers. "But what about your job?" he asked anxiously.

"I'm only on the tills. I can get a job like that anywhere. And it would be good for us. A fresh start." Icy fingers pinpricked his scalp as if a legion of ants swarmed there. He wanted to claw at his head, scratch it until it bled and the sensations stopped. He sat on his hands to prevent himself carrying out the action.

"But everything we have ever known is here!" His wail was too thin, too reedy to persuade her he feared. "I mean there, where we live."

"Maybe that's exactly why we should move!" She picked up their bags and he realised they were back in Birmingham once more. "Come on, we need to catch the other train home now," she said wearily.

"That's my point!" he stood but did not move towards the aisle. "It's home! It's *always* been home… not just the house but the town and everything in it!" he almost didn't recognise his voice. Perhaps the image from the glass had stolen it, swapped it for one of its own, stolen from a little child decades ago.

With her eyes she propelled him forward, ahead of her and out of the train, waiting until they stood together on the platform once more, the sweet, warm scent of the station filling their nostrils. Lucas drank the scent in like it was perfume. Although they lived a train journey away this was his city, his town's nearest great neighbour and suddenly it seemed the dearest place in the world to him, second only to his home town.

"But you don't …" Anna struggled for the right words. "You never seemed to really like where we live. I mean apart from Josh…" she tailed off.

He knew exactly what she meant – apart from Josh he had no friends there, no reasons to stay. "I don't care if we move house but I don't want to leave town!"

She wrapped her arm around him and together they ascended the stairs, moving from one platform to another where they would catch the train home. People passed to both sides of them, entering and exiting the level they were on. For once it didn't matter that he was anonymous; here he was unknown amongst a bunch of people that were all unknown to each other. In a new town, a new housing estate, a new school he would be even more unknown, new and different to the people who were already gelled into a community. At least where he lived he was not unknown to them all, he was just Lucas - different, set apart. But still known.

Somehow the idea of the rigmarole that he would needlessly be put through elsewhere, the burgeoning friendships, the trial conversations before these new people decided he was too unlike them for a sustainable friendship... it was all too much. "I know I haven't made any other friends where we are. But I'm okay with that." He looked his mother in the eye. "Really. I mean I know the kids around us and they know me. I don't want to be a part of their lives and I'm fine with that. But if we moved... if we went somewhere else where the kids were nicer... and... and I still wasn't a part of them, then I think that would be different. I think I would *feel* different."

Anna said nothing but she tightened her arm around his shoulders. It was the perfect moment to ask about his dad. Perhaps because she could see now how alone he was, perhaps because she too was now more alone than she had been before, she would finally give him the answers he sought. But something held him back. Grief and loneliness were not his alone to bear, he did not have the monopoly on feeling very small within the infiniteness of the universe. His mother had lost her best friend, her confidante, the hand that had guided her through life. She too was struggling with where they went from this point onwards and he would not add to that burden. Not this day anyway.

He pulled away from her encircling arm and reached down to take the heavy bags from her. "Come on we need to go to Platform 5. This way!" He strode forward and found the dense crowd separated to flow around either side of him, as if he cleaved a path through them. He waited for his mother to catch up.

*****

The days of the week blurred into one. There had been so much to do, so much to arrange. When he was tired he slept and when he was hungry he ate, although he was tired far more than he was hungry. It no longer mattered if it was dark when he was awake, light when he was asleep, or whether he ate cereal at 4am and sausages at midnight. He didn't go to school for the whole week. Under the circumstances the school were understanding and anyway his mum needed his support.

The worst thing of all was waiting to hear whether or not there would be an autopsy. In the end, whoever made the decision made the right one and the body was released for the funeral without any further investigation. It was horrible to think that his gran might have had to have been cut open just so that the coroner could confirm that she had died of natural circumstances and Lucas was relieved that she had been spared that indignity.

He helped his mum make a list of everyone who had to be contacted and one by one they worked their way through the names. Even though he had spent every spare moment fretting about how he was going to tell Josh about his dad Richard, Josh was the first name on the list. That had been the hardest phone call of all, Lucas thought. Not just because of what he had said but because of what he *hadn't* said.

"Hi," he had said simply when Josh had answered the call.

"Hi," Josh had responded, sounding glum.

"How's your new home?" Lucas asked, partly because he was interested and partly because he was procrastinating.

"S'okay. But the kids round here are older…" Josh hesitated, unable to say that he missed his friend.

Lucas nodded, even though Josh could not see him. "My gran died!" he blurted out, not knowing any other way to tell Josh.

"Aw Lucas, that's bad!" Josh commiserated. "I liked your gran, she didn't take any crap from anyone."

Lucas smiled into the receiver. He had missed the direct to the point way that Josh had about him. "No, she didn't, did she?" He wondered what his gran's advice would have been if she had known that Lucas knew Josh's dad had been lying to him.

"I'm sad for you man!" Jake sounded completely truthful.

Lucas nodded slowly again. "Thanks, Josh. She fell down the stairs and just died. Just like that. Alive one minute, dead the next."

"No crap!" Josh said, thinking about how quick things had changed for his friend. "When's the funeral? I'm sure Mum will bring me."

"That's one of the reasons I'm phoning. It's on Saturday at 2pm."

"Is she being buried?"

Lucas could hear the faint dread in the other boy's voice and an image of a coffin being lowered into the cold, dark earth assailed him. He shivered involuntarily. "No she's being burned."

"You mean cremated," Josh corrected.

Lucas mentally chastised himself for making it sound as if his gran was being tossed into a fiery pit like a barbequed chicken. "Yeah, cremated. That's the word."

"My dad had to play a dead Viking once. They put him on a flaming raft and sent him down the river to film it."

Lucas thought that the nearest Richard Cole had got to being in the movies was in his son's head. He wanted to shout out that it was rubbish but knew he had to break the news more gently to his friend. "So you'll come? To the cremation thing I mean?"

"I'll ask Mum but I know she'll bring me."

Lucas smiled sadly at the thought that he would soon see his friend again. "There will be some food afterwards so maybe you could stay for a while?"

"Maybe." It was noncommittal but that was because it was not up to Josh, Lucas knew.

"I had better go. I've got some of gran's bingo buddies to call next. My mum can't do them all on her own and she's so upset. All she's done since gran died is cry. Sometimes I think she's finally finished and then she starts up all over again!" He knew that Josh could only try to understand. To really understand something like this, you had to experience it for yourself, Lucas thought.

"That's so bad, man. Okay. But when you are finished phoning round everyone, if you want to talk, just about school and stuff, not about your gran... I mean you can if you want to, if it helps that is... but I don't want you to think that you *can't* talk about her..." Josh twisted himself up in knots trying to reach out to his friend.

"Thanks," Lucas said. Soon the situation would be reversed when he had to tell Josh about Richard Cole. However badly his friend took the news, Lucas vowed to be there for him, whether he was shocked or just upset. Josh would always be there for him and he would return the favour. He hung up slowly, crossed Josh's name off the list and moved on to the next one down. Another number to call, another person to inform, another exclamation to listen to. And all the while, time had been moving slowly forwards, merging one day with another, snuffing out the sun's light to let the darkness take over for just a little while before the sun reclaimed the sky once again.

Lucas sat at his bedroom window and watched the night turn into day. It started with a faint glimmering of lightness in the sky. Not so much light, as more the suggestion of light, as if it teased and tantalised before revealing itself fully. It started far, far away and seemed to travel toward him as if hesitant of his reaction. And yet it needn't have feared him. He was but the tiniest thing in the universe with no ability to influence anything. He had no way to stop the progression of the days just as he had no way to alter anything really.

He sat with the laptop balanced on his knees. Normally he wasn't allowed the computer in his bedroom but what was normal anymore? The cursor blinked, waiting. His fingers trembled with a mixture of anticipation and fear as once more he typed in his father's name. This time the plethora of images and references to his dad did not faze him. He found what he was looking for quickly and clicked on the tab. Slowly he read the article to the end and then went right back to the beginning, reading it again, taking time to chew on the information before he interrogated himself to find out how he felt about it.

Hugh Grant had fathered another three children! Two boys and a girl, meaning that now Lucas had two half-brothers and a half-sister. Neither of the two women who had borne him children were engaged or even married to him. He was as single now as he had been when Lucas was conceived. Surely this mean that his heart still ached for his one true love? That no woman could compare to the charms of Anna Pertwee?

Belatedly he wondered if his mother knew about her rivals for his dad's affections. Did she know he had had other children? Was this just part of the secrecy? Part of the reason she was adamant that no good could come of him knowing his father? And how did he feel about the fact that he had brothers and a sister? That his dad was paying money to support them whist he remained ignorant of Lucas's existence? How different could his life have been if only his mother had stood up to his gran?

Valerie Pertwee had surely been the reason that his mother and father had split up. He wondered what the old lady had said or done to bring his mother home, away from London and away from his father. But for all her flaws, his gran had not been an evil or cruel woman. She must have had some reason to fear her daughter's involvement with the actor. Or had it just been that his gran had worried about them being from a different social class? "From a different world," is how he knew she would have phrased it.

It suddenly occurred to him that perhaps there would be mention of his mother in one of the articles. Perhaps it would state that she and his father had been engaged or show a picture of them walking along the street holding hands. But every article omitted the mention of her name. But there was another way to search. He opened another Google tab and typed in his mother's name. *Anna Pertwee.*

Nothing came up. Not a single thing. Not even pictures of some other woman who just happened to share the same name as his mother. He tried again. *Anna Pertwee and Hugh Grant.* This time many of the previous articles about Hugh grant were presented alongside others which had reference to Anna someone or someone Pertwee but no Anna Pertwee. He read them all anyway but they were mostly cast lists or film reviews and in not one instance was the Anna or the Pertwee mentioned, his mother.

As he scrolled through the list daylight burst through the last strongholds of the night, diminishing the shadows in his room and banishing them to the dark place under the bed.

Saturday morning had come at last. The day of the funeral had arrived. Lucas shut down the laptop and slid it under the bed. He probably wouldn't have a chance to go back on it before night fell once more, but at least he would have it to hand and he could look at pictures of his new family whenever he liked. It was a comforting thought.

In the meantime he had the day to get through.

CHAPTER 7

The new trousers and shirt sat uncomfortably upon him, as if they had been picked for someone else. Clothes too new and smart, shoes too shiny and hair too well combed, he looked nothing like his normal self. But that was fine because he didn't feel much like his normal self either.

"The funeral car is here," his mother said, brushing her hand down his hair even though no strands had dared move from where he had gelled them into place. Lucas nodded. "Would you like to see the obituary?" Anna held the newspaper up so that he could read the printed words without having to touch the paper they were printed on.

Lucas wrinkled his nose at the strong scent of ink which wafted in his direction. The words would have been easier to read if he had accepted the paper from his mother but to do so would mean touching the inky blackness and that was not something he could bring himself to do. Ever. And especially not this day. "Can you hold it a little higher?" he asked, trying to cover his nose with his hands to ward off the smell of the paper and the ink.

"Is this better?"

Lucas nodded. "Valerie Pertwee, Beloved Mother and Grandmother. You will be missed all of the days of our lives." It was signed Anna and Lucas in an italicised font as if they had written their names by hand. "It's nice," he said, not really knowing if that was an appropriate comment but not able to think of anything else to say.

Anna tried and failed to smile. Together they walked to the pavement and climbed into the back of the big black car which waited for them there. Most of the neighbours were outside watching. It was supposed to be a mark of respect when people did that, but Lucas thought that in this instance they were probably only fulfilling a morbid curiosity rather than a social obligation. His mother acknowledged each of them as the car crawled slowly down the street, following the progression of the hearse in front of it. "Don't smile at them!" Lucas grumbled petulantly. They were not his friends and he would not take their sympathy, however fleetingly offered.

"They have come out to show their respect to your gran Lucas!" his mother admonished.

"No mum, they are just glad that it's not one of them!" Through the windscreen he could clearly see the coffin in the other car, festooned with floral tributes from family and friends. He supposed it was as good a coffin as any other, although he had not been involved in choosing it.

He wondered what his gran looked like inside the casket. Did she look the same as she had when she'd died? Or was she already showing the first signs of decay and decomposition? Was that why there was a custom of covering the coffin with flowers? To keep the stench at bay? He wrinkled his nose at the thought and turned his gaze away. Then was immediately ashamed at having the thought about his gran. "Josh will be there, won't he? At the place I mean?"

Anna patted his hand. "His mother is taking him directly to the crematorium. You will see him there." Lucas wished that Josh were here now, that he had people sitting on both sides of him who he could trust to look out for him but he would have to content himself with just his mother for the time being.

The journey seemed to take an age and then when they finally arrived at the too-modern looking building, there were too many people wanting to offer their condolences. They had arrived in droves; old ladies who smelled faintly of wee and others who smelled of lavender or other flowery scents; they came up and gave shaky kisses to his cheeks, planting both hands on his arms and holding him in place until they were done. It was almost too much for him to bear, too much closeness, too many words, far too much sentiment. He clenched himself into his core, steeled himself against the feathery touch of their shrivelled-up lips and desiccated bodies.

"I thought there weren't going to be many people here!" he hissed between clenched teeth.

"So did I. But when I told your gran's bingo buddies they said they would spread the word to all her other friends… I guess she was more popular than we realised!" There was a note of admiration in his mother's voice, a pride that her mother had been so well liked and respected. Lucas felt nothing but exasperation. The condolences were taking forever and he just wanted the whole thing to be over and done with. He mustered one final sad smile and pushed his way through the crowd and into the building.

"Excuse Lucas!" he heard his mother apologise to those he barged rudely past, oblivious to the hands held out, the withered cheeks proffered, "This has hit him particularly hard. He was alone with Mum when she had her accident."

Josh was waiting for him inside. A relief at the sight of his friend washed over him. He could face whatever horrors lay ahead now that Josh was here. Neither boy greeted the other, there were no handshakes, no clasps on the back, just acceptance of one another's being was enough. Josh's mum leaned across her son to offer her own condolences. "She was a lovely woman, your gran." She patted Lucas on the knee as if it was the most natural thing in the world.

He wanted to dash her hand away and rub at the spot on the material she had touched but he let it be. Josh might be offended if he gave in to the urge. Music started up from somewhere unseen, speakers that were hidden behind curtains and statues that were designed to look old and weathered.

He recognised some of the tunes. They were old songs, not hymns. Valerie, for all her failings had never been a church-going woman and Lucas was relieved. Hymns about God and the Devil, good overcoming evil, and the rise of mankind to the status of angels would have been too much for him to bear.

His mother slid onto the pew next to him. With her one side and Josh on the other, he felt suddenly stronger. He watched the funeral directors carry the coffin in and down the aisle to place it on an alter at the front. A man stepped forward to the small podium at the side of the alter. His smile was benign, compassionate, and to Lucas at least, transparently false.

"Valerie Pertwee was an unusual woman," he read aloud from the notes Lucas's mother had compiled. "And that has been reflected in how she has been brought into this chapel today. Not first in the line, with her mourners behind her, but last of all with her audience already seated, making her grand entrance to the last party of her time." There were murmured laughs, quiet words of agreement. Lucas tuned them all out. *Nothing lasts forever*, he thought. *Not even death. You die, you rot away and then one day everyone who ever knew you, ever loved you, is gone too – and you are nothing, not even the smallest grain of sand – and it is like you never existed at all!* He shuffled in his seat uncomfortably.

At his side Anna took his hand. His mother's hand was warm and reassuring. From the corner of his eye he noticed that Josh and his mother also held hands. Neither of them had loved Lucas's gran in the way that he and his mother did and yet they were touched by her death. He wondered if it was a sense of loss they felt or whether they were merely touched by the sense of their own mortality, a sense of the fleetingness of life.

He was aware that different people gave speeches about his gran. He knew there was a special word for it but he couldn't bring it to mind. He didn't listen to any of them. Instead he thought about how he was going to break the news to Josh about his father. Then there was music again and an absence of words. Lucas was surprised to see the heavy velvet curtains closing in front of the coffin, shielding it from his view. He looked at his mother, suddenly startled out of his reverie. "What's happening? Where is she going?" The words were issued on a croak as if his vocal chords had lain too long unused.

"It's over honey. Now she goes to be cremated."

"WHAT!" he shrieked and shot up from his seat. Heads turned but he paid them no heed. "THEY ARE GOING TO BURN HER NOW?"

His mother nodded.

"NOW? When she's only just dead?" his voice made an exclamation of the question.

"It's been over a week Lucas. She's been gone for over a week," Anna Pertwee spoke softly.

"What do you mean *gone*? She was gone everyday - gone down the shops, gone down the bingo! She's not FUCKING GONE! SHE'S DEAD!" He heard his voice as if it did not belong to him. He had sworn, not just in front of his mother but actually *at* his mother and he was both ashamed and shocked at himself. A tremble that seemed to start in his toes overtook his whole body and suddenly he felt frozen to the core, hollow and without substance.

Everyone was looking at him. Maybe in sympathy but more likely in horror. He did not dare to meet their eyes to find out which. "Anna if you need any help…" an old man placed a hand on his mother's shoulder.

"Thank you Mr Bulmer but we will be fine thank you. Why don't you go on ahead and we will see you at the pub?" Anna spoke to the man without her eyes ever leaving her son. The man shuffled off. Soon everyone had left, everyone except for him and his mum and Josh and Josh's mum. "Lucas I know how deeply this has affected you but you have got to hold yourself together. Do you understand? It's not what your gran would have wanted. You know that!"

Lucas nodded, embarrassment flushing his face a deep red. Anna turned her attention to Sandra Cole. "You are coming to the send-off aren't you?"

"Yes of course." Sandra's voice was full of pity, soft and unassuming. Lucas thought that she would do well to save her pity – her son was going to need all of her attention in just a little while.

"Do you want to come with us in the funeral car?" Anna asked.

"Thanks but I drove here, so I had better drive and meet you there. But I'm sure Josh would like to go with you and Lucas." Josh nodded.

"Thank you," Anna said, presumably for granting Josh permission to accompany his friend.

The funeral car did not seem so big with another person sitting inside it. It also didn't drive as slowly to the pub as it had on the way to the service, Lucas noticed. He wondered whether that was standard procedure, or whether the driver was desperate to offload him. No one talked in the car, although he was sure they all had a lot to say. They sat together but alone, each steeped in their own silence.

The pub was filled with the same faces he had seen at the funeral service. At the far end of the room, long buffet tables groaned under stacks of sandwiches and plates of pork pies. There were bowls of crisps and plates of fancy little cakes, sausages on sticks and all sorts of dips and salads, all cling-filmed for freshness. The room went quiet as they entered, the conversation not dying softly away but instead halting abruptly mid-flow. Lucas felt his flush re-emerge. Had his behaviour been the main topic of conversation?

Anna cleared her throat. "I'm sure we are all aware that these things are always difficult. Please don't stop your conversations. Don't hesitate to mention my mother in case it will cause offence or upset to me or Lucas. We would be the first people to admit that Valerie Pertwee was a strong character and feistier than a man twice her size could ever have been," Anna laughed but it was a rather pitiful sound as if it was only part humour and part hysteria.

"She would have been the first to come up with a funny tale if she had been here… so tell your stories and let's celebrate her life. And please help yourself to the food… Mum would have hated it to go to waste!" She smiled sadly. "To Valerie Pertwee!" she took a filled glass from a tray on the bar and lifted it in a toast.

Lucas copied her and held his own glass high before swallowing the sweet sherry back in one mouthful, grimacing at the after-burn as the fiery liquid made its way down his throat.

"I have to circulate a little. Will you be okay here with Josh?" his mother asked.

"Yeah, course." He was relieved that finally he would have some time alone with his friend. The information was burning a hole in his brain. The sooner it was out, the better, he thought. Anna gave him a kiss on the forehead and moved away.

Josh's mum was talking to an old lady and seemed engrossed in the conversation. Lucas handed Josh one of the glasses of sherry. "Drink it fast before anyone notices," he instructed. "It's not that nice but it gives you a kind of weird numb feeling for a while." He watched Josh swallow back the liquid. "I have something to tell you," he began hesitantly.

"If it's that someone has moved into our old house…"

"No it's not that," Lucas cut him off abruptly. "It's about your dad."

"My dad?" Josh's lips tightened almost imperceptibly. Lucas wouldn't normally have noticed except that they were standing closer than usual, pushed together by the volume of people in the room and the need to distance themselves from the old folk.

"I saw him. When Mum and I went to buy me these clothes for the funeral."

"You saw who?" Josh asked as if he wasn't following the conversation. Lucas wondered if it had been a mistake after all to give him the sherry. But wasn't that what people gave you when you'd had a shock? But of course Josh hadn't had the shock yet, had he? Lucas had pre-empted it by dosing him up first.

"I saw *him*. Your dad!"

Josh just looked at him like he had gone mad. "He's in Honolulu."

Lucas cocked his head to one side. "The postcard said he was in Hawaii not Honolulu."

"Oh yes. That's it. That was what I meant. Hawaii. Not Honolulu."

This was proving to be even harder than Lucas had anticipated. "Hawaii, Honolulu, Helsinki… it doesn't matter, it's all lies!"

Josh's head jerked sharply backwards as if it was trying to disengage itself with its body but it was his eyes which held Lucas's attention. The pupils did not dilate or contract, the orbs themselves did not widen in surprise and yet they changed significantly. Lucas could not explain it adequately in his mind but it was almost as if shutters came down behind his friend's eyes. "What do you mean it's all lies?" Josh said but it was not a question. It was a challenge.

"I mean he's not abroad. He doesn't work in

Hollywood. He's not a stuntman… he's a salesman in a supermarket," Lucas kept his voice level but firm. He wanted Josh to know how sorry he was to have to break this news to him.

"You evil bastard!" Josh hissed through clenched teeth. "You are only saying this because you don't have a clue who your dad is… you just dreamed up some stupid idea that he is Hugh Grant. As if Hugh Grant would even look at your mum!"

Lucas took a step back away from the vicious words, the hostile attack. "I'm not making this up, I swear Josh!" Lucas tried hard to ignore the intended insult. But Josh was not going to let it go.

"Hugh Grant and your mum… it's fucking ridiculous!"

It was the profanity in the middle of the sentence that hurt, embellishing the word with a sense of honesty that Lucas could no longer ignore. "It's not as fucking ridiculous as your dad getting someone to send postcards from their holiday, pretending to be him, whilst all the time he is chatting up women doing their food shopping in a crappy city centre supermarket!" Unintentionally his voice rose, becoming louder and yet colder with every word.

Each word seemed to hover, quivering in the air before finding its mark. Like bullets he saw the words hit his friend, saw him rebound from the verbal onslaught, face becoming paler as if the blood was drawn from there to a mortal wound. And yet not once did Josh's eyes widen in surprise; not once did he look as if any of this was new information to his ears.

He knew! Lucas realised. *All the time he's been getting the postcards, all the time we've been friends, all these years… he has been lying to me. And lying to himself…*

Lucas never saw the punch which felled him, landing square in the centre of his chin. He staggered backwards, knocking the tray of glasses from the bar and sending them crashing onto the floor, bright shards of glass still covered in a sherry film, the dark red liquid coating the glass like blood. He never felt the hands that pulled him to his feet but he felt them restrain him as he tried to pull away, tried to launch himself at his one-time best friend.

"I think you had better take your son home," a male voice said from behind him, so close that it had to be his unidentified captor.

Lucas thought the man referred to him so was surprised when it was Josh's mum who answered. "Yes, I will." She looked at Anna who appeared beside Lucas, face bloodless and eyes filled with pain. "I'm so sorry Anna. About your mother and now this… I don't know what is going on with these two!"

Anna said nothing. She watched as Josh was

led away by his mother. Only then did she speak, once Josh was out of sight and gone. "Thank you Mr Bulmer. You can let him go now."

Lucas felt his arms released. He wanted to rub at where the muscles had been strained and also his throbbing chin but he would not give the onlookers the satisfaction. "I know how hard this is for you Lucas. But please spare a thought for me! The woman we cremated today was your gran but she was my *mother*. Can you imagine how bad I feel, seeing you fighting at my mother's send-off? Can you even try to put yourself in my shoes? For just one moment? Can you?" tears scalded Anna's face, running in thick streams down her cheeks and dripping off the ends.

Lucas hung his head in shame. "I'm sorry!"

"I know. I know. Look we have to stay here for another hour or so. We have to give your gran the send-off she deserves. Can you sit quietly for a little while? Then we can finally go home and be done with this terrible day!"

He nodded slowly. She pulled him to her and he buried his face in the smooth warmth of her neck. Everything in his world was wrong and he could see no way to ever make it right again.

CHAPTER 8

He reached under the bed for the laptop. It felt strangely wrong for it to be in his room in the middle of the night, when darkness patrolled outside the window like an intruder, seeking a way into the deepest vestiges of his soul.

He stared at it for a moment without switching it on, willing himself to replace it under the bed and knowing he didn't have the courage to do so. He couldn't *know* his father and *not know* him at the same time. He couldn't know his name, his identity, his face and leave it at that, not follow it up in any way. He wasn't brave enough to face the world alone after all!

He pressed the on button and watched the computer flick into life. Without conscious thought he searched for the best way to contact his dad. Twitter seemed the most obvious and instant method, since it was listed that his dad had an account there.

Speedily he signed up for the social media site and listed his details sketchily. It didn't matter that he had no picture listed and divulged next to nothing about himself, he wasn't intending to post tweets; the account was merely a means to an end. He took a few minutes to investigate the site, seeing how it worked and how he could use it to achieve what he desired. There was a direct messaging service, thankfully, meaning that he didn't have to send the message out to the world at large. He clicked on the icon.

What was he to write? How should he begin? With some explanation about who he was? Too boring! His dad would probably not even bother to read further. What if he said he liked his films? Surely that was something every actor liked to hear. But it reeked of a suck-up! He didn't want to suck-up to him, he wanted him to know that he was his father! He positioned his hands over the keyboard. He was over-thinking it. When he overthought anything it always turned out badly. Perhaps it was best to just go with the impulse of gut reaction, or whatever it was called. He typed.

'Hi. You don't know me. But you knew my mother, Anna Pertwee. I know that you will remember her even though it was a long time ago.' He pressed send. Then reread it. Perhaps he shouldn't have put 'knew' perhaps he should have written 'know' instead? Did putting 'knew' make it sound as if she had died, he worried.

There was no answer from his father, not that he expected him to be up, waiting for a mystery message from a son he didn't know existed. He typed again. *'She's fine. Anna I mean. My mother. Anyway I wanted you to know that she never got married or had any more children. Just me. 14 years ago.'* He pressed send. Started another message.

'I know you never got married either so I guess you never met anyone you loved as much as her. And I realise you didn't know anything about me. You didn't know that I was your son. They kept it hidden from you, Mum and Gran. I don't know why but they did. But now you do know.' He pressed send. *'Gran is dead and so you and Mum can get back together now! And we can be a family like we should have been before.'* He hit send again and watched the words appear next to the previously sent sentences.

There was nothing more to say. Without a response to validate them, his words floated on the screen aimlessly. But once his father was awake, once his butler brought him his morning coffee then surely there would be a response. Although maybe not on Twitter. Maybe his father would just jump into his chauffeur driven limousine and race to Lucas's house. Or maybe he would send a helicopter to pick him and his mum up? Whatever the response, Lucas knew it would be life-changing. He closed the computer down. Since he no doubt had a busy day ahead, packing up his things ready for the move to London or New York, wherever his father was currently filming, perhaps he should grab some sleep whilst he could.

Stomach churning excitedly, it was hard to drift off, knowing what excitement lay ahead of him, what adventures and privileges he could not even adequately dream of. He imagined that it was not the pillow which cushioned his head but a soft mound of the whitest sand. Soft waves lapped at his feet and the chirping of the dawn chorus was not a flock of starlings and common sparrows, all dull brown feathers and squat little bodies. It was instead the melodic call of bright white-chested gulls and exotic sea birds, species with colourful feathers and sleek aerodynamic bodies. They flew in circles high in the sky above him, the shadows they cast flowing rapidly over his body.

Someone was talking though. Arguing in a voice that seemed hushed as if trying to suppress the volume that normally accompanied words of anger. His unconscious clamped on to the thought and tried to incorporate it into the dream. It was not words after all, it was the babbling of a troop of baboons, calling to one another from the tops of the nearby trees... But it wasn't baboons! Somewhere down in the deepest part of his unconscious mind the thought resurfaced. It was a whispered argument. Two people. A man and a woman. And the woman's voice was his mother's.

Without being aware that he was awake, Lucas stumbled through the doorway and into the hall, taking care on the steps, lest the same thing happen to him that had happened to his gran. His mother stood in the doorway still in her dressing gown, hand holding the door partially closed, barring the entrance of the man who stood outside, looking inwards. Looking at Lucas. "Hello son," the man said.

"Who are you?" Lucas asked.

The man looked at Lucas's mother then back at Lucas. "Me? Lucas, I'm your dad!"

*****

There had to be some mistake! This wasn't Hugh Grant! Lucas shook his head, desperately trying to clear away his sleep befuddled thoughts. "No. No you are not him!" Lucas shouted. But perhaps he had heard wrong? Had the man said he had come to fetch them for his dad? "Oh! Did you mean you are taking us to him?" a frown pulled Lucas's brows together as he tried to make sense of it all.

"No Lucas what I said was that *I* am your dad!" he spoke Lucas's name like he was unused to curling his tongue around it.

"How do you know my name?" Perhaps it wasn't the most pertinent question but Lucas was beginning to suspect that there was more going on here than he could fathom.

"Because I am your dad," the man repeated, seemingly refusing to tell the truth for some reason.

"So *you* say! But I know you are not!" For a start he was just too ordinary. Average height, average weight, nothing, absolutely nothing about the man was anything more than average...

"Anna what have you been telling the boy?" the stranger's voice had more than an inquisitive edge to it, a sharpness that belied the fact that its speaker was an absolute stranger to both him and his mother.

"Martin calm down! He doesn't know anything about you..." Anna reached forward to the man, placing a hand on his shirt-sleeved arm. Lucas's eyes were drawn to the joining of the two arms; it was not a gesture you would perform on a stranger and yet he couldn't imagine for one moment that what this man said was true. It couldn't be!

"Look there are things we need to talk about," the man looked from Anna to Lucas and then back into the empty street.

"No Martin there's nothing to talk about. What's done is done..." Anna stated.

"I've left her!" he indicated the suitcase at his feet. "Look can I come in or do you really want to talk about this in the street?" he asked pointedly.

Lucas was dumbstruck. There were too many things happening here for him to comprehend, too many words, too many conflicting emotions coursing through him as if on a race to the winning line. Anna said nothing but she stepped backwards allowing the stranger entry. Lucas stepped into the space, barring the man's passage.

"Lucas, step back," his mother instructed. "Lucas, please!" she pleaded, "please let him in and you can finally get all your questions answered!" But there was no joy in her eyes, no light of expectation, just a dull flatness as if her worst fears were coming to life. Lucas stepped back.

"Come into the kitchen." Anna led the way. The stranger followed and Lucas was left alone to close the door. For a moment he stood gazing at its invitation to step out, walk away and leave his life behind. But where could he go? To his dad's house in London? He might not even be there at the moment! The best course of action was to message him urgently; to tell him that an imposter had arrived, claiming to be his father and that if he, his real dad, didn't get a move on, everything might be lost!

Reaching towards the door to push it closed, he noticed movement behind some of the windows which overlooked the front of his house. The stranger's arrival had not gone unnoticed. It wasn't hard to guess what everyone would be gossiping about over the next few days... the stranger who had turned up at his house with a suitcase! He shut the door as quickly but with as much dignity as he could muster.

They were already in the kitchen sitting opposite one another at the table, a vacant sea for him between them. He stood in the doorway looking pointedly at the empty chair, the one so obviously meant for him. The stranger's suitcase had been placed on the floor next to the sink. Lucas wanted to pick it up and hurl it through the closed kitchen window. Then somehow make the man follow it.

"Sit down Lucas." Anna sounded somewhere between worried and resigned.

"I'm not sitting *there*."

"Okay, then sit here." Anna stood up, giving him her chair and moved to the seat between the stranger and Lucas. "Martin, there are things you and I need to talk about but that can wait." Anna turned back to her son. "Lucas I guess I owe you some explanation. This isn't how I thought things would be but..."

"It's not how I ever wanted them to be..." the stranger interrupted.

Anna was suddenly angry. She turned on the stranger with the speed and ferocity of a lioness, protecting her cub. "You! Be quiet!" she said to the man. Lucas's jaw dropped, he had never seen his mother like this before. "You have caused enough damage just by turning up here! Now stay out of it and let me tell him my way!"

The man nodded but Lucas could see that he was not happy with this development. "Lucas this is Martin Jones and he is your father," Anna said.

"But you and Hugh Grant are my parents!"

Anna barked a startled laugh. "How on earth did you get that idea?"

Lucas didn't like the thought which sprang immediately to his mind but he could not silence it. "You mean you were cheating on Hugh Grant with... with... *him*?" The incredulousness in his voice was not lost on the stranger and he raised his eyebrows in response.

"Honey I don't know Hugh Grant! I mean I know who he is and I like his films but I have never even met him."

"But the weekends in London... and all the DVDs! And then why would you never tell me who my father was?" He refrained from looking at the stranger, still unconvinced it was not all some huge misunderstanding.

"The weekends in London were before you were born and they were well... that can wait for another time." She tried to take hold of Lucas's hands but he moved them away from her, needing to keep his head clear of emotions so that he could fully take in what she was telling him. "This man *is* your father. There is absolutely no doubt of that."

"So why has he been gone all these years? And why has he turned up now? And why did you always say that no good could come of me knowing who he is?" There were a million other questions flooding his brain but he suppressed them, trying to concentrate.

Anna sighed. "He has been gone all this time because I sent him away just after you were born…"

"So it was *your* fault!" Lucas turned on his mother, needing a focus, an outlet for his rage. He could have had a loving family all these years if only…

"It wasn't like that Lucas!" Anna washed her hands over her face then clasped them before her mouth, as if about to say a prayer. Lucas felt a deep churning inside of him, a swirling mess of emotions that threatened to drown him in their darkest depths. On the very surface there was some acknowledgement of how hard this must be for his mother but that thought was suppressed by the more pressing righteousness that he felt for his own problems. "I didn't want to tell you like this. I didn't want to ever have to tell you but now I've no choice." She cast a surreptitious glance at his father. "When I met Martin he was already married."

A strange tickling sensation assailed Lucas, as if a legion of cockroaches crawled over his naked torso. It was an unpleasant and deeply disturbing sensation and he wanted to claw at his clothing and flesh until he was done with it.

"We worked together…"

"Where?" he interrupted, not really caring but feeling the need to butt in, to regain the control that he felt slipping away.

"At Anderson's. You have heard me mention it before. The big company I used to work as a receptionist at." Lucas remained silent. He remembered his mum mentioning it once or twice before in conversation. "Martin was the sales manager there. We fell in love. At first I didn't know he was married but then…" she shrugged her shoulders as if that made it all okay.

"He was married but you started an affair with him? Because you were *in love*," he spat the words out contemptuously, "and that just made everything okay, did it? It's okay what we do, who we hurt, because we are in love – is that what you told yourself?" Lucas stood up abruptly, pushing his chair away from the table and catapulting himself out of it. The chair crashed to the floor and lay there, he kicked it away from him, sending it spinning towards the suitcase, knocking it over with a whack.

The sound ricocheted around the room like a slap. "I know you must be hurt by all this… information," Martin said, looking at Lucas as if he actually cared.

"You! You don't know anything! You don't

know me and you don't know anything about me!" Lucas thundered. Every muscle in his body felt tense, coiled as if ready to spring into action. He moved his gaze to his mother. "And as for you…" Words failed him and he suspected he wouldn't have been able to get them out over the huge lump that had appeared in his throat anyway. His mother might not have been perfect but he had never thought her as low as he now did.

"You have done the same thing Josh's neighbour did to his mum and dad!" He ripped his gaze away from her. He could no longer bear to see the pain in her eyes and feel that same pain amplified in his heart. "You had sex with a man who was married to someone else! Where did you do it? In the back of his car? Up an alley?" His tone became more strident with every word.

"Lucas that's enough! Don't speak to your mother like that!" Martin warned, beginning to push himself away from the table.

"Martin, Lucas, please stop!" Anna pleaded, a single teardrop sliding down her cheek to rest on one corner of her mouth. The same mouth she had kissed him goodnight with. The same mouth she had kissed the adulterer with!

"You are nothing but a *whore!*" Lucas hissed, running out of the room and up the stairs, cocooning himself in his bedroom, his safe haven, where the laptop had sent his message to Hugh

Grant, his *real* dad. He threw himself onto the bed and curled into the smallest ball that he could. No one followed him up the stairs and reprimanded him. Neither did anyone come and kiss him and tell him everything would be alright. He already knew that nothing was alright. Nothing would ever be alright. Ever again.

CHAPTER 9

"Why are you here?" Lucas could just about make out his mother's voice through the closed kitchen door. He had lain on his bed for some time, angry and resentful, before he had realised that his mother and this Martin were probably talking about things in his absence that they might not have revealed in his presence. He had stifled his sobs and crept down the stairs. After his dramatic exit, one of them had closed the door so he was able to sit comfortably enough on the bottom step and eavesdrop.

"I left her."

"Yes I gathered that," his mother responded dryly. "But why now?"

"Why not now? I only wish that I had done it years ago... but then your mother..."

"My mother would never have stood in our way if you had really wanted to make an honest woman of me! What she couldn't tolerate, wouldn't allow, was you keeping me on the side, having your wife *and* me and leaving me dangling, never knowing when or where I would see you again."

There was a silence then and Lucas tried to imagine how each of them was reacting to her words. Was he nodding or shrugging his shoulders? Had he taken her into his arms and kissed her objections away? In the silence anything might be happening! Lucas desperately hoped his mother was not weak enough to succumb to the man a second time!

"It was difficult at the time! You know that Anna!"

"You had an excuse for everything! The timing wasn't right! We had to think of your job! There was always something!"

He didn't deny it. "Yes things were difficult at the time but it's different now."

"Different how?" Behind the scepticism, Lucas thought he detected something else in his mother's tone. He strained his ears to catch it again.

"I saw the obituary. In the paper I mean."

"So now my mother is dead you think you can just pick up where we left off! How do you know I don't already have a man in my life?"

"Well do you?" he asked slowly as if the idea had never once occurred to him.

"There have been men... but I found I couldn't trust any of them. Not because of even who or how they were but because of you... because of what you had put me through!" Lucas was surprised at that information. His mother had dated other men? Who? And when? If it was true, it was yet another of her well-kept secrets. He wondered how many more there were.

"I'm sorry!" the man said.

"That's it, is it? You're sorry and that makes everything okay?"

"It was your choice to finish!" he said petulantly.

"I had just had your baby and you were living with your wife! I hardly think that was really a choice was it?" she threw back at him.

Lucas felt the words hit him like a blow. This Martin who said he was his father had known him when he was a baby. He had known he had a child and had still walked away! Lucas felt more adrift than he had ever felt before. Was this why his gran and his mother had resisted telling him all these years? Because they understood that once he knew his father had known that he existed and still had walked away, he would feel worthless, like he was less than nothing?

He felt as though a pit as wide as the Grand Canyon yawned beneath his feet. There was a darkness there that had nothing to do with the lightlessness of the hallway and everything to do with the absence of hope in his soul.

"I couldn't leave her, not then! Not when she had just lost our baby! You really couldn't have expected that of me, surely!" Louder, as if he was getting angry.

"What I expected Martin, was that when you told me you were no longer sleeping with your wife, that it was the truth!"

"It *was* the truth!"

"So how was it that her and I both managed to be pregnant at the same time?"

Lucas gasped at the implications as his mother's words sunk in. The man was not just an adulterer, he was a liar and a cheat. He wondered if there were any children from this marriage, any half-brothers and sisters he might have.

"I swear it was the truth Anna. You have to believe me." He took a rasping breath as if struggling to contain his emotions. "You know that before you and I met she had had a few miscarriages. I had said enough was enough and we stopped trying for a child. Or at least I did. Things changed then within the marriage. She grew distant and I met you. But one night when you and I first started seeing one another she crept back into my bed. She said she had heard a noise and was scared... but... well you can imagine the result. But it was one time! One time only! I swear!"

There was another silence, longer this time. "Then you were both pregnant at the same time and I didn't know what to do. But our baby survived, yours and mine... whilst mine and hers died. What was I supposed to do? I couldn't leave her on her own and you had your mother to help you!"

"Look Martin I do understand," Anna said slowly. "But all these years since... all these years when we could have been together... what kept you away then?"

"I honestly don't know! Pride? Stupidity? The fear that you would laugh in my face or turn me away at the door? The belief that you would already have found someone else... all of those things and none of them. The truth is that I just felt that I had made my bed and that I ought to at least have the guts to lie in it!"

"And now?" she prompted, softer than before, as if she was being worn down despite her reservations.

"And now, what can I say?" Lucas was sure Martin was now shrugging his shoulders. "I saw the obituary and it made me think. It made me think about you and about Lucas and about how fleeting and short life can really be. None of us know how long we have or what fate holds in store for us but to pass up on someone or something you love, just because you haven't got the stomach to chance a knock-back, well that's just cowardice isn't it?"

Lucas hated to admit it but Martin's words were beginning to make him feel sorry for the man. He pulled himself up about it. *Whatever he says about what he did, why he did it, doesn't take*

away from the fact that he let Mum down and he left
her to bring me up with just her mother for help.

"And I never abandoned you. Financially I mean." Lucas wondered what he meant by the comment. "I know I couldn't afford much maintenance, but I paid what I could." Something in his tone changed. "In fact I often wondered why you stayed here with your mum. With the money I sent, you could have rented a nice little house somewhere…"

"You mean this isn't a nice little house?" Anna said acidly.

"No, you know I didn't mean that! What I meant was, well I never thought you would just continue to live with your mother."

"Mum stuck by me. I had a baby and then when I couldn't face having to see you every day and had to change jobs, the best I could get was some shifts at a local store, not even enough to pay for a child-minder. Mum helped out and by the time Lucas was at school, it was her who needed my help! We just got stuck here. Now, with Mum gone… I don't know."

"We can start again Anna. If you will let us?"

She didn't answer his question but instead answered one which he had not voiced. "The money you sent went straight into a bank account for Lucas for when he is older. In case he goes to university or wants to put down a deposit on a flat." Despite the darkness he sat in, Lucas felt his pupils contract in surprise. There were so many secrets. So many things he had known nothing about. Had his whole life been built upon sands that were now shifting?

"That was a great thing to do," Martin said, not pushing her for fear that she would reject him.

"Look Martin. I am not denying that I was madly in love with you. But that was then and to be perfectly honest I don't know *how* I feel anymore. You can't just turn up and expect me to make an instant decision."

"Yes I know. I understand."

"Before I say anything else I need to know two things. Will you answer me truthfully?" she asked hesitantly.

"Yes. Anything."

"Did you have any more children with your wife? And did you tell her about us, either then or now?"

Lucas was almost in physical pain from straining his ears to listen. He crept closer, unwilling to miss either answer.

"We never had any more children. For a long time after you finished it with me I was depressed, angry, filled with mood swings. She thought it was because of the miscarriages, her inability to give me a child. In the end it didn't seem fair that she shouldered all the blame for how I was behaving and reacting, out late drinking and brawling some nights… sometimes not home until the early hours of the morning. So I told her about you. She was angry and hurt but she accepted that I had stayed with her, whatever the reason. It was enough for her at the time."

He sighed. "All these years we have lived separate lives, like tenants just sharing a house. It's been miserable for me and for her. So when I told her that it was time we released one another I actually think she was relieved." He laughed abruptly. "She kissed me on the cheek and it was the first physical contact that I swear we have had in a decade, other than when I asked her to pass the salt." He tailed off, perhaps feeling that there was nothing left to say.

"This is not going to be easy, you know!" Anna warned but there was a warmth to her words that had not been present before, Lucas thought. He wondered what the 'this' that she referred to might be. "As I said, I don't know what I feel right now, and even what I might begin to feel in the future, for you and for us. But Lucas does need a father, now more than ever. Since Mum died he has been angry and there's a pent-up fury in him that sometimes frightens me."

Lucas was surprised to hear his mother speak about him in such a way. A pent-up fury that frightened her? He thought about the fracas at the funeral. That hadn't been his fault surely had it? It was Josh who had swung a punch at him! But then another image sprung into his mind: him smashing his wrist into the porcelain bowl when she and his gran refused to tell him anything about his father.

Had his temper been over the top? Was his mother really worried about him or was it just something that she had said, more spur of the moment than anything else? Certainly no one at school considered him a threat! In fact the very opposite was true! He dreaded going back to school without his friend at his side. Not only that but he was fairly sure that the story of the stranger with the suitcase at his door would be all over the school. The other kids would be sniggering and making innuendos and not even having the decently to wait until he was out of earshot.

"So I can stay?" Martin asked hopefully.

She must have nodded because Lucas did not hear her verbally agree. "But if I change my mind at any time, I don't want any arguments. I want you just to go. Okay?"

"Of course! But I promise to respect your wishes in everything Anna. Just so long as you let me try to make things up to you. I know that might never be possible. But I am prepared to spend my whole life just trying, if only you will let me!"

Lucas was horrified. Was she really going to let him move in? "You can sleep in my room and I will take Mum's for the time being. If we have any chance of making this work we have to make sure that Lucas is okay with it. However hard that is and however long it takes."

"Yes of course. Anything that gives us the chance to be a family," he agreed immediately.

Anything that gives you the chance to be with her again; to be in her bed again, more likely, thought Lucas.

His mother's next words almost echoed his thoughts. "But there will be nothing physical between us Martin. Not until I see Lucas is alright and until I am sure that's what I want too."

"Of course." He actually managed to sound sincere, Lucas thought.

"Okay, then I guess you had better get unpacked and I had better go explain everything to Lucas!"

He heard the scrapes of their chairs as they stood up. Before they had opened the kitchen door he was already up the stairs, safely ensconced in his own room as if he had not moved. He pulled open a magazine and pretended to be engrossed in it as his mother tapped lightly on the bedroom door and came in, closing it softly behind her.

"Are you alright?" she asked worriedly, smoothing his hair back from his forehead. He let her do it even though it annoyed him. It soothed her, made her think that he was more receptive and that suited him. Whatever she thought, he would never be happy that this Martin might be his father. Not after he had believed himself to be the son of Hugh Grant! He felt stupid beyond belief for having built his own hopes so high but he also felt duped, as if by refusing to tell him the truth when he had asked, she had fed his daydream, manipulated him into self-deception.

"He really is your father," she said as if he still doubted it.

He said nothing as if the information had no impact upon him. Anna didn't smile. "He is going to stay here for a while. But only if you are okay with it."

He wasn't sure if it was a question or just a comment. He shrugged.

"*Are* you okay with it?" It was definitely a question this time but he did not feel inclined to answer. He shrugged again. "Is there anything you want to know?" she asked. He stared at her. Was she really offering to answer *any* question now? When she'd avoided them all before, even the simplest things about what his father might have liked or not liked. Whether he preferred peas to green beans... cucumbers to tomatoes?

He realised now they were the wrong questions. What he should have asked was why his father had chosen the dead baby over the live one... the wife he did not love over the girlfriend that he claimed he did love. But these were not questions he could put to his mother, or that she could answer. He asked her one she could. "Where did he live?"

"Do you mean when I met him?" she waited for her son to nod his head. "I don't know if they stayed there but when I met him he had a house a few miles from here. Just outside of Peddlington."

"So he lived about ten minutes from here?" the nearness of his father astounded him.

Anna nodded. "It was one of the things that terrified your gran. That one day we would be forced to tell you who he was and that you would go off and find him. That he would still be married and that he would turn you away at the door. We didn't know if he'd had other children or how he would feel if you had turned up. All your gran and I cared about was that you didn't get hurt."

Her words put a different spin on how he had always seen their refusal to talk. So much so, that he tried to hide his confusion in other questions. "So does he have other children?" he asked, not wanting her to know how much he had learned by listening to their private conversation in the kitchen.

His mother shook her head. "No. No other children. It's complicated I guess. He never really wanted to leave either of us but the situation... well let's just say that for him there was no right answer."

Put like that, Lucas could see how impossible the situation must have seemed. Either way someone would have been hurt, someone abandoned. He could see the impossibility of it but he still wished that it had been the other woman who had been hurt, the other woman who had been abandoned. "Where will he sleep?" he asked already knowing the answer to the question. She surprised him by giving him more information than he had requested.

"For the time being I will sleep in Gran's old room and he will sleep in mine. In time – if we really think that we can be a family – then I guess we will rethink it."

"Will you get married?"

A strange look crossed her face. "I don't know. He hasn't mentioned it and I haven't had time to think about it to be honest but I guess if he got divorced we could." She added quickly, "but only if you were okay with it all of course!"

He wanted to laugh. If he was okay with it? What up until now had he ever been okay with in his life? Life happened and you just had to roll with what was thrown your way, he thought. "I'm sorry I called you a name," he couldn't quite bring himself to repeat it.

Anna nodded. "Okay. So I guess I had better move some of my stuff and then maybe we can have a quiet day, just chilling out." She attempted to smile over the ridiculousness of the situation. "Yesterday we had the funeral and tomorrow you are back at school. I'm not denying things are going to continue to be tough for a while. Let's just try and take each day as it comes." She kissed him on the forehead and left.

Once more he was alone with his thoughts. Reluctantly he pulled his phone off the windowsill. He got as far as bringing up Josh's saved number before he tossed it back onto the sill almost exactly where it had lain before.

Josh would not help him now. He would only mock like everyone else. If Lucas had thought that he was alone in the world before, he had been very mistaken.

This was what being alone was like. And he was hating every minute of it.

CHAPTER 10

He spent the rest of Sunday keeping out of their way, staying in his room for much of the time, only coming out to eat a hurried meal in silence before retreating back to the safety of his bedroom.

A few times they tried to engage him in conversation. He could almost tell it was going to happen directly before it did. There would be a sudden tension in the silence; an almost deepening of the hush, as if it were not just words that were being held back but breath and thoughts too... and then it would come – a question that had been carefully constructed to appear off-the-cuff and spontaneous but was in fact anything but! When these questions came he answered as politely as possible but made sure that he left no room for a follow-up question. He ate quickly and escaped as soon as he could.

Alone in his room there was no one to stop him from logging on to the laptop and checking Twitter for an answer from Hugh Grant but by the time he had checked ten times, he almost *wanted* his mother to come in and take the laptop away. He turned the computer off and waited for the day to end. Maybe Monday would come and he would find that all this had just been a nightmare... but in his heart he knew that was not the case. If he had lived in a dream world ever, it was not now but perversely the time before, when most things had actually been okay in his world. He was not dumb and he watched the news often enough to realise that life for most people was hard, barren of hope and filled with despair. Why should his be any different?

Perhaps his mother came into his room and kissed him in the middle of the night. Perhaps she spoke softly to him in his sleep and tucked the covers snuggly around him... if she did any or all of these things he was unaware of them. His slumber was filled with monsters which chased him and deep chasms which threatened to swallow him deep into the bowels of the earth, crushing his bones to fine powder against their ever-narrowing walls.

He woke, bathed in sweat and leaking moisture from every pore. The bedclothes were sodden with sweat, sour smelling and rancid. He pulled them from the bed and carried them to the bathroom, dumping them in the laundry basket. The mirror over the sink reflected his image back at him. It was the same face that he had always had, only the pallor of the skin and the new dark circles under his eyes were different.

It was earlier than he usually got up but he washed and dressed anyway, slipping out of the house without seeing either his mother or the man she claimed was his father. His stomach rumbled but he ignored it. In a way the discomfort of the emptiness inside of him was a pleasant distraction. It was like a sort of cleansing pain – at once a punishment and retribution for what he had brought upon himself and also a punishment against his mother. In causing pain to himself, he was also causing pain to her and even if she did not yet feel that pain, was unaware of how it lay in wait for her, she would feel it soon.

In the heat of the moment he had sworn at the weekend. But he would never normally be able to behave in such a way in front of his mother. But starving himself, making her see in a very physical way, how she had hurt him - that he *could* do.

The walk to school was as dreadful as he had known it would be. The absence of Josh stung him like a physical pain; each step was drawn from him on limbs of ice, muscles clenched with the misery of abject loneliness. He left the prison of his home and entered the prison of the school.

"Your mother's got a new boyfriend!"

"Bet she couldn't wait 'til yer gran died so she could move her boyfriend in!"

"Who is your mother shacked up with

now?" The taunts came at him from all sides. The school corridors rang with cruel laughter, all of it directed at Lucas. He kept his head down and avoided looking at them. He was only one and they were many.

The day dragged and he wondered briefly how different the next day and the next would be. Would they be repetitions of this first day or would the rest of the children eventually lose interest in him when they saw they were getting no reaction at all?

Break times were the hardest to get through. There were two ways of trying to deal with the short recess between classes but neither worked particularly well. He could hurry out, be one of the first to leave but where would he go? Where was there, that was secluded and safe? Or he could dawdle, be one of the last to leave the class, cutting the time down between one class and the next. But that too had its drawbacks.

He took his time packing up his bag when the end of lesson bell rang. There was one lesson left and then it would be time to go home. One lesson left to get through before he escaped to the misery that awaited him at home... Three other boys seemed to linger over their bags, taking too much care packing their books away, too fastidious to be genuine. Lucas felt himself swallow the spit that pooled in the bottom of his mouth. One of them was Harry Davis, the boy who had tried to block his exit that last Friday Josh had still been at the school. The boy who Josh had stood up to and forced to back down. But Josh wasn't here now and Harry was. And with two friends!

They were alone in the class. The teacher had already scurried off and the corridors were deserted. "Did you know we had a celebrity in our midst?" Harry said in a theatrically loud voice, deliberately ensuring that Lucas heard him clearly.

"Really? A celebrity?" one of the other boys said in a false way, making Lucas realise that the conversation had been staged, set-up for his benefit.

"Yep! A real-to-God kiss-ass celebrity!" Harry beamed as if bestowing the best secret in the world to his pals.

"Who is it then?" the boy who had not yet spoken, Tom Crowling, uttered his line.

"It's Lucas Peepee!" Harry turned a grin on him that was both contemptuous and challenging, daring him to do or say something to refute it. Lucas dragged his gaze back to his bag, unsure what he should do or say or whether he should do or say anything at all! Did the celebrity thing refer to his gran's obituary in the paper he wondered, or was it a reference to the fact that the whole school seemed to be talking about him?

"Peepee is a celebrity Harry? How do you

make that out?" Tom sniggered, already knowing the answer.

"Well it seems that Peepee thinks his daddy is Hugh Grant!"

Lucas felt his breath catch in his throat. Instead of a smooth inhalation, the air seemed to get trapped in his throat somehow, avoiding his lungs and making him issue a staccato stuttering sound as he rasped it into his chest. "What was that? What did you say Mr Grant?" Harry mocked to the accompaniment of guffaws to either side of him.

How do they know? But the answer was blindingly obvious. Josh had told them, or if not them, then someone else and the rumour had spread like wildfire. *How could Josh have done this to me? How could he betray our friendship like this? Why?* But the answer was self-evident. Perhaps they had once been best friends but that time was over. *Maybe I shouldn't have told him about his dad. I could have just kept it to myself. But if he had known something about my dad, I would have wanted him to tell me!*

Even if it had been bad? he asked himself. There was no answer.

"So how is daddy Hugh going to feel when he finds out Lucas's mum is shacked up with some other bloke?" Harry sniggered.

A simmering rage built up in Lucas, an indignation at the unfairness of it all, a fury at the inhumaneness of those around him, that their taunts were designed to wound and hurt, when he had never done anything to cause them offence. It coiled inside of him like a tightly wound spring, concertinaing upon itself, collapsing into the smallest form it could make before unleashing full force on the object of its wrath.

Lucas flew across the room like a thing possessed, fists flailing and lunging into the air, seeking a target that was still too far away. In his mind he saw his fists connect with Harry's nose, felt the thick viscous stream of blood which spattered him and heard the sharp retort of knuckles in contact with cartilage. But in his mind is where the image terminated.

Reality intervened. Two pairs of hands caught him and held him whilst Harry pummelled his fists into his Lucas's abdomen. Lucas felt his empty stomach lurch sickeningly, the force of the blows causing his back to fold in on itself and a thin stream of bile to be ejected from between his lips. He staggered backwards wondering why he was suddenly free, why restraining arms no longer held him in place. All he cared about was that this was his chance. He gathered up his strength and the tattered remains of his dignity and he charged towards Harry, fists held high and at the ready.

Too late he wondered why Harry looked

surprised to see him. Too late did he realise that there were suddenly other people present in the room, people who had not been there just a moment before. It was only as his fist finally connected with the bridge of Harry's nose and that bright red liquid was finally set free, that he saw the smug look up close in his adversary's eyes and knew he had been set-up.

"Lucas Pertwee!" an adult voice exclaimed. Somewhere in the back of his head Lucas recognised it as the teacher. He turned an unrepentant gaze in her direction. "Lucas go right now to the Head's office. And you can explain how you attacked Harry with no provocation!" she bellowed.

"But Miss…" whatever his protest might have been was of no use. The teacher had already turned her back on him, holding Harry's head up towards the ceiling and trying to stem the stream of blood which flowed there.

Lucas left the classroom, closing the door softly behind himself. *What's the use? No one will believe me? But they will believe Harry. Unless…* He pulled his shirt up to examine his abdomen. It was a little reddened but any bruises which might show up later were not yet in evidence. At this moment in time he could not prove that Harry had attacked him first. Once more fate was not on his side. He made his way to the school office.

"What am I to do with you Lucas?" the

Head asked, making him stand opposite her large wooden desk.

He wasn't sure if she really expected an answer but he thought it wise to give one anyway, just in case. "I don't know Mrs Macey," he said truthfully.

"I am aware of your situation. You were off school due to your gran's accident and funeral. And now it seems the whole school is talking about you..." she sighed, "for one reason or another." She picked up a pen from where it lay on her desk but did not use it to write. She held the pen poised and regarded him frankly.

"You have my sympathy about your gran Lucas. And as far as the other situations go, I understand there may be difficulties at home. I am not a hard, unfeeling Headmistress. In fact I pride myself on the fact that I encourage students to come to me if they have a problem. But I cannot condone fighting - for any reason. And an unprovoked attack..." She placed the pen back down on the desk. "It *was* an unprovoked attack, was it not?" She looked him in the eye with a clear, direct gaze.

Was there a point in telling her the truth? He tried to look away but found he couldn't. "Harry hit me first. He had two other boys with him and they held me while he hit me. But then he let me go. And just as I got to him..."

"Your teacher caught you," Mrs Macey

finished for him, either guessing or knowing what had happened. "It's not the first time Harry has been involved in something like this and I daresay it won't be the last either!" she said, surprising him. "I will have a chat with Harry and his parents and I promise you this will not happen again." She pushed the pen and a piece of headed notepaper towards him. "But I need you to do something for me. I need you to write down in your own words, exactly what happened and then I want you to stay away from the likes of Harry. Can you do that Lucas?" she asked.

"I'll try," he answered honestly.

"Alright. Now write whilst I make a call to your mother and tell her that I am sending you home early today." Lucas lifted the pen and brought the paper closer to him. He tried to get on with the writing whilst he listened to as much of the conversation as he could.

"So do you wish to pick him up now?" the Headmistress asked into the telephone, where his mother on the other end, could be heard only faintly. Lucas couldn't catch what the response was. "Thank you Ms Pertwee for your understanding. I will let him know." Mrs Macey hung up the phone. "Your mum says you are to let yourself in and she will be home soon. She has explained a little about what has been going on in your life. If you want to talk to anyone, we have access to trained counsellors at school. I can make an appointment for you. Don't decide right now. Just think about it." She gave him a warm smile and held the door open for him. "I'm always here Lucas." He wasn't sure if it was a threat or a promise.

It was almost an eerie experience, walking home along familiar roads whilst everyone else was still in school. With no reason to rush, and certainly none to dawdle, he walked at his usual pace.

Had the streets been filled with other children he might not have seen it. Had he walked this particular path just an hour later, it might have been too late. At first he thought it was a piece of rubbish on the road – a discarded crumpled up newspaper or chip wrapper – but as he approached, it moved away, cowering from him, drawing its injured body inwards to shield its already broken and battered wings from further harm. A bright red crescent of blood bloomed around its neck and across the area between its wings where feathers and skin had been ripped away to expose the fine muscles beneath.

Terrified, it huddled into the side of the kerb as he towered over it, too terrified to drag itself away, too terrified not to. He saw the indecision flicker under one of its brightly beaded eyes. But more than what he saw, it was what he felt that crushed his heart.

This bird had been beaten and savaged by life – just as he had been. It didn't much matter who or what the perpetrator had been, a car, a cat or even another, bigger bird. What mattered was that life had dealt this creature such an unkind blow and left it abandoned here to die like a piece of trash, discarded and disposable.

With no awareness of what he was about to do, Lucas carefully scooped the pigeon into his arms. It tried to flutter away from him, chest heaving in frenzied gasps, break wide open in a soundless scream. Inside his head Lucas heard its cry. It was a strangely human sound, full of sorrow and misery and desolation.

Only as he brought the bird to his chest, resting it against the beating of his own heart did he recognise the source of the internal scream. It was his own.

CHAPTER 11

It quaked in his hands, thin bedraggled feathers failing to hide the frail emaciated body below, eyes half-closed in anticipation of further cruelty.

"I'm taking you somewhere safe," he told the trembling bird, feeling a satisfying weight of responsibility settle upon his soul. Maybe it was already too late, maybe the bird would succumb to its injuries regardless of what he did now but that would not excuse him doing nothing! It would not excuse him turning his gaze away, pretending he had not seen, nor would it remove the dark stain that would forever mar his soul.

He had been carrying his coat and now he used it to wrap around the bird. Maybe pigeons were supposed to be this cold or maybe this one was in shock, he had no idea, but he figured that it was better to cover it than leave it exposed. Gently he cossetted the bird in the material, using the coat as a buffer against the thin delicate bones and his own harder frame. He walked carefully, trying to jar the creature as little as possible.

The bird's head stuck out from around the wrapper of the coat and for a moment he could have sworn it looked at him with comprehension – an acknowledgement of the fact that he was trying to save it. But the look was momentary, fleeting, if it had even been there at all. He would not fail this bird! And he would not let anyone stand in his way either, he vowed.

Within a few minutes he was home, fumbling to get the front door key out of his trouser pocket whilst still retaining a firm but gentle hold on the bird. Once inside he headed for the under-stairs cupboard. There were boxes in there. He had collected them himself at his mother's request. She had wanted them to store some mementoes of his gran but it wouldn't matter if he took one of them for a makeshift pigeon cage.

The box he selected was a good size and had flaps which could be sealed down, keeping the bird enclosed. He ripped the top flaps off, exposing the box and making it open at the top.

"We don't have any cats or dogs in this house," he told the bird who now seemed to be watching him curiously, not particularly afraid but not at ease either. He guessed that nature had endowed it with the logic that if it was in danger of being harmed or eaten by something, the threat was an immediate one. Now that it had been in his company for at least fifteen minutes and had not been harmed it was probably beginning to realise he was not a threat.

"I'm going to keep the window and the door closed but I need you to rest in the box, not try to escape, okay?" he said, knowing that there was no way it could understand the words. But maybe if not the words themselves, maybe it would get a sense of his thoughts telepathically or something?

Downstairs the front door closed and his mother made her way up to his room. "Lucas I had a phone call from..." At first she didn't notice the box with its resident pigeon, she was so focused on her son. "Oh my God! What's THAT doing here!" Her face was a perfect picture of astonishment, almost as if she had never seen a pigeon before, Lucas thought.

"It's injured," he replied simply.

"That doesn't answer my question!"

"It would have died if I had just left it."

"Lucas it's a wild animal. You can't just bring an injured animal home. It's nature's way. Wild animals get injured and they die."

"Oh like old ladies fall down the stairs and they die and then their daughters move their lovers in?" That was unfair and he knew it but it had welled up in him and he could not hold it back. He wasn't even sure he had tried to hold it back, if he was completely honest with himself.

Tears smarted at the corners of her eyes but

she did not refute his cheap shot. He could see her jaw muscles clenching and unclenching as she tried to hold back her emotion. Part of him felt ashamed that he had let go of his whilst she tried to contain her own but then again she was an adult and as she kept reminding him, he was not.

He tried to bring the argument back to the point. "I don't just bring everything home – in fact I have never brought anything home before. And as for it being nature's way – well nature sucks!" he said forcefully.

"Well we could take it to a vet's?" she offered.

He shook his head emphatically. "They will take one look at it and put it down!"

"Then maybe that's for the best! Vets know about these things," she said softly.

His temper flared. "Whereas I don't know about anything! I'm so dumb I actually thought my father might be someone I could look up to. Not some guy who got his wife and his girlfriend knocked up at the SAME TIME!"

He hadn't meant those words to come out ever; hadn't meant to reveal that he had been listening in to their conversation in the kitchen the night before; hadn't wanted her to know how little he thought of her and her choice of men. But it was out now. The colour drained from her face and her mouth stayed in a perfect 'o' of shock.

There was no going back on what he had said, what he knew. He tried to move forward.

"I'm sorry! For what I said I mean. But not about the pigeon. I am NOT taking it to a vet's and I am NOT abandoning it!"

His mother displayed the frailest smile he had ever seen. "Sometimes the truth is a nasty thing. And sometimes it hurts. All your life I have tried to spare you that hurt and now ultimately I've failed."

Lucas didn't feel like responding and even if he had, he wouldn't have known what to say. "Let's make a deal. You can keep the bird until it is better – as long as it *is* getting better. If at any time it gets worse then you have to agree that we take it to the vets to put it out of its misery, for its own sake."

He nodded. She carried on. "But even if the bird improves, you will have to either release it in one month or take it to a rescue centre or somewhere. A month is long enough for it to be living in your bedroom! Agreed?" she looked him firmly in the eye and he knew she would not bend from this compromise.

"Agreed," he said quietly.

"Is that your coat it is wrapped up in?" Her face said she already knew that it was. "Take it off the bird and put it in the wash. I'll get some old newspaper and we can shred it for its bedding."

"What about its wounds and feeding it?" he asked. Suddenly the task and the responsibility seemed too big for him.

"Well why don't you check out what you should do on the internet? There is bound to be some information there. In the meantime, there is some cooked rice in the fridge it can have."

She was half way out of the room before he had a chance to reply. "Mum, thanks!"

She stopped and turned towards him once more. "Sometimes in life there are things you have to do. Whether other people think they are wrong or right, they are the things that your heart holds onto. Maybe this is one of yours."

He did not respond, not sure of what his answer should be. Maybe she was right. Or maybe the bird was just a timely distraction from his other problems. In a way it didn't matter – the bird needed his help and he would provide it. There was really nothing else.

Inside the box, he unwrapped the bird from his coat and examined it more carefully. This time the pigeon did not shy away from him but instead tried unsuccessfully to lift its wings. It managed to elongate the wings, to stretch them out somewhat but the injured area between the feathers would not allow them to be lifted.

His mother appeared back in the doorway. "I'll take the coat and wash it. I've brought the newspaper and the rice," she passed him the rice in exchange for the coat. But she did not hold out the newspaper. Lucas hesitated before reaching forward, reluctant to let the print soil his fingertips. But the bird's need was greater than his own distaste and he forced himself to accept the paper. He stood with it held rigidly in his hands.

"Have you looked to see how injured it is?" she asked, surprised at his acceptance of the newspaper but choosing not to comment upon it. Lucas shook his head. "Okay, then have a look and while you are doing that I will prepare its box." She instructed, gently prising his fingers from the paper and beginning to tear it into fine strips.

He lifted the bird gently. A few of its wing feathers were missing, torn out from the roots, leaving little holes from which new feathers might eventually grow. There was the already seen damage to the area between its wings, the area that would have been termed the shoulders on a human but he was unsure of the correct terminology for birds. The wings themselves seemed unbroken but there were torn patches underneath, where once again the red muscle showed through. The rest of the bird's body and legs looked normal and undamaged. "Should I clean the wounds?" he asked.

Anna put the last of the ripped paper into the box and carefully laid the dish with the rice on top in one of the corners. "Check what the internet suggests but I would have thought that as long as they are reasonably clean they could be left. Then again I really don't know."

Gently he placed the bird back in the box. Almost immediately it went over to the rice and began to peck. "That's a good sign, that it's eating, right?" He thought it must be.

Anna agreed. "I would say so. We need to give it water. What could we put it in?"

A saucer was fine for the rice but the bird would need something deeper to drink from. "An eggcup?" Lucas suggested and Anna went to fetch one.

He pulled the laptop onto his bed and by the time his mother had returned with the little cup full of water, he was already compiling a list of what to feed the bird and how to look after it. "Is there much information online?" she asked, peering over his shoulder.

"Yes, I think there's enough," he replied. He felt her hand tousle his hair and then she was gone again. There was a faint sound of the front door opening and closing and then someone came up the stairs.

His bedroom door was still open from when his mother had left and Martin used this as an invitation to step into the room, uninvited. "Your mother phoned me at work. Said there was some problem at school."

Lucas cut him off abruptly. "I didn't hear the doorbell ring!" he glared at the man with as much contempt as he could muster.

"Your mother gave me a key," Martin said

without the slightest hint of shame.

"So you have a key Mr Jones, well I wonder what you will have next?" Lucas scoffed, burning inside with a hatred for this stranger who had hijacked his life.

"Look Lucas, I don't expect you to call me dad... but Mr Jones..." his eyes fell on the cardboard box for the first time and he craned his neck to see what was inside. "Is that a... a PIGEON!" he said a little too loudly for Lucas's liking.

"Well done Martin. You have correctly identified the bird," Lucas scoffed. "Do you like that, me calling you Martin, Martin? Is it better than Mr Jones, Martin?" he used the name like an insult, spitting out the consonants like putrid seeds.

Martin ignored the words and the acidic tone they were delivered in. "Anna, Anna! He's got a pigeon up here!" he called down the stairs to Lucas's mother.

As if his mother had been waiting anxiously for her cue, she appeared within seconds. "Yes, I know."

"But its bloody vermin! Those things spread disease!"

Anna said nothing but Lucas stood, pulling himself up to his full height. Even though he had not yet stopped growing, not yet reached his full height, even though he was still shorter than the man who stood before him, he felt taller, stronger, wiser. Martin hadn't stood up to his responsibilities but Lucas would.

"What, like Syphilis? VD? Aids? Chlamydia?" He held the man's gaze unwaveringly. "No, sorry, those are human diseases aren't they? Spread by people who have unprotected sex with lots of other people. You know the sort of people I mean don't you? The sort of people who go around getting other people pregnant and abandoning them. Somehow I don't think anything a pigeon could do could really equal that, do you?" Each word was delivered like an arrow seeking a target and like an arrow shot from a bow, there was an obvious effect.

Martin staggered backwards. "Anna do you let the boy talk to you in this way?" he exclaimed.

"The 'boy', Martin is her son. Yours too if what you claim is true! Pity you never thought about that before you descended upon us!" Lucas fired.

Martin bristled. "You need your arse smacked, Lucas!" He turned to Lucas's mother. "Anna you need to get this boy under control!"

Anna looked at them both for a moment. "No what I need to do is step back. Martin you weren't around for most of his life. You have some making up to do." She turned to her son. "And as for you Lucas. Well you always wanted a father – now you have one!" She turned back to Martin. "I have already told Lucas that he can keep this bird for one month and that there had better be an improvement in it by then. He will keep it in his room and it will be his responsibility to keep it clean and fed. "If you have a problem with that, then I suggest you find alternative accommodation Martin." She looked him directly in the eye as she spoke.

Lucas had never seen his mother so assertive. Neither apparently had Martin.

"Oh right. Well if you have already agreed," he backed down. "But one month mind! And it stays in this room," he said trying to sound as if he had regained some control over the matter.

For his mother's sake, Lucas nodded as if he was accepting the order. "Okay then," Martin said, pride saved and backing towards the door. "Fancy a coffee Anna?" he asked. "I'm parched!" He turned and led the way downstairs as if he had every right to do so. Without another word, Anna followed in his wake. Lucas thought that she had surpassed and maybe even surprised herself. He wondered if she would have the strength to stand up to his father again. Was courage like a muscle that if exercised became strengthened and fortified?

The laptop was still on, still loaded with the page of a bird rescue site. He toggled the screen and brought up another tab. After only a moment's hesitation he logged onto Twitter.

On the top right-hand corner, where the little envelope symbol was displayed, there was a number: 2. He clicked onto it. He had received a message back from Hugh Grant! He clicked on it to open it up. His own sent messages were still there, easily viewed and he cringed when he read them back. The last one was easily the worst!

'Gran is dead and so you and Mum can get back together now! And we can be a family like we should have been before.' The words echoed around his brain. Like vultures they picked at the carrion of his imagination, exposing the shameful stupidity that he had actually thought he could be related to the actor.

He wanted to dismiss the actor's reply, whatever the response had been. But he found his eyes drawn to the few lines below his own message. They might as well have been written in blood, they sat so starkly and boldly on the screen before him. *'Got to think this is some kind of a joke! I may not be the most hands-on father, but I do tend to remember the children I have had!'*

There was a gap then another line below. *'And I **always** remember their mothers' names! I am sorry. I think you have the wrong man! Yours, respectfully, Hugh Grant.'*

There was no point in responding. No point in denying the man's words or even in explaining the misunderstanding. There was no point in any of it really. Lucas deleted his account and shut down the computer.

CHAPTER 12

He spent the rest of the evening avoiding his mother and Martin as much as possible. Not only did the pigeon give him an excuse to be shut up in his room but it gave him a focus.

"Things were different before," he told the bird which still regarded him with bright eyes but seemed less scared as the night went on. "It wasn't easy living with Mum and Gran but I always knew that they loved me. I always knew that we were a family..." he thought back to the final weeks they had spent together, conscience pricked by the thought that the unhappiness of the present was manipulating the memories of the past.

"I don't mean that everything was perfect... but at least it wasn't like it is now!" He felt a need to be searingly honest to the bird as if it possessed some magical power to change things for the better. He lifted at hand towards it, meaning to stroke its little feathered head, but as his hand approached it ducked away, fluttering to the other side of the box. "Sorry," he apologised. "I didn't mean to scare you."

In its haste to get away from him it had upturned its saucer of food. Lucas didn't think it mattered much. The food was mostly gone – a veritable pigeon feast had been gobbled greedily by the injured bird, not just the rice he had first given it but soft, cooked peas and corn and what remained was now a few cold morsels. There would be more food in the morning and the following evening but for now what they both needed more than anything was rest.

Lucas stripped down to his pants, leaving his clothes in a pile on the floor and slid into bed. He hadn't had a shower or brushed his teeth and his body felt slightly sticky and there was an unpleasant furry taste in his mouth. But he couldn't face having to shower in the bathroom that Martin would use. In the *shower* that Martin would use. Not tonight anyway. For this one day he had accepted pretty much all he could. He was filled up to the brim with forced acceptance. Tomorrow was still a sleep away and who knew what could have changed by then? Perhaps his mother would throw Martin out in the morning! Or perhaps Martin would just leave of his own accord. Or perhaps everything to do with the man would prove to be just a bad dream.

But Anna's face came sharp and clear into Lucas's head on the back of that thought, her eyes red-rimmed from crying and her face showing every bit of her pain. Too vivid to be imagination it was a clear memory of when his gran had died. Would Martin leaving hit her that hard? Lucas's heart sank lower than he had thought possible. It was a conundrum and a half! If Martin left them Lucas would be happy but his mother would be miserable and if she was miserable then Lucas would be too... The thoughts rolled around his head even as his eyes closed upon the pillow.

The dreams which came to him in his slumber were neither soothing nor restorative. He tossed and turned within the bedclothes, wrapping and unwrapping them around himself, wrenching them from their moorings and unconsciously kicking them into a bundle which fell to the floor on his next turn. Dragons chased him through the corridors of his dreams. Huge landscapes of burning trees assaulted his sleeping eyes, their flames a bright red and orange which lit up the night sky.

Desperately he tried to turn away from the fire, to shield his face from the intense heat and acrid smell of smoke but wherever he ran it seemed like he was on a treadmill, never advancing into safety but stuck where he was. There was a loud roar and a tongue of flame licked the exposed skin of his shoulder but bizarrely there was no pain. Instead, it was as if the contact was a catalyst and at once the dragons and their flames receded. In the moment before opening his eyes he realised he had been dreaming. He lay there a split-second longer, eyes still closed against the world, almost willing himself to re-enter the terrors of the dream world rather than the reality he had to face.

The room was bright with morning sunshine. The faint warmth on his shoulder which had roused him from his sleep came from a shaft of sunlight which had found its way through the narrow chink in the curtains. It looked like it was going to be a nice day...

The bird! Memory of the injured creature jumped sharply into focus in his brain. Lucas found that he couldn't turn his gaze towards the box which contained it. What if it was dead? What if it too was 'gone'? Or if it was missing, nowhere to be found?

A horrible thought entered his head, an image of Martin sneaking into the room in the middle of the night and taking the bird, perhaps wringing its neck before throwing it into the outside bin or perhaps even the gutter on the road.

Lucas swallowed hard at the idea of the man perpetrating the act on the poor defenceless bird, its feathers painfully crushed into its fragile little body, eyes bulging in fear and terror. His heart wrenched at the certainty that he had not protected it at all but rather had spared it one death only to embrace another. And its last thought would be that he had caught it specifically for that reason!

That belief, that traitorous conviction appalled his brain and his heart – to think that the bird would die thinking so badly of him was a searing pain beyond endurance. It sliced into the core of him and tormented him in its unfairness. Reluctantly he cast his eyes to the box, sure that his gaze would be met by emptiness, an absence of life.

Fast asleep, the pigeon was huddled onto its feet, neck tucked in and eyes shut. Its eyelids were a mid-grey colour, smooth and velvety looking. As if it sensed him watching it became immediately awake, opening its eyes and looking straight at him as if it knew what he was thinking. What he had feared.

"Morning." He said simply, relieved that they had both survived the night. Superstitious that the voicing of his fears would make them real, would elevate them from the depths of his subconscious to the plane of reality, he kept his worries to himself. The bird made no response to his greeting, not even a coo. Perhaps it too sensed the otherworldliness of its situation.

"Fancy some breakfast?" Lucas strove to lighten the atmosphere. The tension he felt would do neither of them any good. The bird tilted its head as if considering the idea. "I guess I ought to name you," Lucas said thoughtfully. "What about

Sasha? Then it doesn't matter if you are a boy or a girl." But the name felt instinctively wrong. "Maybe not Sasha then… Any ideas?" The pigeon made no response.

Perhaps in time it would tweet or coo or make whatever sounds that pigeons made. But that would take time. And patience on his part. What was it that his Gran used to say? Oh yes – 'good things come to those who wait'. He wondered what good things had come to her. Indeed what good thing had come to him, after all his patience? A father who was less honourable than even Josh's dad? Was that the sum total of his luck?

But was it entirely true, he challenged himself? After all, hadn't Martin sent money for Lucas and his mother? Did that go in any way towards exonerating his behaviour? Lucas just didn't know and he didn't have enough clear space in his brain to figure it out. He moved towards the door. "I have to get showered and ready for school. Once I have done that I will bring you your breakfast and then you can rest during the day while I'm gone."

The bathroom door was open, a thin trail of steam puffing out into the hallway. Someone had already had their morning shower, either his mother or Martin. Trying not to think about who had used the room before him, Lucas closed and bolted the door before stepping into the shower.

But before he turned the water on he wondered if he should perhaps rinse the stall out. There was every possibility after all that it had been Martin who had used it last. But what was the point? The guy was clearly here to stay. And if he wasn't? Well that wasn't something that Lucas could consider right now. There was enough concrete things to worry about without adding 'what ifs' into the mix.

He turned the taps on fully so that the combined force of the hot and cold almost swept him off his feet. It was less like a pleasant shower and more like being hosed down by the fire brigade but it served its own purpose. Bright needles of pain struck his body everywhere, lashing the dirt and sweat from him and possibly taking a layer of skin with it. He could only stand the self-inflicted torture for a couple of minutes but it was enough.

He turned the water off, towelled himself roughly dry and brushed his teeth vigorously. Then, wrapping the towel around him, he went back into his room to get dressed in fresh clothes.

He glanced into the box as he dressed. The little bits of corn and peas that had remained from the night before were now gone and the egg-cup of water had been spilled. Carefully he removed the dishes from the box, taking his time and moving slowly. He carried them downstairs to the kitchen. His mother sat alone at the table.

He looked at her and at the empty chair opposite, the one that should have contained his gran.

"Don't worry. Martin has already gone," Anna said quietly, misinterpreting his thoughts. She must have seen something in Lucas's face that made her rethink her words for she quickly clarified, "he has gone to work Lucas… not left us."

Lucas felt the muscles in his face shift from one expression to another. As if he were outside his own body he could not tell what the look on his face had said or what it had morphed into. But he knew what his heart felt, and it wasn't relief.

"I prepared some more food for your bird. There were some leftover potatoes so I chopped them up really small and I did some more peas and corn."

Lucas was relieved to be talking about the bird rather than Martin. "Thanks."

Anna took the dirty bird dishes from him. "But the bird is your responsibility Lucas. I thought I made that clear. You need to read as much about wild bird care as you can."

He nodded. She was right and it was what he had been planning to do until… until he'd had that message from Hugh Grant. He'd read some information, but was it enough to keep the bird alive? He cursed himself for not getting on with his responsibilities. If he messed this up, Martin and/or his mother would make him get rid of the pigeon. Lucas sensed that this would not only be a death sentence for the bird but that in some strange way it would be the death of him too.

He ate his breakfast in silence whilst Anna cleaned up the kitchen around him. He didn't want to talk about the bird and he didn't want to talk about Martin. In fact he couldn't think of a single thing he *did* want to talk about. There was a gulf between him and his mother that hadn't been there before, not even when she had refused to tell him anything about his father. Funny how the sudden knowledge of the man was worse than all the years of not knowing put together, Lucas thought.

Was that because Martin had turned out to be so ordinary? Or was it because it had tainted everything Lucas had ever thought he had known? He finished his cereal and handed his mother the empty bowl. She washed it up immediately and put it on the drainer to dry. The refilled bird dishes were on the side of the sink and he picked them up and turned away. "You have to give him a chance," Anna said softly from behind him.

"I am. That's exactly what I am doing!" he said in surprise. "It's Martin who doesn't want to give him, or her a chance!"

"No Lucas, I didn't mean the bird. I meant you need to give Martin a chance!"

Of course she did, Lucas chastised himself.

How stupid he had been, yet again. Would he never learn? His eyes smarted with unshed tears but he blinked them away. She didn't understand at all and even worse than that, he feared she didn't want to understand.

Back in his room the bird seemed a little livelier than it had the day before. It watched him enter the room and tilted its head quizzically as he bent down to put the food and water next to it in the box. It still shied away as he approached, but he thought it seemed less afraid than before. He tried hard to remember how it had reacted when he first put his hands in the box – its chest area had been heaving and although it was injured it had tried to defend itself from the perceived threat. Now its breathing and heartbeat appeared more regular, or at least there were no visible signs of panic.

He drew his hands slowly out of the box, but even before they reached the top, the bird was pecking away happily at its food. "Brighteyes, that's your name, he told it. Brighteyes."

Disinterested in anything other than the food, the bird appeared unconcerned about its name or the strange boy who had uttered the words. "But she is right. You are my responsibility and I have to make sure you're getting better."

He pulled the laptop back onto the bed. There was time yet to do a little research before school. He looked up various sites which told him what pigeons could safely eat and what to look out for with injuries. There was something called canker that they were particularly susceptible to, he discovered. It was a sort of fungal infection which clogged up their throats so that they couldn't swallow. But looking at the bird pecking away at its breakfast, he was fairly certain that it didn't have that disease. All its heath issues were related to the accident it had had with either a car or a cat.

He looked up what injuries of that type could look like. It didn't take long for him to decide that Brighteyes had more than likely been hit by a car, either in descent of flight or possibly in ascending, not that that mattered. One thing struck a note of fear into his heart. The website stated that if the bird survived the initial shock and if its injuries were not severe enough to kill it straight away, it could still die from infection getting into the wounds!

"I won't let you die, I promise!" He wasn't sure if he actually spoke the words or just thought them but the bird gave no reaction. Once more he closed down the laptop and shoved it under his bed. He snared his school coat from the hook behind the door, where it had been put after it had been washed. "I'll see you later," he told the bird and went to brush his teeth.

His mother was waiting for him outside his bedroom door. "Try and have a good day honey," she said and he knew she meant it. What he couldn't figure out was how she thought this was at all possible with the double whammy of Josh gone and Martin here.

"You too Mum," he mumbled, wondering to himself if he really meant the words and then hating himself for even having the thought. He leaned forward and gave her a kiss on the cheek.

"I only want what's best for all of us," she said, her eyes begging him to understand.

"I know you do." And he did. It was just that he wasn't at all sure that what was developing really was the best thing for all of them… or at least for him anyway. Anna nodded and said nothing more. She watched him descend the stairs and exit through the front door.

Lucas walked a little faster than normal towards the school. There was no Josh at his side to slow his strides with jests and funny stories and there was no reason to dilly-dally. He also had the stupidest feeling that if he hurried to school the day would carry on in the same vein, lessons would be rushed through, break times would pass in a blurred haste and before he knew it, it would be time to come home again.

So he was surprised when, level with the house that used to belong to Josh, the front door opened and someone looked right at him.

CHAPTER 13

It was a girl. Long, waist-length brown hair framed a face that was impish and open. Probably no more than ten or eleven years old, he was struck by the way she held herself in the open doorway; looking out without yet venturing out, as if curious about what the day held in store for her. But not frightened or apprehensive about what that might be.

She is part of the new family that's moved into Josh's house, Lucas thought. Except of course that it wasn't Josh's house at all any more, was it? He looked away, speeding up his pace, wanting to avoid having to acknowledge that things had moved so far on; that *Josh* had moved so far on. "I know who you are," a voice at his side said brightly.

Without even looking down, he knew it was her, the stranger from the house. Taller than most other girls her age, she also seemed to lack their customary shyness. "I don't know *you* and I don't want to know you. And you don't know *me* either," he put in for good measure.

"Well maybe not *know* exactly," she acceded, "but I have seen you."

"Seeing isn't knowing." He ramped up the pace once more, an image of Hugh Grant blazing across his inner vision like an incitement to war.

"I'm Molly. Molly Hickling. What's your name?"

"Go away," he hissed through clenched teeth.

"Well that's a dumb name, Go Away!" She managed to make it sound as if she really thought that was his name. It was only the smallest stifled giggle on the end of her words that gave the game away. "So, Go Away, have you always lived here?" she asked. He ignored her although it had little effect. "You are the boy who thought that Hugh Grant was his dad."

Her tone was flat, there was no mockery, no ridicule intended it seemed, as if perhaps it was not so absurd an idea after all. He felt his legs thrust forward just as quickly as before but there was a softening of his clenched muscles as if in an almost involuntary response to the girl.

"I can understand that. I sometimes wish my dad was someone else," her tone was wistful now and despite himself he was intrigued.

"Do you know who he is?" he asked, refusing to turn and look at her as he issued the question. The conversation was not his choice, she had forced it upon him and therefore he had no obligation to be polite.

She seemed to take no offence. "Yes, of course. He lives with me. It's just that sometimes…well sometimes it just all seems so boring…"

He felt his muscles clench once more. For a moment he had thought that maybe they had something in common, that she was a little bit like him after all, but he had been wrong. She was nothing like him and she never would be.

"But you are the boy who took that pigeon home. What did you do with it? You didn't…" He heard her gulp nosily but couldn't be sure if it was from the effort of talking whilst almost trotting by his side, or something else. "You didn't eat it, did you?" This time her voice was filled with dread and a quiet horror.

For a moment he considered turning to her, macabre grin on his face and saying, 'Yes, and it was delicious!' followed by, 'And if you don't go away, you're next.' But tempting as the thought was, there was another which followed swiftly on the heels of the first. If she believed him, and why wouldn't she, he already had a reputation as a weirdo after all, she would tell the whole school and his life would be even more miserable than it already was!

He stopped abruptly, causing her to almost crash into him, jogging as she was at his heels, only a half-step behind. He turned to her, aware of all the other children behind and around them, making their own way to school. Were they all watching? Sniggering? Had one of them put this Molly girl up to questioning him, so that they could poke fun later? "How do you know about that? Everyone was in school…"

"I wasn't in school," she said. "Well I was, in the morning, just to introduce me to the class. But they let me go home early as it was my first day and I hadn't even unpacked properly from the move to the new house…and there was stuff to do," she gabbled.

So she had been at her window or something and had seen him with the bird. Now it made sense. Like a shutter coming down over his mind, a resolve clicked into place. He would be true to himself – whatever that meant and whatever it cost him. He only had to look down at her from a slight height, but it was enough for the effect he wanted. "So you saw it there, lying hurt and injured on the road, and you just left it? What sort of girl are you?"

She had the decency to look ashamed. "I… it…I mean…" She didn't seem to know what she meant he realised. He continued his close scrutiny of her face as the rest of the kids swirled around and past them. Her lively eyes clouded for a moment and then cleared once more. "It was there and I saw it but I guess I thought it would just fly away," she finished lamely.

"It can't fly. Well not at the moment anyway. It's too injured for that," he said, but although his words had been chosen to sting her, he felt the initial force of them fade away. She was just a little girl after all. "Why don't you just get to school before you are late," he said.

"I don't know anyone there, I'm new," she almost whispered as if this should be a revelation to him.

"Didn't you say you had already been in though?" he asked.

She shrugged her shoulders. "I'm still the new girl!"

"Yes I know. You are in Josh's house."

"Josh?" she repeated stupidly before understanding dawned. "Oh you mean the family who lived there before! The boy who had the football posters on the bedroom wall."

"You mean he didn't take them?" surprise lifted his voice.

"No. My little sister has the other bedroom, the one that Mum says isn't fit to be called a bedroom, it's so small."

He knew the room she was talking about and he thought he would have to agree. The houses on that side of the road were a little smaller than the ones on his side for some reason. "There are two of you?" Somehow the thought filled him with a vague horror; the image of two inquisitive little girls plaguing him.

"No there's only one of me," Molly said as if he was a bit slow. "She's a different person to me."

He recovered himself as best he could, "I thought maybe she was your twin." He started walking again. The bell would soon ring and now there were no other children in sight. It occurred to him that he had not been subjected to the taunts he had been expecting from the other kids. He wondered why that was. Had they suddenly bored of him? Had they found someone more worthy of their derision, unlikely as that actually was? Or was there some other reason?

"No," the girl laughed – a light tinkle of a sound. And as if the almost musical notes lifted some barrier in his head, he thought how long it had been since he had heard genuine laughter. Unaware of the effect she'd had on him she beamed a bright smile, "She's only three and doesn't even go to school yet."

From across the road the school bell summoned them.

*****

The morning's lessons seemed to drag and he had no doubt that the afternoon ones would be no better. But there were no taunts, no sidelong glances and no snide remarks from the other pupils. Whatever Mrs Macey had said or done about him being bullied had obviously had an effect. But the lack of scrutiny and attention he received now was almost as bad as the tormenting had been anyway. Now it was like he was invisible. Like he was so inconsequential in the world that even the pond scum who used to poke fun at him no longer found him worthy of their ridicule.

At last lunchtime arrived. Unwilling to enter the hall early and have to suffer the rest of the school avoiding sitting next to him, he waited until everyone was already seated. Hands on the push plate of one of the big wooden doors, he imagined the reaction he would receive when he walked into the room. Surely everyone would stop and stare, their forks or sandwiches half raised to their lips, their former disinterest in him forgotten momentarily? He hesitated. Perhaps he could eat his lunch in the cloakroom where no one would find him, no one would bother him?

"Hurry in Lucas, or dinner time will be over." Mrs Macey stood directly behind him. Now there was nothing to do but enter. He turned towards the Head, unwilling to divulge how he now felt but somehow hoping that she would not force him to enter. "You won't have any more trouble, I promise," she said kindly, placing her hand above his and forcing the door open a little. Now people could see him standing there with the Head directly behind him, like his own personal guardian angel! If he hadn't looked like a loser dork before then he definitely looked like one now.

He turned back towards the open door. All faces were studiously averted from where he stood, as if there had been an announcement that anyone who met his gaze would be turned into a pillar of stone. All faces, except for one. The Mandy girl or whatever her name had been; the girl who had followed him to school. Lucas's heart sank.

Like a prisoner on death row, he shuffled forward to meet his fate. Almost imperceptibly he felt the atmosphere in the room change. People seemed to shuffle in their seats, to draw themselves closer to their tables so that their circle was closed to him, impenetrable. Even the kids on the benches seemed to spread themselves out just enough that they took up all of the spare space whilst not leaving enough of a gap between them that he might be able to sit down in.

Spare chairs lined the walls of the room but it was clear that no one was prepared to make a space for him to put one down. A golf-ball of saliva formed in his throat and he almost couldn't breathe. There was no sudden silence to greet his arrival, no lessening of the normal racket that usually echoed off the wooden walls but the sound seemed more strained than usual, as if all the kids were merely actors on a stage set and were trying their very best to look real. Except of course that it *was* all real – horribly, horribly real!

The sound of metal chair legs scraping across a wooden floor cut across the conversation as surely as a rapier blade would have slashed fine paper. Mandy was standing up and waving him over to her as if they were best buddies. Come to think of it, considering the amount of time he had spent with her in one day and comparing that to the handful of words he had spoken to everyone else here in the last few years, it wasn't so inapt a description. A gently placed hand in the small of his back pushed him forward. No doubt that was Mrs Macey but he didn't look back to check.

As if the suddenly hushed conversation was a huge tidal wave on the ocean and he was a boardless surfer, caught in the majestic brutality of it, he floundered like a drowning man past the seated pupils to where Mandy had placed another chair next to her own. "Hi Mandy," he said quietly.

"It's Molly, remember?" She didn't seem in the least offended that he had misremembered her name.

"Yes, sorry." He didn't want her as a friend. He wanted Josh back. He wanted his gran and his life and *everything* back the way they had been.

"These are my new friends," she said brightly, indicating a group of astonished looking girls who looked uncomfortable in his presence. "He lives across the road from me," she explained to them before uttering in a stage whisper,

"What's your name?" to him.

"Lucas," he whispered back, not really knowing why they were whispering. He was struck by how ludicrous the situation was. Here he was, a fourteen-year-old sitting with a bunch of ten or eleven-year-olds. Inwardly he cursed the architect of the flagship school, whoever he had been, for having the brainwave of linking primary and secondary schools on one site through the use of a huge communal dining hall. Sitting next to a group little girls was infinitely worse than being ignored by the whole school.

He ate his sandwiches in silence. After a few tense and uncomfortable moments, the girls seemed to forget that he was even at their table and began to chat about the latest boy band as they had no doubt been doing before. Lucas chewed and swallowed and let their words wash over him. Did it really matter if he was a social pariah? Did it matter if the only person in the world who seemed pleased to see him was a little girl?

Yes! Yes it did! Shame burned at the forefront of his brain. But before the humiliation could consume him, reducing his sense of self to a charred heap of what-ifs, an image came to his mind. Inquisitive beady eyes regarded him from a sleek feathered head. In his imagination he furnished the remaining details, the smooth plumage how it would look once Brighteyes had healed, the iridescent shimmering colours of the feathers as the bird sat on his window ledge, preparing for flight.

Maybe to all these kids he was just a freak, but to Brighteyes he was a friend, a protector, a saviour! As if she was reading his thoughts he heard Molly tell her new friends about the bird. "It's injured but he's going to make it better, aren't you?" she exclaimed, forcing him to enter the conversation. He nodded.

"How?" one of the girls asked. It was a very good question and one he didn't really know the answer to. But he thought he might just know a man who did.

*****

The science teacher was in his lab, as Lucas had suspected he would be. He was eating a ham and pickle sandwich and dropping crumbs all over the Bunsen burners that he appeared to be checking at the same time. "Excuse me sir," Lucas began, stepping into the room. Mr Levy looked up in surprise at the interruption.

"What can I do for you Lucas?" a frown parted the upper half of his forehead from its bottom half.

"Can you make penicillin?" Lucas asked. "At home I mean?"

Mr Levy looked surprised. "Can you be

a little more specific Lucas? Is your question whether or not *I* can make penicillin at my home or whether anyone can make it in their own home?"

Lucas didn't really care which of the definitions his words had to the teacher – he just wanted an answer. "Either," he started to say and then thought to elaborate. "I mean is it easy to make?"

"Well that depends. I mean it was more or less discovered by accident, so therefore there is very much a natural element to its development. That said however, not all mould is penicillin."

Lucas wasn't sure if his actual question had been answered. "Perhaps if you explain your interest," Mr Levy suggested, setting the last of the burners down and popping what remained of his sandwich into his mouth.

Lucas really didn't want to go into detail but did he have a choice, he wondered. "I have this pigeon. And it's hurt. I thought if I gave it some penicillin, then it would get better."

"I see. Why not just take it to a vet?" the teacher asked.

"Because they will put it down!" Lucas felt himself getting frustrated once more.

"Well if a vet would put it down then perhaps that would be best for the bird."

"NO! No it wouldn't! But even if they didn't put it down, if they even said that they thought it *ought* to be, that would be enough of a death sentence that my mum would make me hand it over…" he wasn't sure if he was completely right about this. Hadn't his mum said that she would give him a chance with the bird? But he also knew that she would listen to the vet's opinion and that it would override his own to her mind.

"Well without going to a vet you wouldn't know what dosage to give the bird," the teacher reasoned. Lucas grimaced. He hadn't thought of that.

"But say if I could find that information from the internet…"

"It's still not that easy to grow pure penicillin. You could kill the pigeon rather than cure it."

"So what can I do?" Lucas asked. It was a horrible no-win situation. If he asked for help he could well be condemning the creature to a death sentence, if he didn't, it might die anyway.

"Well Lucas, I am no vet. But I am a scientist first and foremost. Have you ever heard of something called Chaos Theory?"

"No." Lucas hoped that the conversation wasn't descending into one of Mr Levy's lectures about scientific principles.

"Well Chaos Theory is a particular field of study in mathematics which has implications in the scientific world. Perhaps you have heard of The Butterfly Effect?" Lucas shook his head.

The teacher looked crestfallen. "It's of no matter. But both theories teach us to always expect the unexpected and that one small, insignificant change can, over time and space, lead to a monumental shift in circumstances somewhere else."

"I'm sorry Mr Levy but I don't think I'm following you," Lucas sighed.

"Your racing pigeon…"

Lucas interrupted to stave off further confusion. "It's not a racing pigeon. It's a normal one I found in the street. It had been injured by a car I think."

The teacher clapped his hands delightedly. "How wonderful! How perfectly wonderful Lucas, for this serves to explain the theory even better!" Lucas didn't see how that was possible but he kept his mouth shut. "Let's assume that the bird would have died were it not for your intervention. That after all would have been the most likely outcome. But now you have intervened. The bird may die or it may not but ripples have been formed by your actions – ripples that might have far reaching consequences!"

Lucas still didn't know how this helped him in any way. "But what do I do?"

That's the whole point. You do nothing now other than carry on looking after the bird – whatever happens next is down to Chaos Theory – or fate if you would like to call it that!"

Lucas backed out of the room leaving the chortling teacher behind. No one could help him and no one else could help the bird. He really was alone against the world.

CHAPTER 14

When Lucas got home from school the house was empty. He let himself in and pocketed his key. Unoccupied, the house had a deserted feel to it, a despondency which seemed to leak out of the brickwork like treacle, as if the house felt emotions such as loneliness and melancholy. He paused at the foot of the stairs, remembering how it had been when his gran was alive; the house had never felt this empty then. Now it felt like a hollowed out shell, a cracked and broken egg with its insides sucked dry by the bitter wind of life.

But the house wasn't entirely empty. Brighteyes was in his bedroom, a tiny and fragile life-force. Unless..! Lucas raced up the stairs and flung the bedroom door open. Fear sucked at his cheeks, gouging them out and making his heart beat double-time.

The bird looked startled by his sudden entrance and tried to flap its wings at him. It arched its shoulder muscles as it had tried the day before, but this time he was almost sure that the injured wing was raised a little higher than it had been on the previous attempt. He stood unmoving for a moment to let the bird settle and become re-accustomed to him before entering the room.

"Are you feeling better?" he asked. The bird continued to stare at him. The skinned and de-feathered area looked drier and firmer than before and a scab had formed over a large part of the surface. But when the bird had attempted to lift its wing, the scab had cracked and now a thin line of blood oozed from it.

Lucas fetched some clean tissue from the bathroom and gently dabbed it on the wound. "According to my science teacher you are some sort of experiment the universe is holding. I think that's rubbish but just in case it's not..." he finished mopping up the blood from the bird which surprisingly made no attempt to flee from him and looked up at the sky through the bedroom window. "If you take this bird, you had better be prepared to take me with it."

He had spoken to the sky, the clouds, the universe and whatever sentient thing which perhaps lay behind it. Whether he challenged a deity or his words merely echoed off the inanimate walls was really neither here nor there. What mattered was that the challenge had been issued and that its words were carved in his heart.

The door opened and his mother's head poked through. "Did you say something Lucas?"

she asked.

"I was just talking to Brighteyes," he lied. "I didn't hear you get home." He looked at the time, "You're home early."

She smiled. "Brighteyes. That's a lovely name for it. Does it seem any better at all?"

He nodded slowly, wondering if she was avoiding his implied question. "A little bit better I think!"

"That's good. I'm home early because Martin picked me up from work. No more waiting around for the bus!" she smiled again, radiance shining through her eyes like a sunbeam through plate glass. He could see so easily how deeply hurt she was going to get. He wished he could protect her from life as much as he was trying to do for Brighteyes but it was impossible.

As if she read his thoughts through the mask of his face she looked worried. "Things happen when you are an adult Lucas. They happen and you make a decision based upon what you think is right at the time. But no one really knows. And sometimes it's a choice between your heart and your head and even then, sometimes whichever way you jump, you lose." Her eyes seemed suddenly too bright, too filled with a brittle hope. "Do you understand even a little bit of what I'm saying?"

He nodded although he wasn't really sure he did.

"All those years ago I made choices and so did Martin. Those choices can't be undone. All we can ever do is learn to move on from them. And hope for the best. And if one day, a situation arises that puts you back almost exactly in that same place then perhaps you take the other choice, the one you didn't take the last time, the one that your heart wants." A tear slowly slid down her cheek. And he understood that her words were her challenge to the universe, just as his has been.

She wiped the tear away and smiled shakily. "I thought after tea we could watch a DVD? I bought some popcorn and there are still some chocolate biscuits in the tin." She laughed shakily, "Should I avoid a Hugh Grant film?"

He bit his lip. He understood that she was trying hard to smooth things over but the whole Hugh Grant thing was still raw. He averted his eyes so she couldn't see the pain that flared there. "No it's fine." But the words burned through him.

"Okay good." She sounded relieved that there had been no argument. Had she realised too late that the reference to the actor was in bad taste? Or had she expected him to ask if Martin would be watching with them? Probably at least one of those, if not both. Well there had been no point in asking, he already knew the answer. And as for challenging the Hugh Grant comment, well enough salt had already been rubbed in that particular wound, he thought. "I'll let you get on

with your homework whilst I get the tea sorted."
She closed the door quietly.

Before starting on his homework Lucas used
the internet to find out some more about wild
pigeons and how to care for them. Surprisingly
there was rather a lot of information on the
subject and most of it was very helpful. But one
of the things that surprised him even more was
that there were other people across the world who
were intent on doing the very same things as him.
There were pigeon rescuers everywhere, from
Mumbai to Mississippi, France to Falkirk! There
was a whole community of them online!

But one thing still separated them from
him – they were adults. Able to make their own
decisions in life, they had a freedom of will that
was as yet still denied to him. And yet seeing
them affected him deeply. Perhaps he was not as
alone as he felt after all. Something occurred to
him. If he was to help Brighteyes at all, if he was to
be of value to this community and able to hold his
head high, then he would have to do a good job.
To make a change he would have to instigate the
change. Starting with himself.

Normally he did the homework for the
subjects he enjoyed first and then raced through
the ones he hated, which included maths. But
this time he started with maths, in particular the
dreaded algebra. He bit on the end of his pencil,
brain tying itself in knots, trying to figure out the

valve of the elusive x. He stared at the equation, almost willing it to form and manipulate itself into other lines, ones which miraculously revealed the answer.

The equation was not unlike life he thought, there was something missing from his life and he didn't know exactly what that was. He thought about the stuff that Mr Levy had been on about, the chaotic theory or whatever he had called it. What it really boiled down to was that no one *really* knew what would happen in life – you could hazard a guess and you could work at trying to make it go your way, but there were no guarantees.

In reaching inside his head for this understanding, his eyes had become unfocused on the book before him. He sharpened his vision bringing it back to the stark black and white symbols on the page. And suddenly he understood the value of algebra, the meaning and the specific need for it. It was all about trying to understand what was missing, trying to find the bit of the jigsaw puzzle that had been lost. It was about trying to make sense of life in its very own way!

Like a chambered bullet within a gun, he heard an audible click in his head as something shifted, some barrier was unblocked, some restriction of his own making was lifted. All the other pieces of the puzzle were there, he just hadn't seen how they were connected before. He pulled the pencil from his mouth and began to write. Figures and numbers were scrawled untidily on the page, arrows linking one symbol to another. He was sure it wasn't the method he had been shown but by the end of it he had come up with a value for x.

He slotted the number into the original equation and worked it forwards and backwards. It worked! And worked and worked! Somehow he had devised his own method of solving the problem. He moved onto the next one in line. This time his working out was faster, more assured. He moved on again and again. Finally there were no more equations left to solve. He closed the book and moved onto the next piece of homework.

With Brighteyes watching his every move, he blasted through the set work as if it was of a level given to a much younger child. He couldn't believe how easy the work had suddenly become! Had his teachers finally given up on him and decided to assign him easier work?

He flicked back the pages of every book, looking at the homework of previous days, previous weeks. He re-read the questions which had been set and the mathematical equations he'd had to solve. He remembered toiling reluctantly over them, sometimes moaning to Josh down the phone about how difficult and pointless they were and hearing the same disgruntled remarks back. And yet in every case, the solution or answers seemed blindingly obvious now. What was happening? Had his mind been invaded by aliens? Had he been abducted in his sleep and been given a mind transplant? It just didn't make sense!

A tiny voice from the back of his head fought to be heard. *It just didn't have any importance before, any relevance... but now it does!* It was because of Brighteyes! Because of the bird, he had a reason to make sense of the world. He thought that the need had always been there but had perhaps lain dormant. Having the bird and the responsibility that it brought had given him the key to unlock his resolve. If he was too dim to understand how his actions would impact the bird, then Brighteyes would not survive. Whatever happened would be his doing and his alone.

Into the search engine on the laptop he typed the words 'chaotic theory' and watched as it brought up the phrase 'showing results for Chaos Theory'. He clicked on it and read the explanation. It was much more complicated than Mr Levy had suggested, but he thought he got a small measure of the idea. In the back of his maths book he copied down some of the explanation. He didn't know why he did this and he didn't care to question himself too much.

He had a slight headache and suspected

it was actual brain ache from his mind's sudden expansion. He wondered if it had physically grown inside his head; whether the circumference of his head was slightly larger than a mere half hour ago. Or perhaps when the brain grew it folded and compacted into itself even more, so that it became denser without being larger?

He thought about looking it up on the internet but either way it would only cause more growth and probably a bigger headache, so he left it for another day. But before he abandoned and perhaps lost the thought entirely, he wrote the question down in the back of his science book so that he could look it up another time.

"Lucas! Dinner!" his mother called up the stairs.

"Gotta go Brighteyes, but I'll be back later. Get some rest." The pigeon blinked in response. Opening his bedroom door, the smell of hot vinegar wafted towards him. Forgetting all about Martin for a moment, he descended the stairs eagerly. Three huge bags of fish and chips had been laid out on the table, still in their paper wrappers, steam rising from them as if they'd been but a moment out of the hot chip fat. The vinegary oiliness was irresistible and his stomach gave a deep growl of appreciation.

"Martin thought it would be nice to have a chip-shop tea," Anna said pointedly, forcing him to acknowledge his evening's benefactor.

Lucas smiled politely and forced out the words he hadn't wanted to say. "Thank you!"

Martin smiled and held something wrapped in a paper bag out to him. "I stopped off at the pet shop first. This is what they sell to pigeon fanciers, you know the men who keep racing pigeons. They said this is the highest quality food." He held the bag out to Lucas.

Lucas was torn. He wanted the contents of the bag but he didn't want to take it from Martin and he certainly didn't want to have to thank the man for a second time in almost the same breath. He reached forward and grasped the proffered bag but Martin did not immediately relinquish his hold. They stood for a moment like two warriors, each weighing the other up. Lucas swallowed the saliva which lay in his mouth, letting it take some of his pride with it. *This is for Brighteyes*, he told himself as he forced the words of thanks out between narrow lips.

"That's okay," Martin said magnanimously and something in his eyes said that he knew how much it had cost Lucas to say the words and that he was both pleased and relieved. "Don't let your fish and chips get cold." He smiled genuinely.

"Ahem, have you washed your hands?" Anna asked.

Lucas tried to remember if he had washed them after wiping away the birds oozing blood.

He couldn't imagine that he wouldn't have done so but could not truthfully remember either washing or drying his hands.

"Okay, well why don't you give the bird - Brighteyes," she remembered, "some of the special food and then wash your hands afterwards and have tea with us. That way the bird can eat in peace."

It seemed a sensible suggestion so Lucas did as she asked. He was only gone a minute or two but by the time he came back into the kitchen, Martin and his mother were already discussing which DVD they would watch. "My favourite is actually 'About A Boy'," Anna said. "But perhaps we should watch a different type of film?" she suggested, looking at Lucas.

Lucas thought that the plot of the film was a little too close to his own unfolding life in some strange and warped way. If he had to endure watching Hugh Grant befriend a boy who was not his son, whilst Martin and Anna sat next to him on the sofa, he thought he might choke to death on the very first piece of popcorn. But he couldn't tell his mother that. So instead he said, "We have seen that over and over. What about the one where Sandra Bullock is his lawyer but he doesn't know that he's in love with her?" It was actually his least favourite of his mother's collection but he knew that it would have been her second choice and therefore his get-out card. Picking a non-Hugh-Grant film wasn't really an option, he didn't think they actually owned any other DVDs.

"I didn't think you were keen on that one Lucas. You always said it was mushy!" Clearly she hadn't realised exactly why he had chosen it.

He shrugged aiming for nonchalance. "It's okay. And it's better than some of the others." This would in the past have been a dangerous thing to have said and would have launched Anna into a full discussion about the various plots and merits of each and every one of Hugh Grant's films. But now she merely nodded. Once they had finished eating and whilst Anna was clearing everything away, Martin located the disk and slipped it into the DVD player. He was engrossed in the task and didn't seem to notice Lucas scrutinising him.

"If you keep staring like that, you will burn a hole in the back of my head!" Martin said without turning around, bending down and pressing a button on the machine.

Lucas wondered how he had known he was being watched. "I was just wondering if you liked Hugh Grant the way Mum does?" What he had actually been wondering was how if his mum fancied Hugh Grant so much, she could ever have fancied Martin in the first place, as he was nothing like the actor, neither in looks, attitude or style.

"Lucas quite frankly, *no one* likes Hugh

Grant the way your mother does! Do they Anna?"
he asked good humouredly.

Anna laughed and it was the most girly
coquettish sound Lucas had ever heard her utter.
"I don't know what you are both talking about!"
But her eyes twinkled and a real joy lit up her face
at this momentary respite from hostilities.

"I wish Gran was here with us," Lucas said
then could have kicked himself when he saw the
short-lived joy disappear from his mother's face.

"Yes, I do too Lucas," Anna said softly. But
although she said the words as if she really meant
them, Lucas harboured a doubt. Did she really
wish that? If Valerie Pertwee had still been here,
then Martin most certainly would not have been.
Lucas would have staked his life on that.

He snatched a handful of popcorn from the
bowl on the coffee table and forced as much as
he could into his mouth. If he couldn't manage to
keep some thoughts to himself, then the evening
would become very unpleasant very quickly, he
thought. Martin passed him the bowl. "Here you
go, knock yourself out Lucas." The words were
not said unkindly. Did Martin realise that the only
way Lucas could keep from blurting something
out was by stuffing his mouth too full to talk?
Maybe!

With them both still standing, an
awkwardness presented itself. The living room
contained a large sofa and two armchairs, all in

a deep brown material. Anna had already seated herself at one end of the sofa, leaving the middle space and the end one free. Lucas didn't want Martin to sit next to his mother on the sofa but the only way of preventing that for sure was to sit next to her himself, which then left open the possibility that Martin would sit the other side of him, effectively putting Lucas in between them.

Bowl of popcorn in his hands, Lucas turned and looked at Martin. They were still both standing, both equidistant from the seat at Anna's side. Momentarily a moving picture image sprang up in Lucas's head. He could throw the popcorn at Martin and whilst he was momentarily blinded or confused by the salty puffs of grain, Lucas could dive, head first onto the seat, thus sparing himself from having to watch them sitting together.

It was a ludicrous image and he almost laughed aloud, only just managing to stop himself in time. He didn't think either his mother or Martin would have been impressed if he had been forced to tell them what he was laughing so hard about. Just before he steeled himself to make a decision about where to sit, Martin moved to one of the armchairs and flopped down into it as if the thought of sitting on the sofa had never even crossed his mind.

"You can sit here, we don't bite, do we Lucas?" Anna said, patting the cushion next to her. Lucas wasn't sure if he could hold himself to her promise. He might bite if Martin sat there! He might bite very hard indeed!

"No, I'm fine here. Besides I like the armrests," Martin explained and placed both arms along the sides of the chair in demonstration.

"But you can't see the TV so well from there," Anna tried again.

"Honestly Anna I can see fine," Martin said but Lucas knew he was lying. He had sat on that chair many times when his gran and mum had sat on the sofa and he knew that although you could watch the TV from there, it was a weird angle and you couldn't get caught up in the plot in the same way as you could from the sofa.

Lucas sat down on the sofa but for some reason it didn't feel right to be there. On the seat next to him, his mother radiated nervousness and all the ease of a tightly coiled spring. She pressed the play button on the remote and the opening credits rolled over the screen. Lucas kept his attention swivelled away from the other occupants of the room and prepared to endure what he suspected would feel like the longest film showing of his life.

CHAPTER 15

About halfway through the film, Martin stood up and disappeared into the kitchen. He was gone for only a matter of minutes but it was enough time for Lucas to wonder what would happen if he didn't come back in. Would his mother be angry if she thought that Martin had been too bored to continue watching the film? Would his walking out on it spell disaster for the relationship?

But just as Lucas began to have some hope that this might actually happen, Martin reappeared carrying a tray, loaded with snacks and drinks. He set it down on the coffee table and picked up his own pint glass without further comment. Anna reached forward for the large glass of wine that Martin had put on the tray for her. She took a sip and selected a chocolate from the open box. Lucas noticed that the box contained only dark chocolate – his mother's preference. "What a treat!" she cooed, "Lucas there's some coke for you too!"

He was gutted that she would now expect

him to be grateful to Martin. Again! Before she could prompt him, he dived in himself. "Thanks," he muttered, still refusing to look the man in the eye but nonetheless reaching forward for the drink.

"I know your mother prefers dark chocolate but it's not to everyone's taste," Martin responded warmly as if he believed Lucas's thanks to be genuine. "So I got you a couple of chocolate bars in case you'd like that better."

Lucas was flabbergasted. Was there no end to what this man would do to get into Anna Pertwee's good books? To get into her bed? And what should he, Lucas, do about it? He stole a sidelong glance at his mother who seemed to be so riveted with the film that she was unaware of the tension and few lines of conversation around her. Within the confines of such a small room, Lucas knew that was actually impossible. His mother was continuing to do what she had promised – leave them to it to forge a relationship with one another. Or not – if that was an option. Lucas wondered if that was possible, if they could live in the same house, hating each other for all eternity, passing things and comments politely back and forth whilst seething with an inner rage.

Martin took Lucas's silence for indecision. Or perhaps he just used it to make himself look even better. "I bought some crisps too in case you would prefer those, but you could have them all really. A growing boy like you doesn't need to worry too much about what he eats once in a while. Why don't you go into the kitchen and choose what you want?"

Lucas nodded but he couldn't bring himself to say thanks and he couldn't shake the feeling that it was a ruse to get him out of his position on the sofa. Perhaps if he ventured into the kitchen to find whatever might be there, he would return to find Martin and his mother snuggled up on the sofa and himself relegated to the armchair with the bad view of the TV.

But it seemed that his brain had already informed his stomach of the sugary and salty snacks that were on offer, making his stomach give a long, low, protracted growl. He could feel the waves of peristalsis that racked his intestines and demanded he venture forth and seize the treats that had been bought for him. He nodded and stood up, edging away from the sofa towards the door without straying into his mother's line of vision.

In the kitchen, three popular confectionary bars had been laid out next to a packet of salt and vinegar crisps. The pack was one of the extra-large ones, one size below the family size and therefore meant for him alone and not for sharing. He was overwhelmed with relief at this simple thing. He was already being asked to share way too much – his home, his life and worst of all, his mother's love and attention. Sharing the crisps, small and insignificant as that might be, may well have been the straw that broke the camel's back.

He selected two out of the three chocolate bars and the crisps and re-entered the lounge. Nothing much had changed from when he had left, except perhaps that both Martin and his mother appeared to have downed quite a lot of their drinks. "Thanks," he mumbled, feeling the words stick in the back of his throat.

Martin smiled, "No problem. But whilst you are up, Lucas, would you mind fetching me another can from the fridge and the bottle of wine for your mum?" It was a question without being a question and not one of those rhetorical ones that supplied their own answer either, Lucas thought, his temper simmering quietly. It was a demand, an order nicely given but one which he could not refuse, at least not without seeming rude and churlish.

He put his snacks down on the table and went to fetch the drinks. Who was Martin to be ordering him about? Who was he to be using the fridge to store his beer as if he had every right to be there? As if he had a right to be buying Anna chocolates and wine; buying Lucas chocolates and crisps? But the answer was self-evident. If his mother was to be believed, and quite frankly

Lucas couldn't see why she would lie, then Martin was his father... and the only one he was ever likely to have.

Unwilling to hand Martin the can, he placed it on the floor beside the armchair and put the wine bottle on the floor next to his mother then settled down to watch what remained of the film with the snacks in his lap.

He ate his way through the dialogue and the scenes, not really needing to pay attention to the screen to know what was happening in the film: he had seen it so many times before he almost knew the lines by heart. He popped a crisp into his mouth, savouring the strong vinegary coating before letting the wafer thin potato almost dissolve on his tongue. Here was the scene where Sandra Bullock made an impassioned speech and here was the one where Huge Grant raised his eyebrows in amazement at his passionate and forthright employee.

Was this how it had been between Martin and his mum? Suddenly he was considering the film in a whole new light. Had there been this chemistry, this energy between them when they had worked together before he was born? Had it been inevitable that they had fallen in love and had an affair? Was it no more than the hand of fate that had pushed them together, a warped destiny that had taken no account of the fact that Martin was married? He finished the crisps and moved on to one of the chocolate bars. In the end the film would be happy; all issues resolved the characters would admit to each other and to themselves how they felt and that would be that. Real life was rarely that simple Lucas realised.

The clink of glass upon glass called his attention back to his mother who was pouring herself another glass of wine. He hoped she wouldn't drink too much, relax and let Martin kiss her or worse. Focused on her actions, Anna did not immediately notice Lucas watching her. He could see why Martin was sticking around. Apart from the obvious that he had nowhere else to go, Anna was still an attractive woman.

Unused to thinking of his mum in that way, Lucas mentally compared her with the other mums who turned up at the school on parents' evening. Trim and slender but too curvy to be thought of as thin, she was younger and fitter looking than most of the other mums, even though they were more or less all the same age.

Yes, his mum was her own version of Sandra Bullock, ordinary enough to fit in with the crowd whilst also exquisite enough to be noticed within it. But Martin? Lucas had already realised the man was no Hugh Grant... but there *was* something about him which made him noticeable too, something almost unapologetic about him, as if he understood and accepted his failings and therefore felt no need to seek anyone else's acceptance of them. Lucas ate the chocolate as he contemplated, not really paying attention to the film at all. By the time he had finished the second bar, the film was also finishing.

"Well I enjoyed that!" his mother exclaimed although whether she meant the wine or the film or even the combination of the two was unclear. "Time for bed Lucas," she declared, getting up and collecting the sweet rappers and glasses onto the tray.

"But I have to check on Brighteyes first and make sure the water bowl is still fresh and everything," he said, worried that he would be made to go to bed before he had done these tasks for his feathered companion.

Anna nodded. "Of course, that's your responsibility. But as soon as it's done, then bed!"

Lucas nodded. "Okay, night Mum," he bent and kissed her cheek. Straightening up there was a moment of tension when he wondered if he could just leave the room without acknowledging Martin, but before he could try, he caught the warning look in his mother's eyes. "Night Martin," he threw the words over his shoulder, hoping that would be enough to satisfy his mother, at least for now. "And thanks again for the snacks," he felt obliged to say.

"No problem Lucas, I'm just glad you enjoyed them." Delivered from behind his back, Lucas couldn't detect any sarcasm or derision in

Martin's voice and yet he was almost sure it was there. Almost.

He climbed the stairs and went into his room. He had left the bedside lamp on when he went out and therefore didn't need to switch it on. Brighteyes had appeared to be asleep when he first pushed open the door but was instantly awake and regarding him as curiously as ever.

Very slowly he reached into the box. The bird backed up to the furthest corner to try to avoid his hands but it didn't attempt to bat them away with its wings. Gently he lifted it and brought it close to his face to be examined. "I read some stuff about you lot today," he told the bird. "Pigeons I mean. You mate for life." He thought that its injures looked a little better and that the bird itself seemed stronger, less hollow than it had before. He placed it on the windowsill for a moment. The window was closed so there was no chance of it flying or falling from it and although it was now dark outside, he thought that the bird would appreciate a safe view of the world it had so nearly permanently departed. "It's a shame the same can't be said for humans."

Brighteyes tilted its head at the darkness for a moment before turning its beady gaze back to Lucas. It appeared to watch as the boy cleaned out the dirty paper in the box and replaced it with fresh strips of torn newspaper and then topped up the food. "I'll get you some fresh water," he said, taking the eggcup and moving towards his door. He stepped into the hall just as the door to the bedroom Martin was using closed. He didn't see who shut it but he had a suspicion it wasn't Martin.

A quake started somewhere inside him and soon consumed the whole of his being. He sloshed the bird's water down the bathroom sink and refilled it with fresh water from the tap. But he was reluctant to step back out into the hall. Perhaps his mother was just having a chat with Martin in the bedroom; perhaps she was helping him with something. His mind struggled to think what that something could be, other than the blindingly obvious. His head thumped with tension. But perhaps he had been mistaken and even now his mother was preparing for bed in his gran's old room.

Eggcup in hand, he knocked softly on what used to be Valerie Pertwee's bedroom door. It was hard to gauge the rap of knuckles against wood – too softly and his mother would not hear, even if she was in that room, too loudly and she would hear even if she was in Martin's room. And if she *was* in the other bedroom with Martin, the very last thing Lucas wanted to do was to witness the advancement of their relationship. To be provided with concrete proof.

There was no answer to his knock. Unable to prevent himself, Lucas pushed open the door.

The room was in darkness. Either his mother was already in bed, asleep, or she wasn't there. "Mum?" he whispered into the darkness, knowing in his heart that his words fell on empty space. She wasn't there. And she wasn't downstairs either. The floor below him lay dark and silent. Everyone in the house was upstairs. Which meant that Anna was in Martin's bedroom.

Lucas shook his head in anger and frustration. It wasn't Martin's bedroom! Calling and thinking of it as that gave too much permanency to the relationship, as if Martin was definitely there to stay. For good. It was in fact his mother's room. So therefore Anna had merely gone into her own bedroom. Except that for the moment at least, Martin was sleeping there!

Lucas shunted the thoughts around in his head as he popped Brighteyes back into its box and prepared himself for bed. He mashed and moulded the evidence, cut and shaped the deliberations, trying to make them fit what he wanted to believe. But there really was no other explanation. His mother and Martin were sleeping together. If they hadn't been up until now, they were certainly doing so tonight... and maybe all the nights from this one onwards!

He slid into bed and shuddered at the coldness of the sheets and the emptiness inside of him. His mind supplied the susurration of a whispered conversation; words which were inexplicable to him; voices that were secretive and private; hearts that were shuttered away from him. The last image which filled his inner vision before sleep claimed him almost broke his heart: it was his mother walking arm in arm with Martin, whilst he, Lucas, was nowhere to be seen. Lost. Lonely.

Abandoned.

CHAPTER 16

Days passed, as time generally did. People said that time was a healer but Lucas wasn't experiencing that at all. If anything, time for him was an aggressor, making everyone around him feel that things were moving on, that life was getting easier, when it wasn't getting any easier for him!

He heard her sneak out that first morning. Heard her make her way to her own bedroom so that she could pretend she had been there all night. And to his shame he had gone along with the pretence. Had averted his eyes and his mind of thoughts of what exactly had gone on in the darkness and privacy of the bedroom Martin slept in. But like the pounding of a fierce headache, the feelings conjured up by the thought of them together would not go away.

He felt sickened in his soul. He wasn't dumb, he knew what adults did in bed together. But the thought of his mother and Martin…! It was gut-wrenching beyond belief. But there was so much more to it than that too. He knew that if he challenged his mother she would say that she loved Martin and he figured that she probably did. And maybe that was exactly what was wrong with the situation! It wasn't just sex and companionship she was experiencing this time, it was love. Love that was supposed to ease the soul and lift the heart. Love that supposedly conquered all. Well it wasn't conquering him!

It would have been so much better if he had been sure that it was *just* sex between them, just a carnal desire being fulfilled, devoid of any stirrings below skin level; empty of promises of love. But he knew damn well that was not the case.

He could see how radiant his mother was becoming, how glowing and somehow more at ease with herself she was getting on a daily basis. At first it was subtle things which changed about her, a certain light that mysteriously lit up her eyes when she was thinking about something. Something he knew nothing about. Then other more obvious changes began to appear. She began to dress differently – only a little but it was noticeable. Her skirts began to get shorter than she usually wore. Instead of the mid-calf gypsy style skirts she normally favoured, she began to wear ones that skimmed her knees. Hardly minis he had to admit but certainly shorter than before.

Her tops changed too. Now she seldom wore the loose, floaty ones she liked but instead sported fitted tops which clung to her curves. And perfume! She had never worn perfume in the day before but she wore it now! He would bend to kiss her as he left for school or went to bed and the sweet smell would clog in his nostrils like cotton wool, hampering his breathing and making him feel ill.

And with the change of clothing came a boldness that frightened him. That first morning she had put up every pretence of having slept in his gran's old room and he had put up every pretence of believing her. But the next morning she had tried a little less hard to look as if she had done nothing wrong and he in turn had pretended a little more that he didn't know what was going on.

He hated it! He hated what she was doing with Martin and he hated that she was virtually lying to him with her pretence of innocence. But more than that, he hated that the pretence was deliberately being eroded away, being slowly deconstructed on a daily basis so that presumably the whole thing wouldn't come as a shock to him, but would instead be a gradual realisation that she was sleeping with Martin. Of course if that was *all* she had been doing – sleeping – there really would not have been a problem but he knew that was not the case at all.

This morning she was more blatant than ever. Martin had to make an early start and

Lucas heard them talking as they came out of the room together. He was already up and had put Brighteyes on his bedroom windowsill as he cleaned out the box and put fresh food in.

The pigeon was coming along well and every day took more of an interest in the world outside the window. She would turn her head to watch other birds fly past but now, instead of trying to press herself through the glass as she had done the first morning he had placed her there, she would watch for a while and then turn to him as if to say, 'That will be me one day, won't it? You *will* set me free, won't you?'

He always replied verbally to her look. "Yes Brighteyes, that will be you too one day." His mouth said the words even as his heart tried to retract them. He could no longer imagine being in his room without his little feathered friend to keep him company. The pigeon was growing more and more comfortable with him every day and there was a feeling of teamwork between them, as if it was actively helping in its own rehabilitation.

Daily he examined the wounds to make sure they continued to improve. At first scared of him, the bird would try to cower away but now it spread its wings as if to enable him access to its injured areas. Somehow it knew that he was no threat and in return he gave it more freedom when he was home, taking it out of the box and letting it wander around at will.

It still couldn't fly though. Too many lost feathers and too much injury inflicted on its muscles meant that the journey back to flight would not be a quick one but Lucas was almost relieved at the thought. It gave them a little more time together if nothing else.

He glanced at the view the bird was currently enjoying through the window pane. The morning was bright but perhaps not as bright as the one before had been. Darker days and colder nights were fast approaching. He wondered how sensible it would be to release the bird during the unforgiving harshness of winter. If the bird was ready to go by then would he be justified in holding onto it until the spring? The question thundered around his brain but he couldn't find the answer within himself. And maybe that was okay, maybe things would work out by themselves.

He gave the pigeon a light pat on its head. "C'mon Brighteyes. Back to your box. I have to get my teeth brushed then go to school. You get some rest while I'm gone," he said. He placed the bird back in its box and smiled as straight away it began to eat.

His mother was in the bathroom brushing her teeth with the door slightly ajar. Lucas was about to go in and wait his turn until he realised she was not alone. Martin was in there with her, using his electric shaver at the special power socket. From where Lucas stood he could see them but they could not see him. He watched horrified and mesmerized as Martin playfully slapped his mother on the bottom. Anna laughed and in return poked a foamy toothbrush at the man's midriff.

There was so much easy familiarity between them now. Lucas's throat constricted with envy. There was no room in this little tableau for him and he felt like he was the stranger, the outsider who had no place to be there. Then, just as she turned back to the sink, Anna caught sight of her son. "Morning honey! How did you sleep?" she asked.

Lucas considered telling the truth for a moment. 'I slept okay until I heard him grunting in the middle of the night and you groaning Mum!' he could have said but he couldn't steel himself to be *that* aggressive, *that* vile. "Okay," he mumbled instead.

"Well Martin has had an idea, haven't you Martin?" Anna prompted. Martin nodded. Lucas watched the man's head bob up and down and wanted to smash his fist into it.

"I thought we could go on a bike ride," he said enthusiastically although Lucas was sure that the enthusiasm was summoned for Anna's benefit only.

Lucas tried not to look horrified at the

prospect of spending time alone with Martin. "My bike has a puncture."

"Yes your mum mentioned that, so I bought you a spare tyre and we can look at the puncture at the weekend and see if it can be repaired." Martin beamed as if he couldn't wait.

"I've got homework..." Lucas said quickly, desperate for another excuse.

"I'm sure you can take one night off from homework and catch up tomorrow night?" This time it was a proper question. Lucas thought about denying that possibility but his mother would have been angry and perhaps Martin would have been offended. Not that he was concerned about offending the man but if his mother thought that he had... It just wasn't a good idea, he decided.

"And there's Brighteyes too, she will be alone all day *and* all evening then!" he tried to keep his voice level, to not betray the desperation which leached from his soul. All of this was happening because Josh had left! He knew that wasn't a logical belief but he was sure of it nonetheless. When Josh had lived across the road, Lucas's world had been calm, it had been orderly, it had been *good.* But now? Josh was gone and wouldn't even speak to him on the phone, his gran was dead and cremated, there was an annoying girl living in Josh's old house who seemed determined to befriend him, Hugh Grant had turned out *not* to be his father and Martin had, arriving like cholera into a third-world country and infecting everyone he touched with his own special brand of falseness!

Unaware of his inner hysteria, his mother had an answer for the problem of Brighteyes. "I'll take her into the living room with me and we can keep each other company."

From the look on her face Lucas could see that she thought that was a good idea. "No, the noise from the TV and the flashes of light will scare her..." He knew now they would not accept any excuse why he couldn't go out on a bike ride with Martin but Brighteyes was a genuine consideration. "She likes being on my windowsill," he said. "I suppose if I put her there before I went out and you just came in every so often and checked on her, she'd be fine."

Anna nodded. "That sounds like a good idea." She came out of the bathroom to let him brush his teeth. "Right then, I'll see you after school," she gave him a peck on the cheek, breath minty-fresh and jarring with the muskiness of the perfume she wore. Lucas submitted to the kiss but did not enter the bathroom, waiting for Martin to exit first.

The man carried on shaving. To Lucas he appeared already closely shaved but Martin continued to run the electric razor over his skin. "It's okay I just need to finish here. I don't need the sink." He indicated the empty space Anna had just vacated. Lucas really didn't want to be brushing his teeth whilst sharing the bathroom with Martin but he didn't seem to have any choice in the matter. He brushed furiously, desperate to get out of the situation and out of the house.

Molly was waiting for him to walk to school with her. Just as she had most mornings since moving to the street. She was fiddling with her shoe laces as he came level with her house and he had more than a suspicion that she had only been pretending to be doing them up or tightening them or whatever, lingering until he came past. It was clearly not going to be his day.

"How's your pigeon?" she asked brightly.

"It's not really my pigeon is it?" he replied sharply.

"Well if it isn't yours, whose is it?" she asked, falling into step beside him.

Lucas was frustrated with the girl, who seemed determined to hang around him. What was it with her? Why wouldn't she just go away and play with other little kids her own age? "No one's really. It's a pigeon. It can't be owned by me or anyone!"

She was undaunted. "My mum said that when she was my age her dad had pigeons. She said-" she appeared to be readying herself to quote her mother, taking a deep breath, "'my dad owned over twenty racing pigeons.'" She delivered the quote in a slightly more mature voice which she clearly thought sounded like her mother.

Lucas was getting more annoyed by the minute. "Well if they were *racing* pigeons, that's different isn't it?" Although he wasn't exactly sure if that was true or not. "Why don't go find another little girl to walk to school with anyway? Why are you hanging around me?" The words came out a little more harshly than he had intended. He stole a covert sidelong glance at her. He didn't mean to hurt her but he really did wish that she would just go away.

Molly said nothing but continued to keep pace with him. Lucas tried again. "You know just because Josh was my friend and you have moved into his old house, doesn't make you my new best friend."

Molly nodded but her mouth had turned down slightly at the corners he noticed. "No, it doesn't, you are right. But who else have you got?" she pushed the point of her answer into his heart, the truth of it piercing him and bringing him to a halt. "You see Lucas, I have just moved onto this street and to this school... but already I have made friends. And they *wanted* to walk to school with me." She looked him dead in the eyes.

"But do you know why I didn't walk with them? Do you know why I stood outside my house and waited for you to arrive?" she paused and he wasn't sure that he wanted to hear the answer anyway. "I did that not because I don't have any friends but because YOU don't! After all those years in that school with the same kids there every day, you don't have a single one to call your friend!"

He wanted to protest that she was wrong, that he did have a friend, that Josh was his friend, but he knew she was right. Not only was Josh no longer his friend but now that he was gone from both the street and the school, there was no one he could even pass the time of day with!

He had neither the will nor the temerity to try to contradict her. "I'm fine with that," he said quietly instead, hating how it felt like giving up on himself. They began to walk again, this time at a more measured pace.

"You really expect me to believe that?" she asked incredulously, not moving her gaze from his face as if she could physically pull the truth from him.

"What are you? Some kind of ten-year old Jeremy Kyle?" he asked.

"Maybe, maybe not. Maybe I'm just your best bet of being normal," she responded a little too undiplomatically for his liking.

"I am normal!" he exclaimed, beginning to be angry once more. "Anyway that's just a word… what does being normal mean to anyone?"

Molly shrugged. "I guess being normal is having people around you who like you, people you want to spend time with."

When she put it like that he thought that maybe she was right after all. There was no one in his life now who fitted that description. "But I can't hang around with a ten-year-old girl," he said a little too disparagingly.

"Oh yes, 'cos you have queues of people lining up to hang out with you!" she snorted. Once more she had stung him to the core. "Y'see you are looking at this all wrong." She sounded so grown-up and confident of her point that he was intrigued. "If you kinda treat me as a kid sister then you are not really hanging out with me as such."

"I still don't get how that works in my favour." He thought for a moment. "Or even in yours."

She smiled and her face lit up. "Well I just think you deserve another chance. I mean you're like that pigeon of yours... you're kinda in the gutter with no one to help you," she waived her arms dramatically, "they're just all passing you by without taking notice."

"Apart from you," he said, beginning to get an inkling of how she was thinking.

"Exactly!" she beamed. "And so just like you did with the pigeon, I noticed and I tried to interview to help you."

"I think you mean intervene," he corrected.

"Interview, intervene, whatever! What I mean is that this time I am you and you are the pigeon."

In a more than slightly warped way her words made sense to him. Saving the pigeon had made him feel good, it had given him a purpose in life. Maybe that was what she sought too? But it still didn't answer the question of how she could actually help him in any way. "Okay, say I treat you as a kid sister, then what? How does that make me more popular?"

Molly snorted. "I never said it would make you more popular, what I said was that I could help you be more *normal*." She waved her hands in the air again as if needing their help to explain her point. "I can't *make* people like you Lucas, though I can't see any reason why they wouldn't once they get to know you. Under all that moodiness and stuff I mean."

"Gee thanks!"

She laughed again. "Don't take everything so personally," she said.

He raised his eyebrows. "I'm sorry but you have spent the entire conversation insulting me and I'm not supposed to take it personally?" She really did take the biscuit, he thought.

"Exactly! It's just a seeing thing, a whatdoyoumacaall it, a thingy…"

Lucas thought hard. The conversation was

going off track and he was losing the thread rapidly.

"When you watch something and you see it!" she was getting annoyed with herself that she couldn't remember the word.

"An observation?" he supplied.

"That's it! That's the thing I meant – an obstication! That's what it was!" she was almost skipping with excitement now.

"Ob*servation*," he supplied again.

"Whatever," she waved the word off with her hands. "The point is that you have to let them get to know you before they can like you."

Lucas thought that most of the kids at his school already knew too much about him and none of it was stuff that evoked any admiration in them, let alone offers of friendship. "But how is our hanging around together going to achieve that?" he asked.

"Because dumbo, those girls *I* hang around with – well most of them have big brothers and sometimes their mums let them go places 'cos their brothers are there to look after them…"

Lucas cottoned on. "But you are not allowed to go 'cos you don't have a big brother looking after you!"

She nodded. "Yup! And some of these boys are older than you. If you made friends with some of them, the rest of the boys in your year would look up to you."

It suddenly all made sense. By hanging out with younger kids he would be introduced to older ones, ramping up his street cred in a way he would never have thought even remotely possible.

"Come on little sis, get a move on, or we'll be late for school," he teased and thought that maybe the day might not be so bad after all.

CHAPTER 17

School turned out to be the same as usual and yet infinitely different from how it had ever been before. There was a new girl in his form class, rounding the class number back out from twenty-nine to thirty and taking Josh's vacated place.

Claudia King was everything her name suggested and more. An incandescent beauty, she merely had to look around her to have immediately captured the heart of every boy in the class. "Claudia will be starting school with us today." The new girl stood next to Mrs Macey at the front of the classroom, looking not the least bit awkward. "Perhaps you would like to tell everyone a little bit about yourself Claudia," the Head Teacher prompted.

The girl smiled and Lucas felt sure that somewhere outside the school walls, a rainbow lit up the dull and gloomy neighbourhood. "Hi. My name is Claudia and my family and I have just moved here." Her voice was the most beautiful sound that Lucas had ever heard. Neither too loud nor too soft to be heard, it was melodious yet carried within itself an edge of sharp intelligence, like she was sure of herself but not in a cocky way.

Without looking, Lucas suspected that the other girls in the class would be jealous to the point of deliberately looking bored or maybe even outright aggressive. He wondered if Emily Matthews would have her pencil sharpener out again, feigning disinterest. Dragging his eyes away from this vision of loveliness he cast his glance around. To his amazement he saw that the girls were just as entranced by this Goddess in their midst as the boys were.

Claudia flicked her long golden locks out of her eyes. Lucas's brain slowed the action into a series of slow-motion stills, the slight initial incline of her head, followed by the toss that made her hair billow around her face like some golden halo and then the descent of those golden, silken strands which came to rest as perfectly as if they had been set there by the most accomplished hairdresser.

"I have just started to play the violin," the girl tinkled out a self-deprecating laugh. "My dad says it sounds like a strangulated cat! But I think I'll keep practising anyway..." she shrugged her shoulders.

"Thank you Claudia for telling us a little bit about you. I'm sure your teachers will help you settle in and feel at home right away!" Mrs Macey dismissed the girl as she indicated the empty chair Claudia was expected to fill. He wished it was the actual one that Josh had vacated but that space remained an open void between himself and the rest of the class. "And Class I expect you to make your new classmate very welcome!" She turned on her heel and left.

Somehow Lucas didn't think that Claudia would have any cause for complaint. All faces were turned towards her in warm adoration. The girl would be swamped with offers to be shown around by both the girls and the boys. There was no point in him even trying to talk to her, she was so far above a mere mortal like him. Even so, he spent the rest of the day in a mild swoon.

Claudia turned out to be in the same set as him for Maths and a few other lessons and Lucas couldn't help but be aware of how different he felt when she was around. And he thought that he was not alone in experiencing these feelings. Everywhere she went people seemed eager to make way for her, shuffling themselves tighter onto benches to make a space for her, or cramming themselves into corners so that she might have the best seat.

Even though she evoked the same desire in him as she seemed to in everyone else, a fierce longing to be even a small part of her world, to breathe the same air as she did, he was a little sickened by the outright fawning that was taking place around her. *It's because she is so beautiful*, he thought to himself. *It's not because of who she is inside, but because of what she looks like on the outside!* But wasn't that what had entranced him too?

Instead of falling at her feet, Lucas kept a safe distance between them. Even where in some classes they were seated close enough that he could have stretched out and touched her, had he been so inclined, he kept himself away. And not once did she look in his direction. It wasn't that she was ignoring him, more like she was the sun to his moon; she shone so brightly she attracted the attention of most everything nearby, her light and beauty eclipsing all else. He was just a pale comparison, lacking both the force and the impetus to draw people to him in the same way, lacking the brightness to attract *her*.

Just as the moon orbits the Earth, which in turn orbits the Sun, the moon still spinning alongside it, so was he forced to witness this adulation first-hand. It was all he could do to prevent himself from being sucked into the *Claudiamania* which seemed to sweep the school. Even on the journey home, there was no escaping the mention of Claudia's name.

"We had a new girl in class today," Molly chirped. "She has a big sister in your year. Her name is Claudia, have you met her yet?" Molly looked expectantly up to him as they walked, her school bag swung precariously from one shoulder.

"Mmm."

"Mmm? What does that mean? D'you mean you haven't met her or you have?" Molly persisted.

"Yes I've met her." He was suddenly curious about what Claudia's little sister was like. He wondered if she was the same as the older girl in any way. "What's the little sister like?" he asked casually.

"Her name is Keira and she's funny!"

"I meant what does she look like?"

Molly looked at him strangely. "She's got dark blonde hair and wears glasses. Why? What does her big sister look like?"

Josh hated how Molly seemed to be always able to cut to the heart of every issue; how she seemed to have this ability to look *inside* him, not to what he had said but almost to what he had *thought*. It was unnerving to say the least! "She's quite pretty, I guess," he said, but from the way the younger girl arched her eyebrows, this time he thought *he* knew what she was thinking. "I mean if you like that sort of thing!" Still Molly said nothing and he was forced into a half-admission. "Well at least most of the class thinks so anyway."

"But not you, right?" She regarded him honestly and he thought there was a flicker of disappointment in her large eyes.

"Well she is pretty... but..." he was uncomfortable about having to admit it. He walked slightly faster, eager to be home.

"I'll see you tomorrow. Maybe we can hang out after school then, but tonight I have to visit my grandma." Molly also seemed eager to get home. She flicked her bag off her shoulder and didn't even wait for him to say goodbye before she skipped through her front door and was gone.

Lucas knew she hadn't meant anything by her comment about visiting her gran; she hadn't said it to upset him or to rub his nose in things, but nonetheless her words brought forth a painful surge of remembrance and regret. Talking to his own gran was now a thing of the past, a vestige of another time, another life - another Lucas. He walked the few remaining steps to his own front door, noticing that Martin's car was already parked outside the house.

Martin was alone in the kitchen, a single mug placed in front of the boiling kettle. "Ah back from school already," he said cheerfully and flicked the kettle switch to off as if he didn't have the audacity to make tea in Lucas's home right in front of the boy's eyes. Lucas grunted in response and prepared to dump his bag on the floor. "I fixed the new tyre onto your bike so we are all ready to go."

Lucas reached above the fridge to the biscuit tin and selected a couple of custard creams before replacing the lid and storing the box away again. Was Martin really expecting an answer? A refusal? Could Lucas give him one?

Martin surprised him by speaking again suddenly. "Look son, I understand how you feel. But we have got to get along for your mum's sake… and if we try, well you might just find that you actually *like* me!"

Lucas snapped the last biscuit in half then put both halves immediately into his mouth. '*Son*'? Who the hell was Martin to be calling *him* 'son'? He chewed ferociously, turning the biscuit into a creamy paste that stuck to the roof of his mouth and clung to his upper molars. Without saying a word, he picked his bag up once more and headed for his own room. He would have to go with Martin, his mother had made that perfectly clear but no one could make him enjoy it or be pleasant company. So he would change into old clothes whilst he let Martin sweat it out downstairs, wondering if he was coming or not.

He said hello to Brighteyes, who he thought looked a little pleased to see him. "I have to go out tonight," he told the bird apologetically, "but you will be fine and Mum will check up on you." Carefully he lifted the bird onto the windowsill and gave the box a quick clean and the dishes a refill. He had built up a real routine now and the whole procedure took less than ten minutes.

Dressed in jeans and a top he took the bag

with the bird's dirty bedding in it downstairs to deposit in the outside bin on his way out. Martin was already waiting outside on his bike; Lucas's bike was propped by the front door. Its new tyre shone blackly against the rest of the frame, the only new thing about the oldest bike in the world. "It's seen better days I think," Martin nodded towards the old bike.

Lucas swung the bag into the bin and deliberately let its lid crash back down. "Mum worked hard to earn the money to buy that!" he said, knowing that he was being deliberately antagonistic.

"Well yes," Martin acceded, "I'm sure she did and I bet it looked a lot better then," he fumbled for the right words, "but we could get you a better bike now, couldn't we?"

Lucas's skin prickled with severe distaste for the man. "*We* are quite happy with this bike!"

"Oh okay, just a suggestion." But Lucas knew it hadn't been a suggestion, it had been a dig about how life had been before, *before* Martin and how it would be from now on.

It was only a short ride before they could get onto the canal towpath but it was along busy roads so they rode in single file. Lucas was grateful that it meant there was no conversation between them but all too soon Martin had pulled off the road onto a canal path that was wide enough for them to ride side-by-side. "That's better!" Martin said cheerfully. "Now you can tell me about your day at school."

Lucas thought for a moment. The scene all around him was so beautiful, the few boats on the water quaintly painted with flowers and names embellished in flowing script. Here and there a few ducks swam serenely on top of the water, or dived momentarily beneath the still, glassy surface, their movements causing little ripples all around; ripples which grew wider and wider before fading to nothing once more.

Across from the towpath were fields of the lushest green grass where cows grazed sedately and gazed at him as if he were the oddest looking thing they had ever seen. Set against a blue sky which held only a hint of the darkness which would later descend, it was a surreal scene and he felt as if he were not witnessing it for real, through his own eyes but instead through the medium of oil on canvas.

It was somehow too perfect to be real. And it was about to be spoiled by having to talk to Martin! "What do you want to know?" he asked reluctantly.

Martin seemed buoyed up by the words. "Well you can start by telling me what lessons you had and how you enjoyed them."

Lucas wondered if Martin had expected him to remain sullenly silent during the ride. Lucas had of course contemplated it but he had also calculated the fallout from his mother if he stuck to it. "I did maths and English in the morning…" for a moment he considered telling Martin that there was a new girl in school. But the man would not have been content with whatever Lucas was prepared to tell him, he would have asked more questions, demanded more facts. Both things that Lucas either didn't have or didn't want to divulge.

Martin cut into the little silence that had been left at the end of Lucas's words. "I always enjoyed English. I liked finding all the new ways of expressing myself."

A stab of anger pierced Lucas's soul. *Pity you didn't find a way of expressing to your wife that you didn't love her and that you were having an affair!* The silently thought words bit into him as if they were microscopic piranha fish which resided in the chambers of his heart, each nibble eating away a little more at that vital organ. "I don't really like English," he said instead, knowing that it wasn't strictly true, that he had no real feelings for the subject either way but determined to be as different from Martin as he could.

"Well we are all different in what we like, aren't we?" asked Martin, taking no offence from Lucas's statement. "Anyway did you have a good day?"

Lucas shrugged. "School was school."

Martin nodded. "Your mother told me what

happened with Josh."

Lucas's front wheel wobbled. She had no right! No right to tell her boyfriend about Lucas's personal problems! He felt a temper that was hot and hard flare up in him. He pushed the ball of his foot down harder onto the pedal, making the wheel spin faster and the bike spur up the path faster than before. Beside him he sensed Martin struggle to catch up with the sudden increased activity.

Lucas pushed the bike harder and faster, feeling the pedals fly round almost as if by their own volition, ignoring the shafts of pain which licked up his legs like flames. Between gritted teeth he shot out his response. "Don't *you* mention his name to me!"

Martin was either slow witted or he completely failed to understand that he had pressed on this most tender of points. "Who? Josh?" His eyebrows knitted together in an attempt to work out what was going on. A thin bead of perspiration wove its way down from his hairline, across his forehead and into his eyes.

Stopping pedalling so abruptly that they almost crashed into one another, in one smooth leap Lucas was off the bike and standing in the middle of the towpath, his bike abandoned on the grass and mud. "Yes. Josh! And don't you ever say that name again! It's all your fault! Everything! Josh not speaking to me, Gran dying, Mum never moving on with her life but keeping us living in that stupid little house, living our stupid little lives… And me! I am your fault too! An unwanted and unplanned baby, raised by a mum who barely existed and an old woman! I am a freak! I have no friends – everyone hates me and I don't fit in! AND IT'S ALL YOUR FAULT!" Lucas felt the rage boil in him, filling his face and his words with equal amounts of hatred, each word crafted in poison, forged in a furnace of hate.

And yet as the words left him, he was filled with a strange calmness, a quieting serenity descending from the top of his head down towards his toes, as if in getting all the anger out, he had actually vented some of the poison from his system. He replayed the words in his head. They were true on the whole. He did hold Martin responsible for the overall situation but it was a bit unfair to blame his lack of friends on the guy. And in truth he had loved his Gran and missed her very much. It was also true that he had the ability to make friends, Molly had proved that with her persistence. So why had he not made any friends in the past other than Josh?

The answer was clear when he looked for it. It had suited him and it had suited Josh to be exclusive friends. Both with absent fathers, their situations had been similar enough that there had been an immediate bond but that hadn't necessarily excluded others from this friendship... no it had been their attitude which had done that for them. Memories flickered through his head, odd occasions when someone else had tried to join in on their conversation or game of football.

On all of these occasions Josh had subtly hinted that it had been better when it was just the two of them, that the other boy didn't understand their particular shared point of view, that his ball skills were worse/better/different to theirs... that in short, they didn't need anyone but the two of them! As if scales had previously covered his eyes, scales which were now wrenched away with the suddenness of a knife through jelly, Lucas blinked rapidly and looked at his father.

Martin's eyes were filled with tears but rather than even attempt to hold them back, the man stood unashamedly crying in front of his son. "I know I have done you wrong... you *and* your mother... and believe me, if I could turn the clock back I would! But I don't have that ability Lucas, none of us does! But will you let that hatred of me keep you pushed to the ground for the rest of your life? Will you let it threaten every relationship you have? Poison every opportunity you have? Because that's exactly what you're doing!"

Martin's words sounded sincere. "You are not a freak Lucas, even if you really think you are. You are a normal fourteen year old boy who has lived in an unusual situation. I know that maybe you can't see that right now but that gives you a lot of advantages. You have more to talk about, more to think about and more to get on with in your life, than probably most of the other kids at your school. Haven't you ever thought of it that way?" Martin held his gaze but it was not a challenge.

Lucas's anger had almost completely dissipated. He wanted to hold onto it but with the realisations that he had been forced into, his resolve had waivered and been replaced with a sense that not only were things around him changing at a rate that he found hard to keep up with, but that *he* was changing too.

The question was, what or who was he changing into and would he even recognise himself by the end of the process? More than that... would he *like* who he had become? The thought was both scary and exhilarating.

CHAPTER 18

Martin gave Lucas the choice of returning home or carrying on. Lucas surprised them both by choosing to continue on with the bike ride. It was a lovely day and the canal path was easy going and if he was forced to admit it, it wasn't *awful* being with Martin, though obviously Hugh Grant would have been his preference.

They talked about nothing, the small stuff that has no real meaning, until Lucas almost couldn't stand it anymore. "You do love my mum, don't you?" he asked, voice constricted with anxiety. He hadn't tried to sound casual - that would have been wrong – it was far too important a question for that – but he also tried to sound not too solemn.

"Yes. Very much. I always have. And I love you too."

Lucas wished Martin hadn't added that last part. The question hadn't been about him, nor had he wanted it to be. "You don't know me," he said quietly hoping that would be an end to it.

"No I guess not. And you don't know me

either. But that doesn't stop me loving you… and in time I hope that we will know each other very well and that you might start to love me back."

Lucas squirmed a little on his seat and pushed harder on the pedals. "It's not about me. I just need to know that you won't leave her again."

"I'll never leave your mum. Unless that's what she wants of course." He sounded sincere and Lucas couldn't see that situation ever arising.

"Will you marry her?" He wasn't sure if that would make things better or worse. Whichever was the case, it would certainly give a permanency to the situation.

"Well I would like to but there are things we have to get sorted first." Lucas assumed that Martin meant his divorce. "You know when you're young things sometimes seem simple. Black or white, short or long. But when you're older you realise that there are an infinite number of shades things can be and maybe more than one of them is right or maybe they're all wrong."

The conversation was becoming a little too philosophical for Lucas's liking. He tried to manoeuvre it back to practicalities. "If you get married will we move house?"

Martin thought for a moment. "I don't know. If we all wanted to I suppose… but you and Anna have built a life there, would you want to leave that?"

It was Lucas's time to think. He cycled up a

steep bank to the lock above. The canal stretched out for miles and miles but he could only see as far as the next lock, the rest was hidden from view. *Just like life itself*, he thought. He caught his breath and turned his cycle back the way that they had come, aware that Martin was still waiting for his response. He didn't want to give an answer because he didn't know what the answer should be.

He raced past Martin, the wind taking his t-shirt, billowing it out behind him and causing it to make a light flapping sound like a loose tent in the wind. He sped along the path, faster and faster away from where he had been but this time it was not speed fed from anger and resentment but rather a desire to move on with time, to forge a new destiny for himself. Even buffeted by the wind as he was, he felt his face break into a grin and what felt like the tiniest drop of joy seemed to pulsate its way into his veins, expanding to envelop him.

"Last one back to the road empties the bins for a week!" he called back to Martin. If he lost it was no real hardship, emptying the bins was always his chore anyway. But if Martin lost then Lucas could lord it over him for a while. Like pistons, his legs shot up and down, round and round, and yet his pace slowed almost imperceptibly, allowing Martin to catch up if not actually overtake him.

"That's not fair, you had a head start!" Martin complained good-humouredly.

"But you have a better bike," Lucas threw back, upping his speed just a little when Martin threatened to overtake him. The road was just ahead and Lucas was set to be the clear winner. Forcing his legs onwards for the final stretch, he felt Martin fall behind ever so slightly. The man didn't appear to be particularly out of breath or struggling and yet he slowed his speed and allowed his bike to fall behind Lucas's back wheel. He let Lucas win.

Knowing that the contest had been rigged a little, Lucas still did not feel put out. Sure at the end Martin had let him win, but that said more about the man's desire to be a proper father than it did about his sporting prowess. And hadn't he himself slowed the pace so that Martin could catch up? A confusing mix of emotions swirled around him, ebbing and flowing as he tried to grasp even one of them. Unsure how he felt, Lucas was relieved when Martin said it was time to head for home and he rode back as subdued as he had been at the start.

When they arrived back at the house, Anna was sitting at the kitchen table with the laptop plugged in and lit up in front of her. She was logged into several sites at once and the screen flickered brightly as she moved from one site to another, either comparing them or trying to find something on them. She barely looked up as they came past her, both of them hot and sweaty and needing a shower.

Lucas hoped he could get in before Martin. Going in after was not a comforting thought. "Hi Mum," Lucas said, thinking that he had never seen her take an interest in the internet before, unless she was looking for something specific. At the sound of his voice she seemed to snap out of whatever fugue she had been in. Her smile was distracted and somehow empty.

"Hi you two," she said, eyeing them up and down and taking in the mud splattered clothing and the hair that was stuck to Lucas's scalp. "Did you have a good time?" there was an obvious anxiety in her voice. Was she concerned that they had bickered the whole time and that they were no further forward in establishing a relationship than they had been before? Underlying her words was the unspoken '*did you manage to sort anything out between you?*'

Lucas answered her spoken and unspoken words with a grin. "Yes we had a good time but Ma-" he faltered and looked down at the floor. He couldn't call the man Martin forever but Dad seemed far too wrong. Perhaps it was something he would have to work up to? A dad was someone who had loved and looked after your welfare from birth. What Martin was more strictly, was his biological father in the most correct scientific terms. But he balked at using the word.

"He thinks he is in better condition than he actually is." It had been hard to evade but not impossible. Lucas rushed out the rest of the words on a breath, eager to put conversational distance between himself and the near miss. "So he'll be emptying the bins for the next week!"

The look that passed between his mother and Martin was impossible to ignore. A glance which spoke volumes but carried no sound lingered between them. It was broken only when Martin held his hands up in the air as if in defeat. But Lucas saw the small smile that fastened itself onto the man's lips.

I'm not forgiving you for the past just yet, Lucas thought silently to himself, *but I am prepared to wait and see how you cope with the future. It's as much as I can give and as much as you should be asking for! Under the circumstances.*

"Oh!" There was no hiding the happiness which showed in his mother's face but for some reason Lucas couldn't fathom, it was short-lived. Why was she not ecstatic that Lucas was thawing towards Martin, even a little? "Poor Martin," she said in mock commiseration. "But at least it's only for a week." She turned to her son. "I looked in on Brighteyes quite a few times but she hadn't moved from the windowsill and seemed quite happy there. Go and have a shower and then we can have dinner."

Lucas nodded, he was starving and he was relieved that his mum had given him the instruction, meaning that he could get in first, before Martin. "I'll go put the bikes away," Martin said but Anna put out an arm to halt him.

"Can you wait a minute?" she asked, pulling out the chair opposite her. Halfway out of the door, Lucas only managed a glimpse of the paper which had been half hidden under the laptop. He could see that it was an official letter of some kind, although not who it was from or what it was about. He tried to slow down but Anna gently whacked him on the rump, a false smile on her face that didn't climb her cheeks to her eyes. "Off with you into the shower, young man!"

Perhaps Lucas's face too easily reflected her own for suddenly she tried harder to fake the smile, mouth widening but eyes never losing their worried look. Lucas had no choice but to exit through the door, leaving them alone with the mystery letter. He trod heavily on the first few steps then silently crept back to stand just outside the door, pressing his ear against the wood and trying to figure out what the new mystery was about.

"This came in the post!" There was a slight paper crackle as if it was passed from one hand to another. A moment of silence in which the letter might have been being read by Martin followed. "Can they do that Martin?" his mother asked anxiously. "Can they just throw us out onto the street?" Her blatant fear communicated itself to Lucas and he felt his whole body tense. What was she talking about? Who was trying to throw them into the street? And why?

As if he was there in the room with them, Lucas 'saw' Martin's shoulders shrug and his mouth purse in contemplation. He couldn't see the adults but he hoped that Martin had put an arm around Anna to comfort and protect her from whatever threat the letter contained. "I don't think they can just throw us out." There was a slight emphasis on the word 'us' Lucas thought. "But there are things that will definitely need to be sorted out here. Was the tenancy held in your mother's name as it states here?"

Perhaps his mother nodded, Lucas couldn't tell, but her voice was filled with fear and apprehension when she gave her answer. "Yes. A couple of times I said we ought to get it changed but Mum always said that whilst she had breath this was *her* home."

"Foolish old lady!" Martin responded. Lucas bristled. His gran had been many things, stubborn and irritable and sometimes too outspoken, but foolishness had not been one of her failings. "If you had explained the circumstances then to the council it would probably have been quite easy to sort out. But now…"

"But it was me who paid the rent, me who organised for any repairs and me who went out to work to ensure that the bills were paid!" Anna cried softly.

"To them that's irrelevant. As far as the council is concerned your mother was their tenant and now that she is dead, they want the house back."

"What am I going to do?" Anna asked but her voice was so low it seemed she almost didn't expect an answer.

"We will phone them in the morning and explain. Worst case scenario, we might have to get a lawyer involved to show that you have rights as you have lived here so long, though proving that might be difficult." Lucas wished that Martin would choose his words more carefully as they didn't seem to be having the calming effect he desired.

"What if they won't listen or we don't win the case, then we will be homeless!" Anna wailed once more. "And destitute from the lawyer's fees! We can't afford that!"

"Anna these things take time. They can't just happen overnight, so whatever and however things turn out, we will have plenty of warning – plenty of time to make other arrangements."

"What about your house? We could live there!" Lucas thought he caught a hint of something else in the desperation of his mother's words, some slyness, some calculated needling as if there was an undercurrent of tension strung through the words.

"You know that's not possible." Delivered flatly, there was no room for discussion on the topic; it was a closed book.

"No, because *she's* still there!" The venom in the spat-out words took Lucas aback. "You wouldn't want little *wifey* upset, would you? Wouldn't want her to have to leave her comfortable home! You would rather see me and our son out on the street with no roof over our heads than have to make her move!"

"Anna that's not true and you know it, you are just upset. I told you before that I am applying for a divorce and that my house will be sold. When it is, the share of money I'll get will go straight to you and Lucas, I promise. But I can't just make her leave her own house, can I?" he was pleading now. Lucas wondered whether Anna had shrugged him off.

"But it's not just *her* house is it? It's yours too!"

"Yes, it was mine and hers together. But I left! I left to be with you! And now I can't just throw her out!" he argued. "Be reasonable Anna! I mean would you really want to live there anyway?" he sounded as if he already knew the answer. "Sit every morning in the kitchen she used to cook in, watch TV at night in-"

She cut him off with an example of her own, "Go to bed every night in the bedroom where you made love to her...?" there was a question wrapped up in the ferocity of her words but Lucas could not fully comprehend what it was.

"It wasn't like that Anna. It wasn't how you think of it at all. But we were married and so yes we went to bed together, it's what married people do after all... but I never once stopped loving you, stopped thinking of you..."

"Oh well that's comforting, isn't it then? To think that whilst you were with her, *sleeping* with her, you were thinking of me!"

Lucas recoiled from the door. They were moving into territory he knew he should know nothing about. But there was always the chance that they would come back to the topic of the letter. His conscience vied with itself, quietly battling morality against ignorance. The stronger side of his brain won and he pressed his ear to the door once more.

"I didn't mean it like that and you know it! Why are you picking a fight with me, Anna? Don't you already have enough on your hands? The council want to evict you because as far as they are concerned you are a squatter in your mother's house. Your son is adjusting to a life without his gran and his best friend in it and having to come to terms with a father who has turned up out of the blue! Isn't that enough to have to get your head around and to sort out without making things even worse?" Lucas heard Martin sigh softly. "I am not your enemy Anna. I never was and I never will be. And if you give me the chance, I will stand at your side for the rest of my life, proclaiming my undying love for you."

There was a loud sob and Lucas knew that now his mother was crying. Martin's voice changed, becoming less forceful. "Because I love you Anna. And I love Lucas too."

Lucas felt a burning in the ear that was pressed to the door, as if it was pushed there too harshly by an invisible hand. But as quickly as the burning pain entered his ear, it passed through it, finding its own inexplicable route to his heart where it burned with a new intensity. He didn't know what Martin's words meant. Or rather he did *know*, he understood the definitions of the words very well, what he didn't understand, *couldn't* understand was the truth of them. Did Martin really love him? It certainly seemed that way, if his recent actions were anything to go by. In fact was there anything else to judge by at all?

"I know, I know…" Anna was crying loudly now. "It's just such a mess!"

"And that's my fault!" Martin said. "But I will make things right Anna, I promise. And when my divorce is through and the house is sold, if it's what you want, we will buy somewhere away from here. Somewhere we can make a new life for ourselves."

Lucas wondered if his mother was nodding or shaking her head. "But if you want to stay here, either in this house or just in this area, then that will be alright too. Whatever you want Anna. It's your choice."

There was a silence that lasted a few heartbeats. Were they kissing or just looking at one another? "You promise?" Anna asked quietly.

"I promise," Martin affirmed. "But in the meantime we'll get this tenancy sorted okay?"

"Okay." It was a brighter sound than Lucas had come to expect. The conversation appeared to be over and in case one or both of them came through the kitchen door and found him still lurking there, clearly spying on them, he tiptoed up the stairs to his room.

Brighteyes was still on the windowsill where he had placed her. He came and stood next to her, looking out at the fields which had been her entertainment for the whole day. The scene was pretty much the same as it had been that morning, only the position of the sun and the different angles of the rays it cast lending the scene any sense of the passage of time. He put one hand on the windowsill, not meaning to frighten the bird but merely to feel as if he was rooted somewhere, anywhere. The world seemed to be sliding out from under his feet once more and he could not clearly see what lay ahead.

"It sounds like the council don't want us here," he told the bird who stared at his fingers, spread across the white paint of the sill. "The council own the houses and I guess they get to decide who lives in them," he explained, as if the bird was attempting to follow the conversation.

Brighteyes looked up once at him and then pecked gently at his fingers. For a moment he was too startled to do anything. The peck was not painful or even uncomfortable, instead it was like the bird equivalent of a cuddle. Slowly he turned his palm over to indicate that it was empty. The bird pecked gently into the cup of his hand. Each time its beak came away empty but each time it returned, as if nibbling some invisible sustenance from the lines and creases within the skin.

Slowly so as not to scare the bird, he tried to reach across to the plastic tub that sat on top of his bed. His mother had half filled it with the birdseed Martin had bought and he had been using it to supplement the peas and corn he had been feeding the pigeon. He managed to grasp the tub one handed but couldn't prise off the lid. Very slowly he withdrew the hand from the windowsill and removing the lid, snatched a small handful of the grains. He slid his hand back onto the windowsill.

Brighteyes pecked cautiously at first from his hand and then with increasing confidence. Lucas stood very still and watched the little feathered head bob up and down within his hand. A feeling of ultimate power rose within the core of him, perhaps from his soul, if such a thing existed. He recognised that he had been afforded the greatest honour by the pigeon – a recognition that he was its giver and protector – and that it felt completely safe. Was this how Martin wanted to feel with him and his mum? Was this how Martin wanted *them* to feel about him?

Soon the seed was gone but the bird did not move away. Lucas resisted the urge to try to stroke the creature. It would have been too much, too soon. The bird would indicate when it was ready for that, he realised.

He replaced the lid back on the tub and gently lifted the bird back into its box. "I am going to get washed and have my tea. I'll see you later Brighteyes. But don't worry, whatever that letter says, whatever the council think they are going to do, we will be fine." And with that he stepped into the hall and closed the bedroom door softly behind him.

CHAPTER 19

Sleep came easily to Lucas that night, even though he worried what the future might hold. Perhaps the thought that it was not just him and his mother alone in the world anymore which helped; perhaps it was also the knowledge that only an arm's reach away slept a wild creature which was growing to trust him. Because if that could truly be accomplished, if he really could get a wild bird to love and trust him then what else was possible? And what little could be *im*possible?

His mother never mentioned the letter to his face and he never let on that he knew she and Martin were undertaking a battle with the 'powers-that-be' as his gran would have said. In front of him they strove to be happy and normal or at least as close to a semblance of normal as he thought they could achieve. What they said in private, he no longer wanted to know. Sometimes knowledge could be a worm that squirmed inside your stomach, making you ill and eating away at the very core of you from within.

The school hours passed in an equal haze.

No one bullied him or even tried to but neither did they extend any friendship – it was almost as if he had ceased to exist, so little impact did he make wherever he went. Only Molly continued to take any interest in him, waiting for him every day for their walk to school and for the journey back.

Today, when he stepped outside the school she was already there waiting for him at her post by the school gates, one shoulder slumped against the wall as if she was having to hold it up. "Come round to mine after your tea tonight," she said, casually swinging her bag containing her school books and whatever other rubbish ten-year-old girls took to school. Lucas thought it was probably filled with folder posters of boy bands and pink pencils with fluffy, feathery bits on the top. He said nothing about the request but the look on his face must have been dubious at best. He began to walk and she fell into step beside him.

"Look we talked about this before and you agreed you needed to make friends. So start tonight!" She sounded a little exasperated. "I've got a couple of friends coming to call, then we are going to the park." She rummaged in the bottom of her bag then popped a piece of bright pink bubble-gum in her mouth and offered him the last piece. He declined the offer and she shrugged her shoulders, dropping the piece back into the open bag. Lucas wondered if she was even concerned that it would stick to one of her books or furry pencil case.

"You want me to go with you to the park?" he asked suddenly doubtful once more about the plan.

"Hmmm okay maybe that's a bad idea... but you could meet us there!" she exclaimed as the idea popped into her head. "If you get there before us or just after... and I will call you over and ask about the pigeon... what's it called again?"

"Brighteyes," he supplied.

"Okay so I will ask about Brighteyes and then you can just kind of hang out. Like I said, a couple of the girls aren't allowed to go to the park without their brothers, so they will be there too."

"Okay." Even to himself he sounded more than reluctant.

"Well if you don't want to," she said as if she wasn't bothered anymore, but the sudden pop of her bubble-gum suggested otherwise.

"No, you are right. At least I think you are," he conceded.

"See you later then!" she swung away from him towards her own home.

Tea was over quickly and it didn't take long to clean out the pigeon's box and refill its water and food containers. "I'll be out for a little while now," he told the bird, positioning it on the windowsill as usual. But instead of merely turning to the glass as it usually did when placed there, this time it raised its wings and sort of shuddered them. It was the closest thing to a human shrug that he had ever seen and it made him laugh. "Does that mean you don't care, Brighteyes?" he asked jokingly.

The bird did the strange shuddery, shrugging movement once more but this time it also extended its wings and gave them the smallest, almost-not-there sort of flap. Already its wounds had dried up and healed and there were the very first signs that feathers might be beginning to regrow. Fine empty quills jutted out from the dark skin with a promise of fresh bright plumage. *Maybe things change so slowly that it just sort of happens without you noticing*, he thought. *And then suddenly you do notice and everything is different, maybe better than before, maybe worse – or maybe just different.* The thought made him uneasy and he tried to banish it, concentrating instead on what he should take to the park, aiming to look casual.

He considered taking a football but thought that might look a bit strange being as he was on his own. The bike was a better idea. That way he would at least look as if he had a valid reason to be there. "I'm going up the park on my bike," he told his mum and Martin who were washing and drying the dishes together as if they had done it all of their lives. It was weird seeing them doing a task together.

"Hang on a minute," Martin said, drying his hands on the tea towel and dropping it onto the kitchen table. Lucas tensed. Was Martin really going to start questioning him about where he was going? Trying to stop him from going out? "Why don't you take my bike for a change," Martin said. "You're big enough for it and I'm not using it."

Lucas wasn't sure how to answer. It was true that his own bike was tired and old and that in various places the paint had been worn or bashed off the rusty metal beneath, but he was relieved that Martin had diplomatically not pointed this out. And the bike he was offering for Lucas to use was not only top of the range, it was virtually brand new! He hesitated. He wanted to ride Martin's bike but didn't want to have to admit that to him. "I'm fine on my own bike," he mumbled.

Martin flicked the tea towel over his shoulder and turned away as if accepting Lucas's answer. "Whatever you like. I just thought you would be doing me a favour by riding it…"

"Doing you a favour? How?" Perhaps there was a way he could ride Martin's bike and still keep face?

"Well it's a new bike. I haven't had it long. The saddle is still not worn in and the brakes are tight… it could really do with a little more use just to make it more comfortable for my old bones!"

Okay so Martin had laid it on a bit thick but put like that Lucas could see how he could be helping Martin break the bike in. "Well I guess I could take it tonight," he said slowly, trying to appear not too enthusiastic. "If you're sure it will help you out that is!" he ended.

Martin smiled. "Oh, it definitely would!" For a moment he was so genuine that Lucas forgot that the man had fabricated the reason. Then again, did that matter? All that really mattered was that he would be riding a new bike.

Martin turned back to the dishes as if the matter was settled between them. Anna had said nothing the entire time and hadn't even turned round from the sink where she continued to wash the dishes. But as Martin returned to her side, Lucas saw her posture change; her back which had been held rigidly straight, now curved a little, as if the was exhaling a long held breath. She looked over her shoulder at him and her face was radiant. "Just be careful on the roads, honey."

It wasn't a long ride to the park but if it had been ten times as much it still wouldn't have been enough to have made him regret his decision. The bike glided over pavements and grass alike; every gear shift and cog change was a mechanical wonder. Where his old bike clanged and protested over every change in terrain or speed, this bike seemed to almost challenge him to throw more at it. *Is that the best you can do?* it seemed to mock.

There was no way that Martin could have lost any race with him when they were on their own bikes, which made that evening at the canal seem all the more significant. It would have been so easy for Martin to have overtaken him at any time and yet he hadn't. Had Martin also felt the force of the bike that night? Had he felt the bike's need for speed, need for control of the road, dominance over the ground and yet managed to hold back so that Lucas could win? If so it said a lot about how important it was to him that they established a relationship.

Molly was already at the park when he arrived. She was hanging around by the monkey bars and chatting to a bunch of girls. He headed over towards her, trying not to look as if he had reached his destination. Slowing his pace as he approached he saw her grin widen as she spotted him. "Hey Lucas!" she called and waved.

"Hi Molly," he called back, still cycling and almost on the brink of passing her by.

"Hey, hang on. I wanted to ask you something," she called as he passed her, feet pumping on the pedals as if anxious to be off.

He pulled on the brakes. "Oh okay," he said. "What is it?" he asked, as if the conversation was not set up.

"I... I wanted to know if," she began.

A loud voice interrupted her. "Is this guy giving you trouble?" An older boy inserted himself into the group of girls. He seemed to have asked the question generally, but Lucas noticed how he looked at one of the little girls in particular as if it was her opinion he was interested in.

"It's okay Jason," Molly said. "Lucas lives opposite me, kind-of. He's like my big brother... I mean if I'd had a big brother that is." Lucas hoped she would end there before she got herself tied in knots trying to explain how they knew each other without giving the whole game away. He tried to act natural and keep his eyes from boring into hers which would make them both look suspect. "Lucas this is Jason, he's Sara's big brother," Molly finished the introductions, indicating one of the girls in the crowd.

"Okay cool, as long as there's no issue," Jason said, eyeing up the bike Lucas sat on. Lucas nodded, unsure what to do next. With the introductions done and the fact established that he was no threat to the girls was the exchange over? Should he just ride away? He couldn't really just hang round could he? He tensed himself to push off. "Cool bike!" Jason said admiringly.

Lucas looked down at the bike. "Actually it's not really mine." He could have kicked himself. What a dumb thing to say!

"So who owns it then?" the cautious look was back on the older boy's face. Lucas had seen him around but hadn't even known his name until now. A couple of years older than himself, Jason's face was a mass of erupting pimples and angular stretched skin, as if the bones below were growing almost too fast for the skin to keep up.

"Well...um," Lucas thought for a moment how to answer the question. The plain truth was that Martin did, but if he just said that, Jason would be sure to ask who Martin was. And it was this part which Lucas was stuck on. What was he to say? My mum's boyfriend? Partner? Lover? Or the less contentions but still unpalatable truth that Martin was actually his father? "He's our lodger!" the words came out without him even deciding on them. Molly's eyes widened, that clearly was not what she had been expecting him to say.

"Your *lodger*?" the other boy asked incredulously. "Does your mum run a bed-and-breakfast place then?"

Lucas tried to extricate himself with humour. "He's not really our lodger. Mum just calls him that when she says he doesn't help out around the house enough!" *Lame, Lucas, really, really lame*, he berated himself.

"So if he's not your lodger, then who is he?" Jason persisted.

"He's my dad," Lucas said, managing not to choke on the words.

"He's got a well-fit bike, your old man!" Jason stroked a hand over the front wheel. "Doesn't he mind you using it? I want one of these but they're so expensive."

Lucas shrugged like the comments meant nothing to him. "Do you want to try it out?" he offered, already beginning to climb off. Jason didn't need to be asked twice. He leapt into the saddle and disappeared through the trees.

Molly shot Lucas an anxious gaze. "What if he damages the bike?" she asked in a nervous whisper. Lucas didn't know how to respond. Belatedly the very same thought had invaded his mind and he worried how his stupid generosity could be explained to his mum and to Martin.

"It'll be fine." Mentally he crossed his fingers. "And if he doesn't come back, I will just have to take his sister hostage!" It was just another of his dumb remarks he should have kept to himself, he thought, seeing Molly's rapid glance towards the other girl.

But she needn't have worried. It seemed her friend thought the remark funny. Sara laughed, "*He* wouldn't bother about that, but Mum would make him sorry!" She crossed her hands over her mouth, giggling contagiously so that Molly was forced to join in. Still Lucas held his breath until the older boy reappeared with the bike, other boys following in his wake.

"These are my mates," he informed Lucas, as the group of older lads crowded round the bike. "Do you mind if they all have a go?" he asked.

Lucas was grateful that at least the question had been put to him. It would after all have been so easy for them to have just taken the bike and either have discarded it when they were done, or taken it home with them.

"It's not my bike, it's my-" he hesitated unwilling to call Martin his dad again. But upsetting your dad was bound to be more officially worrying than upsetting your mum's boyfriend wasn't it? "It's my dad's," he said, biting down on the faint taste of bile that rose to his lips, "and I don't think he would be keen on everyone just riding it…" he worried that the explanation would anger them or that they would find him prissy and refuse to talk to him again. But he couldn't let the bike be wrecked. He held his breath again, worried that he had just ruined everything.

"Yeah, that's cool man," one of the boys said. "If I had me a bike same as that, I'd feel the same way." He smiled broadly at Lucas. "You are a cool guy. What'd you say your name was?"

But before he had a chance to answer Molly piped up excitedly. "His name is Lucas and he lives opposite me, sort of." Lucas could cheerfully have strangled the girl. After all her hard effort of getting him to agree to this and then setting it up, she had gone and ruined it for him. He held his breath worried that she would let slip the story of his 'new dad' but she didn't.

The other boys laughed. "Seems like you got a fan club Lucas!" Jason joked but there was no nastiness there, Lucas realised. "You want to hang out with us tonight? We are over on the ramps. You know?" He indicated the skateboard area, just behind the small thicket of trees. "That's if you're not here with friends."

Lucas tried his best shrug. "I'm here on my own tonight. So sure, I'll come over."

Jason turned to his sister. "I'm gonna be just over there, so if you need anything... and remember, I'll be watching you." It was half-threat, half-statement. The little girl nodded.

The boys walked off and Lucas rode slowly at their side. He would have given anything for Harry Davis and in fact the entire school to have witnessed what was happening.

CHAPTER 20

Jason and his friends turned out to be even cooler than Lucas had hoped. Spinning bikes 360 degrees in the air and somersaulting on skateboards there seemed to be nothing they didn't know or were afraid to tackle. Lucas watched them with a growing sense of awe.

"Take my bike man," one of the boys said, handing it over to him. "Don't damage your old man's bike trying to stunt on it, it's not made for that. But this one is."

"Really?" Lucas asked in disbelief. "You'd let me try your bike?"

The boy smiled and there wasn't a single bit of pretence in it. "Sure. A guy's gotta learn sometime, right? It took me months of practise to get the flip just right." He patted the saddle. "Give it a go."

Lucas placed Martin's bike carefully on the ground on climbed onto the other bike. It had a different feel to Martin's – not so fast but kind of bouncier as if the shocks were souped-up. He tried the ramp, coursing down one side and up the other. He arrived at the top faster than expected and almost fell right off the edge, only just stopping himself in time. Colour flamed high in his cheeks as he rode back to the other boy. "It's a knack. You have to keep trying," the boy said, waiving him away for another try.

Lucas circled the ramps once, trying to gain both momentum and courage. Then he rode up a ramp and flew back down it towards its mirror image on the other side. This time at the apex he executed a quarter turn, landing fairly squarely, without too much wobble. Nothing stupendous but it was a start! He cycled back to the other boy.

"You know I think you might just have a natural talent there," the boy said.

Lucas didn't know if he was being kind but figured he shouldn't push his luck before the older boys got bored of him. "Yeah, you think so?" He looked at his watch. "Oh I gotta go…" He came up blank with a credible excuse but it didn't matter, the boy had already turned his attention elsewhere.

"Hey Jase," he called, "what's with the single flip? You chicken?" He cycled back to the others, Lucas already forgotten.

He didn't mind being dismissed, the fact that they had given him the time of day was enough for him. Molly had been right, this was exactly what he needed to do! He cycled back to her. "I'm off home. Are you coming?" He hoped she would say yes. He didn't want to leave her to walk home alone and he also wanted to tell her what had happened.

She nodded and said goodbye to her friends. "I can't walk as fast as you can ride…" she said, half-jogging beside him. Her cheeks were puffed red and her arms were pumping like pistons at her side. Much as it was kind of funny to see her like this, it really wasn't fair. He thought about telling her to hop on but was afraid their combined weight would damage the bike so instead he got off and walked, pushing the bike along. "Well?" she asked excitedly.

Lucas shrugged. "I had fun," was all he said. It was strange because he had thought that he was bursting with excitement to tell her… but the moment she asked, he realised something. The boys had been interested in him today, because of the bike. What would have happened if he had gone there on his own bike? What *would* happen when he went there in his own bike?

"Good. That's good," she said, sounding older than her years. If she realised he was being evasive, she didn't let on.

He moved the conversation onto more comfortable ground. "Has your mum unpacked everything now?" he asked.

"Pretty much but now she says our old stuff doesn't go in the new house," Molly sighed as if this was a major source of discontent for her.

"And she keeps saying I need to keep my bedroom tidier now. I don't see what difference it makes to her, I'm the one who has to sleep in it."

Lucas thought about his own conversations with his mum on that same subject. They rounded the last corner into their own road. "Mums are weird like that."

Molly laughed and skipped off up the street. "I'm never going to be like that," she declared. Lucas laughed and shook his head, watching her go. When she was finally gone he cycled the last bit down the street to his own house. Carefully he stowed the bike back in the shed. Martin and his Mum were watching TV when he entered the house.

"Did you have a good time?" his mum asked.

"Yeah, fine," Lucas mumbled, not inclined to tell her what had happened. Not wanting to let slip what riding the bike had allowed him to do. Trying to keep it casual. Without looking directly at Martin he said, "Thanks for letting me use your bike. I put it away." It was polite but carried no particular warmth.

Martin nodded. "No problem Lucas, it's there to be used."

"Are you coming to watch TV?" Anna asked.

Lucas shook his head. "I'm tired and I've left Brighteyes alone long enough. I'm going up." He hoped it was a good enough reason to not look rude.

"Okay then. I'll pop in to see you before bedtime," Anna promised.

Brighteyes was fine and didn't seem to hold it against him that she had been left alone all day and all evening. "Sorry," he apologised to her. She inclined her head towards the growing darkness outside the window as if in understanding of where he had been.

Watching her smooth movement of feathered head upon shoulders, he felt even more guilty than before. Like a jailer who had locked and imprisoned her whilst he went wherever he desired. With a heavy heart he carried her to her box. "It's not forever," he told her and at once wasn't sure if he referred to her captivity or to his own sudden freedom.

He went through his routine to get ready for bed, purposely not thinking, keeping his mind blank as much as possible. But when finally he drew the covers up that thought resurfaced. He heard it inside his head, issued on a voice that was light and almost-not-there; the sort of voice a pigeon would have if it could talk.

'Nothing is forever,' he heard it whisper as his eyes closed.

*****

"How did it go in school today?" Molly asked as he arrived for their walk home.

It was so close in words and intonation to his mother's daily question that Lucas snorted out a laugh. "You'll make a great mother some day," he said, only half –jokingly.

"Hmmph! I'm not ever going to have kids. We saw the video in school and its icky!" Her face crumpled in revulsion. "Hey you changed the subject!" her eyes widened as she realised how neatly she had been side-tracked. "I was right wasn't I?" she gloated, not appearing to need his confirmation.

"Yes Molly you were right," he half-droned, unwilling to give her the full recognition she thought she deserved. He suspected she would be totally unbearable if she knew how well her plan had in fact worked.

"SO?" she pushed.

"So… a few kids from my class were at the park the same time as us." He was reluctant to give too much away but her eyes seemed to soak up his words as soon as they were uttered.

"They saw you hanging out with the older kids didn't they? And now they all want to be your friends!"

He laughed. "I wouldn't go that far." He thought for a moment. "At least not yet. But they weren't ignoring me anymore." He thought it was much more than that really but in case it was a temporary thing or just a figment of his imagination, he was reluctant to dwell upon it.

Things could so easily and quickly revert to how they had been before. And then where would he be if he had built his hopes up?

"And they never will again. You'll see!" Molly chirped with confidence. "I'll meet you at the park again tonight, after tea!" She was gone before he had a chance to agree or disagree. He walked slowly to his own end of the street.

His mum was already home when he got in, rubbing some sort of butter onto large red chunks of meat. "Is that steak?" he asked eyeing up the thick, juicy slabs of beef.

"Yes." She smiled, fingers working the seasoning into the meat. Lucas tried to count how many slices were on the board in front of her but her hands moved too quickly for him to be sure. It was only when she lifted one up, preparing to drop it into the pan that he saw there was only one left on the board.

"What am *I* having for tea?" He tried not to sound despondent. Steak was expensive and it was natural that Martin wouldn't want to spend his wages on providing it for Lucas too! And he didn't begrudge his mother the treat... if there was anyone in the world who deserved the finest steak it was her!

Anna stopped what she was doing and looked at him strangely. "You are having steak and chips Lucas, the same as me and Martin."

Lucas could feel tears smart at the corners

of his eyes, even as a thick pool of saliva formed under his tongue at the thought of devouring the steak with a pile of crispy, golden chips waiting on the side. "Really?" his voice came out as a squeak.

Anna nodded but she didn't laugh. Instead very slowly, so that he caught her meaning she said, "Martin said to give the biggest one to you. He said that you are a growing lad and that you need your energy."

Lucas felt a little lightheaded. Then common sense kicked in. Martin saw him as a means to an end. "He only said that so you would be impressed. So that you would keep letting him into your bed every night." He managed to make the words sound accusatory without being overly sleazy.

Anna's expression changed subtly; it was as if something almost imperceptible shifted beneath her skin, tightening muscles in her cheeks and temples and relaxing her shoulders so that they slumped a little. "Give him a chance Lucas. He's doing all he can to make things right for us."

Her voice was so soft, so full of love and of hurt that he was almost ashamed of his words. But not ashamed enough that he couldn't use her words against her to get what he wanted. "Do you think he will let me borrow his bike again tonight?" he held his breath awaiting her answer.

He wouldn't have blamed her if she had forbidden him from borrowing it but she surprised him with her answer.

"I'm sure he won't mind." She put the other steak into the pan and shuffled them all around with a fork, making them sizzle and spit hot, fragrant fat into the air. "He'll be home in five minutes, why don't you ask him then?"

Funny how she managed to use the word home so subtly, Lucas thought. But what exactly did she mean by it? That Martin would be arriving in the home Lucas shared with his mother? Or that she now considered it Martin's home too?

By the time Lucas had spent a few minutes with Brighteyes and washed his hands, Martin was back. Lucas hurried into the kitchen, the aroma of steak filling his nostrils and found Martin already seated at the table. "How was your day?" the man enquired cheerfully as if they had had this conversation many times before.

"Um okay," Lucas muttered, wondering how to broach the subject of the bike.

"You know it's a nice night again... why don't you have another ride out on my bike?" Martin suggested. Lucas glanced at his mother. Had she already pre-empted his request or had Martin spontaneously suggested the idea?

"Actually I was going to ask you if I could do that! Are you sure?" For a moment he forgot who Martin was, forgot that he was probably just trying to win him over. Martin nodded.

Delicious as the dinner was, Lucas didn't waste much time in finishing it off. Trying to chew quickly whilst still savouring the meal was difficult but not impossible. He chewed, extracted as much flavour as possible and swallowed. Before the others were even half-way through, he had cleaned his plate and excused himself from the table. "I've never seen you so eager to go out before," his mother remarked. "Just make sure you are not neglecting your homework. Or your pigeon!"

"I finished all my homework before school this morning," he said. But he still felt a stab of guilt. Was he neglecting Brighteyes? He really didn't intend to leave the bird alone for so long but then again was it in its best interests to make it too tame either? What would happen once it was released to the wild if it was too used to human company?

Lucas worried about the rights and wrongs of the situation as he peddled to the park. Brighteyes seemed to be getting better, growing stronger every day. And that was a good thing – no, actually that was a *great* thing! But she also seemed to be becoming more accustomed to him every day, a little less afraid, a little more accepting of his sudden movements, less startled when he spoke… and sometimes recently, he had noticed that she seemed to be paying more attention to him, almost as if she considered him to be part of her flock.

He was honoured by the bird's acceptance but he was also more than a little worried. Would she pine for him when she was back in the wild? Would she feel betrayed? Abandoned? Alone? And him – how would he feel having to give her up to fate, not ever knowing if she was alright?

He put the thoughts aside as he spotted Molly and her friends. The older boys were a little distance away, in the skate park as they had been before. Jason had just come off the ramp at high speed when he spotted Lucas. "Hey over here Lucas," he called.

Lucas hesitated. It was the reaction he had hoped for and yet he felt strangely uncomfortable at leaving Molly once more. He looked at her but said nothing. "They're calling you over," she said brightly.

Lucas nodded. He watched one of Molly's friends blow a huge pink gum bubble which obscured most of her face. The unknown girl popped the bubble with one finger and folded the stretched gum back into her mouth. "Are you okay Molly?" He wondered what he meant by the remark.

"Yeah I'm fine here. Go and meet your friends," she said without any hint of nastiness or evasiveness. The smile she gave him was even and good-tempered. He did his best to return it but some uneasiness coiled in the pit of his stomach. Something felt wrong about the scenario. But he couldn't put his finger on what it was exactly.

Slowly he rode over towards Jason who stood within a larger crowd than before. Once more, the bike Lucas rode was the centre of attention with everyone wanting to ask questions about its performance. But just as he was in the middle of explaining how smooth it was, there was a sharp scream followed by a deafening silence. Instinctively Lucas looked towards Molly but she was no longer where he had left her.

A little girl lay prone on the ground, an empty swing still oscillating above her, moving back and forth, back and forth on its metal chain. There was something ominous about the movement of the empty swing. Lucas felt his eyes drawn to it as if there was a deeper meaning there that was his, and his alone to clasp. Had this been what he had been unconsciously been afraid of? That there would be some sort of accident?

Lucas spun the bike around and raced over to the girl. Everything felt slowed down again, as if he was the only person who could maintain normal speed. Adults and children rushed to the scene from every direction, but none of them was Molly. *What does that mean?* he demanded of his befuddled brain. Did it mean that Molly *was* the girl on the ground? His heart leapt up spiking pain into his chest with every strangulated breath. He threw himself off the bike and felt it crash to the ground unheeded.

"Let me through! Let me though!" Lucas pushed the crowd aside and burrowed his way to the centre. Within seconds he had reached the girl, who was cradled between two adults on their knees, who seemed to be doing their very best not to panic. It wasn't Molly. The girl's face was a strange puce colour and there was an unnatural stillness to her which brought unwelcome thoughts of his gran to the front of his mind.

Not again, not again! his fevered brain screamed. All at once the image of his gran faded away to be replaced by a more recent one… this same girl blowing a huge pink bubble. Popping it only to start the process all over again. Could that be the reason she didn't appear to be breathing? Was the gum stuck in her throat? Uncaring as to how his actions were received, Lucas dragged the girl from the adults' arms. Strangely they did not put up much resistance. They think I am her brother, he realised. It was of no consequence at that moment in time, nothing other than the girl had any significance to him at all.

Grasping her firmly around her rib cage he hauled her halfway to her feet. Unconscious, she was floppy and couldn't stand but as she was so much smaller than him he could still prop her upright. He only hoped it would be enough for what he was about to do. Locking his arms tightly around the girl's torso he heaved upwards and inwards. The girl's body jerked with the movement but there was no other obvious change. Again and again he performed the manoeuvre aware that time was beginning to run out. Still the girl lay lifeless in his arms. Lucas sank to the cold, hard ground, the little girl motionless in his arms.

Beside him, Molly was crying, thick tears coursing down her face and some of the adults were shaking their heads at one another as if lamenting a lost cause. Lucas took a second to look at the little girl, at her dark blonde hair and thick glasses which gave her a kind of cute bug-eyed look. Had her life really ended so easily? Here in a swing park on an evening that should have been no different to any other? Was life really that cruel?

And then he remembered Brighteyes, remembered how cold and thin the bird had felt in his hands that day... He pulled himself and the girl up once more, uncaring how roughly he handled her, how bruised her flesh might be from this mistreatment. Once more he performed the Heimlich manoeuvre with every ounce of his strength.

This time the force of the exhaled air dislodged the gum from the girl's windpipe and ejected it from her mouth on a jet of saliva. Round, pink and moist, the gum glistened on the concrete as finally the girl drew one rasping breath after another.

She looked a bit dazed and there was a trail of blood which ran from one nostril, trickling in a thin crimson stream over her lips and chin. A bump the size of a small egg protruded from her forehead and her knees were scraped and bleeding. "You're not Molly," he said, as if she had been masquerading as his friend and he hadn't already realised that Molly stood at his side. Perhaps it was a dumb thing to say under the circumstances but no one laughed.

A voice spoke from his side. "I'm here Lucas. I'm okay. This is Keira, the new friend I was telling you about. I think she let go of the swing and just fell." Molly gave the explanation not just to him but to the rest of the crowd who still gathered around.

"We ought to phone the ambulance," one of the women who had been holding Keira said. Previously purple, Keira's face was now parchment white, paler than a ghost. She seemed shaky on her feet and leaned against the swing frame for support. Her glasses were no longer straight on the bridge of her nose and one leg of the spectacles seemed to sit higher on her ears than the other one. "Please don't!" she said. "Please don't make me go in an ambulance!"

Lucas couldn't tell if they were real or forced teardrops that glistened like giant orbs, magnified beyond reality behind the thick lenses of the lopsided glasses but he was fairly certain that the wobble in her voice was for real.

"Well you make sure you go straight home… and tell your mother that your friend's brother saved your life today," the woman said before departing. She bestowed a smile on Lucas. "That was quick-thinking what you did there."

Lucas nodded, embarrassed a little by the attention. Finally everyone was gone, back to where they had originally come from. But still Lucas felt eyes upon him, people waiting to ensure they went home together. "Will you help me get home?" Keira asked, her eyes flitting from Molly to Lucas and back again.

Lucas wanted some answers. "Why didn't you want them to call an ambulance?"

"Because they would have taken me to hospital and then I would never be allowed out on my own again." Her voice wobbled once more and Lucas thought that she was only just managing to hold herself together. Had she been aware of how close she had been to suffocating? To dying?

"Don't you have *anyone* here to look after you?" he felt himself emphasising the word unintentionally. Keira shook her head. "I only have a big sister and she's at home."

Inwardly Lucas sighed. He didn't want to

leave Jason and the older boys but he couldn't just abandon the girl either. "Okay, look wait here a minute and I'll be right back." He picked up Martin's bike from the grass. Luckily it was unscathed and other than a few blades of grass caught between the spokes, it was none the worse for him abandoning it. He pedalled back over to Jason, wondering how he would explain what he was doing.

"I have to take Molly's friend home. She fell off the swing and…" he began but tailed off, not sure how the older boy would react. Would he laugh or say something derogatory?

To Lucas's surprise Jason patted him on the back. "I'd be the same if it was my sister," he said.

Lucas felt doubly awkward. "She's not my sister. But she is Molly's friend and she doesn't have a brother and I am supposed to be looking out for Molly…so…" He didn't want to have to explain it further, he didn't think the idea would hold up to the older boy's close scrutiny.

"It's okay. You do what you have to do and when you are ready to come back, whether that's tonight or another time, we will probably be here," he gave Lucas a reassuring smile. "Oh and another thing. You don't need the bike."

"What?" Lucas was confused. Was Jason suggesting that he leave the bike behind? A moment of panic assailed him once more. He couldn't leave Martin's bike behind whilst he took the girl home! Anything might happen to the bike. He might never even get it back!

Jason patted him on the back once more. "What I mean is that you are a cool kid Lucas. You don't have to be on a fancy bike to hang out with us, you are welcome anytime."

Lucas was dumbfounded. Was it really that easy to make new friends? Without even really trying? Jason shrugged. "Molly told Sara about your pigeon rescue. And Sara told me. She said it would have been dead if not for you. And that no one else had bothered to try to help." Jason eyed up his friends in the skate park. He looked back at Lucas. "I'm not into pigeons myself but I can see what you are trying to do. And it's cool. It's helping nature and that's *mega* cool."

Even Jason seemed uncomfortable with the level of comradeship he had extended. He dropped his arm from Lucas's back and turned away, but not before he had given the younger boy a thumbs up sign.

Lucas's heart swelled. Perhaps when Josh had abandoned him and he had felt that his world was ending, it actually had... but maybe it was also the start of a new world, one in which he was accepted for who he was and not what he had or didn't have.

He cycled back to the girls with a grin on his face. Together they hobbled out of the park, him pushing the bike with one hand and propping up the injured girl with the other, whilst Molly held her up at the other side.

The journey was painfully slow due to Keira's unwillingness to move at anything faster than a snail's pace. Her knees were still bleeding and the dark smudge of a bruise now coloured her cheekbone below the egg-shaped lump. Lucas wondered if perhaps he should have phoned the girl's parents to come pick her up but he hadn't thought of that at the time. Besides he didn't see how that would have helped Kiera's case at all.

"The next road on the left is mine!" Kiera's pace sped up a little now that the end was in sight. Only five minutes walk from his own and Molly's road, the houses on this street were a million miles apart from his humble abode. Here the front gardens were a proper size with lawns and flower-beds and tarmacked drives for car parking. The houses were wider than they were on his street and somehow looked as if they stood straighter and prouder – as if they recognised their mortared superiority.

Lucas felt almost embarrassed to be walking along the pavement there, as if the neighbourhood recognised that he did not belong, that his clothes were too old, too unfashionable to be gracing its streets. He felt the white-rimmed eyes of every building rest upon him as if to mark him out as different. Vertical blinds seemed angled towards him, curtains fluttered as if someone hid just out of sight.

"That's my house there," Kiera pointed to the most immaculate house in the street. Pained a lush cream with a glossy red door it stood out as freshly decorated and lovingly cared for. He thought of his own shabby house front, the paint that had been there a million years, the weeds that had crept up between the paving slabs now that his gran was no longer there to keep them at bay. The houses were worlds apart. And if the houses were, then no doubt the occupants were too!

Eager to deposit the girl he hustled her over to the front door and indicated to Molly that she should ring the bell. A faint jangling could be heard through the door and Lucas wondered what the reaction of Kiera's parents would be to him when they answered the door. He realised they might not be very happy that their daughter had been brought home by a strange boy a few years older than she was. He steeled himself for their reaction, hoping that he would have a chance to explain.

But when the door opened it was not an adult who stood there before him; it was none other than Claudia King! Of course! He almost slapped himself as he remembered now that Molly had told him Kiera had an older sister and that she was new to the school.

Claudia looked at Lucas then at her sister

then at Lucas again. "What happened?" she asked anxiously, reaching forward and pulling Kiera into her embrace.

"I fell off the swing!" Keira explained. "Molly and Lucas helped me home," she continued as if that part was not self-evident. Then with some apprehension she added, "I choked, Claudia. I had some bubble gum and when I fell I sort of swallowed it. Except it didn't go all the way down!" Safe at home now, the telling of her near-death experience brought renewed feelings of helplessness and panic. Her voice rose into a hysterical wailing, interspersed by hiccupped sobs.

"Oh my God, Keira!" Claudia gasped, wrapping her arms around the younger girl.

"Lucas saved her. He sort of squeezed her till she spat out the gum and then she was okay!" Molly explained.

Claudia glanced at Molly but it was on Lucas that her cool blue gaze lingered. He thought that she was perhaps grateful and mystified in equal measure. But she asked no more questions. "Thank you Lucas," she said simply as she led her sister into the house, her eyes never once leaving Lucas's until the door was softly closed and she was gone.

Lucas stood gazing at the door without moving. Did Claudia stand the same way, the other side of the dividing door, he wondered. It was the first time that they had really *looked* at one another, even though they were in some of the same classes together. And the intensity of it had scorched him. Claudia was like a lit match, beautiful to watch and no doubt just as deadly. He on the other hand was a plain little moth. She was so clearly out of his league.

"Lucas?" Molly was already a few houses down from where he still stood. He hurried to catch her up but every step he took seemed to move him further away from where he wanted to be.

CHAPTER 21

By the morning Lucas had almost forgotten what had happened the night before but he still hadn't managed to get the picture of Claudia King's face from his mind. Alive and well she haunted him, invading every thought, watching over everything he did, until he began to feel as if they were telepathically connected.

He had set the alarm for an hour earlier than normal so that he could get his homework done and perhaps that way get a jump on the weekend. As usual, Brighteyes watched him from the window sill, alternating her gaze between him and the fields outside.

The sky promised another nice day and even the prospect of a whole hour of homework could not dampen his spirits. He flew though the set questions in fractions and decimal points with ease, regardless of whether they were purely numerical or worded ones, reshaping them in his mind to have reference to the bird. 2.5 multiplied by 3.8 became two full adults and a baby bird requiring 3.8 mls of medicine each. 5

and 7/8 divided by 2.9 became five adults and a teenage bird who had to share almost 3mls of water between them… suddenly everything had a relevance, a purpose that he understood.

Even his English homework had a significance that it hadn't had previously. In his freestyle assignment he chose to write an investigative report on how pigeons were maligned by society, vilified because of the erroneous belief that their faeces was harmful to humans. And to his surprise he loved every moment of the work, arguing his point with ferocity, an unassailable logic and a clear and precise rhetoric.

He was so engrossed in the research, flicking through several open tabs on the laptop that at first he didn't notice the slight breeze which seemed to brush across his cheek, and ruffle the papers on the bed. But when the soft breeze fell away, he noticed it in its absence. Where had the short-lived gust come from? Horrified at the implications, he could not at first bring himself to look at the window where Brighteyes should have stood. Had the catch somehow come loose and the window swung open? If he raised his eyes to the sill would Brighteyes be gone?

He couldn't look but he couldn't ignore it either. Fear pounded through his veins as he moved his gaze to the window. The bird was gone! Panic galvanised him into action and he thrust the laptop onto the bed, leaping up to stand by the window. It was only then that he noticed the window was latched firmly shut. So where was Brighteyes?

Lucas looked on the floor and all around the bed, even crouching on all fours to look at the space under the bed but the bird was not there. He stood up mystified. "Where have you gone Brighteyes?" he said to the empty room. A thin squalling sound answered him. His ears fixed on the sound and rotated his eyes up to the top of the wardrobe where the pigeon perched. Head twisted almost all the way around, the bird was preening itself, drawing the new feathers which had emerged from the injured area through its beak and priming them for use. The slight breeze had been the air being displaced by the bird's movement through it.

"You can fly again!" Lucas exclaimed as if a minor miracle had just taken place. "You can fly Brighteyes!" But as his words sank in, Lucas recognised that it was a double-edged sword. The bird was almost ready to go, which meant that the time to say goodbye had almost arrived. How had he not noticed these feathers? How had they grown from the quills, spreading and strengthening without him being aware of them? There was a strange tightening sensation in his heart. Because he had been otherwise occupied! He had been busy with his new life... Once the bird had been his whole life, his only reason for going on, but he recognised that was no longer the case.

For a moment he listened to the quiet of the house, the profound stillness of it. Soon when his mum and Martin got up the peace would be shattered... not in a bad way, but just with the sounds of everyday living. Only for this moment was time itself suspended – as if it was possible that things would never change, the world would never move on. But of course it would. It always did.

And he would have to tell his mum that Brighteyes was so much better. No doubt she would be relieved, albeit for different reasons to his own. On impulse Lucas stood on his bed, legs planted wide apart for balance on the soft mattress he held his arms above his head, palms flat and facing upwards. He pursed his lips and made a sort of cross between a chirping and a kissing sound. Immediately the bird stopped its preening and moved closer to the wardrobe's edge. Looking down it seemed to gauge the distance between itself and Lucas's hand with only one eye, head titled at an angle towards him and jutting sharply up and down. And then suddenly she was in flight, wings extended and flapping in his direction.

It was only a brief swoop before she alighted in his hand but it was enough to show that she was still favouring the damaged wing a little, keeping it a little lower than the other one and perhaps not beating it quite so hard.

Lucas felt the little talons scratch gently across the palm of his right hand and he moved his left across to give the bird more purchase on the skin. His eyes were filled with tears and he no longer knew if they were tears of joy or of sadness. Gently he brought the bird up to his lips and kissed its little head. "I guess these past few weeks we have both been healing." The truth of the words hurt his heart a little but there was a clean sharpness to the pain.

He placed the bird back on the windowsill for what might be one of its very last times. The landscape outside the window had changed since he had first brought the bird home but until now he had barely noticed. Now the trees had begun to look bare, their greenery shed in huge piles beneath their boughs. Had so much time really passed without him being aware of it? He shook his head in wonder.

Someone knocked then began to push the bedroom door open. "I thought we could fix that puncture on your tyre later today then you could use it as a spare," Martin said. Lucas nodded, dragging his gaze away from the window. "How's the bird getting on?" Martin seemed genuinely interested.

"Slow but steady," Lucas lied.

"Well that's not a bad thing," Martin said. "How's the homework going?"

Lucas shrugged. "Fine I guess." He wondered why he was so reluctant to tell the man anything. Did it really matter if Martin knew that he was getting on better at school?

"Okay, well I'll get the tyre repair kit out when I get home from work." Martin closed the door behind himself and left Lucas alone with Brighteyes once more. When Lucas returned his gaze to the windowsill he found the bird regarding him with what seemed like a stony stare.

"What?" he shot out indignantly, pulling his school uniform on. "You think I should have been more talkative? That's rich coming from you!" Even though or perhaps because of the fact that it was his subconscious which had supplied the bird's comments, Lucas felt ill at ease. He saved his work on the laptop and closed it down, putting it under the bed for safety. Thinking that his mother might still be asleep, he made his way quietly downstairs, careful to make as little noise as possible. But just as he prepared to push open the kitchen door, he heard voices clearly from inside the room.

"So he didn't even mention the Parent's Evening to you?" Anna Pertwee sounded a little upset. There was no verbal answer from Martin so Lucas could only assume the man had shook his head. "But he knows it is tonight! And he must know you would want to come with me!"

Lucas felt a knot well up in his stomach. He wasn't deliberately eavesdropping but now he was there he was reluctant to make his presence known. Had that been the specific reason that Martin had asked him how it was going? To give Lucas the opportunity to tell him about Parent's Evening? It wasn't that he had deliberately not told them about the event… not as such. He had given his mother the letter school had handed out weeks ago. He just hadn't reminded anyone that it was coming up. It didn't matter to him what the teachers thought of him; what they might say. All that mattered was that he knew that he was finally doing his best. Whether that was good enough for anyone else, it was good enough for Lucas.

When he spoke, Martin sounded as if he was just on the other side of the door. "He's clearly not ready for that Anna. I will just have to give him some more time."

"Time is something we haven't got on our side, Martin," his mother said.

What does she mean by that? Lucas thought.

"You don't know that yet Anna," Martin protested.

"I know that the council are not interested in the fact that I have been living here all these years. I know that they still want us out! And I know that if we are forced to leave here, Lucas will somehow make all of this your fault!"

Lucas frowned. Were they really going to be homeless? Forced to leave the only place he had ever lived and just at the exact time that he was finally making friends, starting to gain the tiniest bit of respect from the kids in school? Had it really all been for nothing?

"The solicitor said we had a good case, Anna, and that we would probably know within a few days. So let's not worry until then. Anyway I'd better get going."

On the verge of being discovered, Lucas dashed back over to the foot of the stairs, coughed loudly and jumped hard on the spot, as if he had taken the last two stairs in a single bound. He walked towards the kitchen just as Martin pushed open the door to the hall, nearly colliding with the man. "Oh sorry," Lucas said innocently as if he had not been standing listening to the conversation for the last few minutes.

"I'm off now. See you later," Martin said, leaving Lucas alone with Anna. Lucas waited until the door was firmly closed behind him.

"You are coming to Parent's Evening aren't you?" he tried to sound casual and failed.

Anna took a long time answering the question. "Yes of course, but I thought that it would be nice for both of you if Martin - your father -," she added unnecessarily, "came along too." Her raised intonation at the end of the sentence turned it into a quasi-question.

He wished he hadn't asked. He had landed himself in the very position he had wanted to avoid. "Well…" he stalled. How could he avoid the issue without hurting his mother? He was saved from further conversation by the strident ringing of the telephone. His mother hurried away to answer it.

"Hello," he heard her say, followed by, "speaking," after which there was a very long pause as if she was listening to instructions. Lucas made himself a bowl of cereal and sat at the kitchen table. She didn't say much at her end of the conversation so he couldn't try to piece together what it was all about. He waited. "Important call?" he asked when she returned.

"Hmm nothing for you to worry about," she fobbed him off. "But about Parent's Evening… I would really like it if Martin came too…" she phrased it as if it was Lucas's decision even though he suspected she would not allow him to protest the point. He said nothing, hoping that his silence would be more effective than words. "So we will all go as a family together then! Great!" She kissed him on the top of his head. "Right! Well I had better go get ready for work too." She lifted her mug of tea and was gone before he could think of anything to say that might change her mind.

*****

School turned out to be different too. Running a little later than usual, most of the class were already in their seats by the time Lucas got himself into the room. There was an expectant hush as he hurried to his seat and he wondered if he was later than he thought. Was he about to get a detention? He held his breath and looked around him. All eyes were turned in his direction. That was not a good sign.

"Good morning Lucas," his teacher said. "Is there anything you would like to tell us?"

"I'm sorry for being late," Lucas stuttered, hoping that the apology would appease the woman. Against all his expectations the teacher smiled. She smiled even more when Mrs Macey entered the classroom.

"Well Lucas, I hear that you are something of a hero!" the Head stated. Lucas stared. How did she know what had happened? "Molly Hickling told me you saved Kiera King's life when she choked on some bubble-gum! Well done on your fast thinking and actions young man!"

Lucas felt himself go the colour of beetroot. *Great. Molly was annoyed that I was too late to walk her to school, so she went and told the Head in order to embarrass me!* The kids in his class would once more have a reason to poke fun at him!

"Because you acted so selflessly, taking Kiera home and making sure she was safe," the Head droned on, making Lucas wish he had a scarf or a golf ball to hand, anything he could stuff in the woman's mouth to prevent her from making things worse than they already were, "I have decided to reward you. There will be a surprise for you personally later, but so that everyone recognises the tragedy that you prevented, I have declared the afternoon free from work for the whole school!"

Her final words were almost drowned out in the cheer that arose from the class. Mrs Macey raised her hands until everyone was quiet once more. "You will work as normal this morning. But after lunch there will be games in the playground and a film showing in the hall – you can all decide which of those things you would prefer to do." She smiled at everyone and then just at Lucas, and he thought that he could read her unspoken meaning. By rewarding the whole school she had turned the situation completely around. Instead of Lucas being mocked and taunted for what he had done, everyone would be praising him. Thanking him. He had only one last niggling doubt.

"Mrs Macey," he hurried out of the classroom after her, catching her up half-way down the corridor. "Molly told you, I guess… but did she…" he couldn't find the right words.

"Molly is a bright girl Lucas. Don't ever underestimate that. She was aware that you wouldn't want anyone to know because of what might happen. It was actually her idea that I rewarded the whole school – I just added the specifics of the reward." She patted Lucas on the shoulder. "Now get yourself back to class young man, before I have to reprimand you!" but there was humour in her voice.

Dazed, Lucas made his way back to class and somehow got through the morning lessons. There was a jollity throughout the school that wasn't normally there and as he passed along the corridors heading from one lesson to another, he was hailed over and over again by kids who normally wouldn't have stopped to pee on him had he been on fire. "Great work Lucas!" one boy said, grinning his way past.

Another high-fived him. "Great job, man!" he heard over and over.

In maths class, Claudia was the only one who did not congratulate him yet he didn't feel put out. Her thanks had been more personal and had been given at the time. And yet sometimes, when he had his back to her, he had the oddest sensation that she was watching him. But every time he turned around she was wrapped up in some other task.

The end of the lesson bell signalled the end of the morning and the class whooped with glee.

Lucas smiled and bent to focus on putting all of his books and pens away. A shadow moved by his side but he didn't immediately look up.

"So Peepee is a hero now," Harry hissed, clearly a little worried about speaking too loudly.

Lucas laughed, surprised at how genuine it felt and sounded. "Yup, sure looks that way, doesn't it? Shame it will never happen to you!" He deliberately pushed past the other boy, leaving him wondering if he meant that it was a shame Harry would never experience being a hero, or perhaps that it was a shame he wouldn't choke.

Someone came up close behind him, perhaps Harry, closer than was usual and Lucas steeled himself for a blow, spinning round and readying himself to attack rather than defend. But it wasn't Harry who stood so close behind him. It was Claudia. "Thank you Lucas," she said softly but her eyes amplified the words to a thousand decibels in his head.

"You already said thanks yesterday," he reminded her.

"Yes but that was before I got the full story from Keira. I didn't realise that she really had nearly died! I just thought she was," she waived her hands in the air, "exaggerating!" Her voice caught with emotion and her lovely face clouded with fear.

"Well anyway it's done now," he said, unsure how to follow on.

She nodded. "Well I guess I'll see you later." But she didn't move.

It was his turn to nod. He watched her walk away. But just before she turned the corner out of sight, she turned around and smiled. It was the best smile he had ever seen.

CHAPTER 22

Molly was waiting for him in her usual spot. "You told Mrs Macey," Lucas said. "Thank you."

"You are so welcome Lucas," she chirped. "I bet everyone was pleased with the result! Do you know what she is giving you as a reward?"

Lucas shook his head. "I'm not bothered about that right now... my mum wants to bring Martin to Parent's Evening."

Molly thought about that. "Well I guess he is your dad after all..."

Lucas cut in, "Yes for the last five minutes of my life!"

Molly thought again. "And all these guys in school who want to be your friend now – where were they before? Huh? Sometimes you just have to move with the times Lucas, you know?" And of course she was right. He wasn't going to turn down his new friends just because they hadn't been his friends before, was he?

"Mrs Macey told me you were smart today, but I don't think that even she realises how smart you really are!" he said.

"Really? So how smart am I then?" her little face was open and he couldn't resist pulling her leg.

"Smart enough to know that if I catch you, I am going to throw you in the duck pond!" He laughed and lunged for her at the same time. Shrieking playfully she veered away from him, twisting and turning as she ran, evading him all the way to her front door.

"Later!" she laughed and swung herself through the doorway, leaving him to amble the last few yards home.

Tea wasn't on the table, nor was it in the oven but there was a fresh apple pie laid out on the table. Leaving the kitchen door ajar as he had found it, Lucas made his way up to his room.

Brighteyes was on top of the wardrobe again but before he could do or say anything there was a knock on his door and his mother entered. She was still in her work clothes but had applied fresh make-up and perfume and brushed her hair. The door was still open behind her and she made no attempt to close it. Too late Lucas realised what was about to happen. Before Anna even had a chance to say anything, Brighteyes had noticed the open doorway and spreading her wings wide, she sailed through the opening, flying down the stairs like a torpedo and alighting somewhere in the kitchen out of sight.

Anna sucked her breath in in surprise.

"You never said it was so much better Lucas!" Was there a hint of reprimand in her voice, he wondered.

"I was waiting until I thought that she was completely better," he said softly.

"Well it looks completely better to me!" his mother said with a trace of irony. "Where did it go?"

"Into the kitchen, I think," he muttered, leading the way down the stairs. The kitchen door was still ajar and he had more than a suspicion of what he would find when he pushed through it.

Brighteyes stood in the middle of the pie, talons balancing on the crust, beak dipping into and out of the deep apple filling. It must have been a tasty pie for the bird had already pecked a huge hole in the centre and evacuated its bowels all over the kitchen table in order to make room for the delicious new food. Lucas was horrified but not as horrified as his mother, who turned huge saucer eyes towards him. "I just brought that home!"

It was such a shocking scene that Lucas almost found it funny. Unfortunately his mother did not feel the same! "That bird should have been released now Lucas!" she said angrily. "How long has it been fully recovered?"

"It's only been flying since this morning!" he protested.

"Well that seems to have been long enough!"

she said, shooing it off the ruined dessert. "The pie is no good for us now but clearly the bird needs to be back with its own kind. Everything needs its own kind Lucas, that's just the way it is."

She was right but that didn't make him feel any better. "When?" he asked.

"Well," she responded, "there's no time like the present!"

Lucas stared at her. Was she really suggesting that the bird went right that very minute? With no time for him to prepare himself?

"Martin will be back soon… he's coming to the school with us remember. And I thought that maybe you wouldn't want an audience when you let it go." He realised that she had already thought it through. And she was right, he didn't want Martin standing watching when the bird flew away. It just wouldn't feel right, he decided.

Brighteyes was still perched on the table, clearly unwilling to move too far from the pie. Lucas placed his hand flat on the table and whistled to the pigeon. As if it had been trained for this precise thing, the bird hopped onto his hand. Lucas closed his other hand around its wings, folding them flat against the little body. "It's time to go Brighhteyes. Time to find your own flock again," he told it, throat hoarse from trying to hold back the emotion.

Anna placed a hand on his back. "It's the

right thing to do Lucas. You have given it the gift of life. Now let it live it." He knew she was right but it didn't help somehow.

With his mother opening doors for him he found himself suddenly outside in the back garden with the bird still clutched tight against him. Brighteyes twisted her head back and forth, looking up close at the things she had been seeing so long only through the bedroom window. Lucas wondered if the air smelled fresh and new to her too. "Do you want me to go back inside?" Anna asked.

Lucas shook his head. This was one of the hardest things he had ever had to do and he didn't want to have to do it alone. "Fly free Brighteyes and maybe one day, if you are ever around here again, you will stop by and say hello." The words almost would not come; crafted in love and hope they were finely coated in fear and tinged with loss so that they appeared barbed, each syllable sticking in his throat and wrenching through him.

He spread his hands. For a golden moment the pigeon stood surveying its surroundings, head twisting from side to side. He almost thought that it might not leave, that it might just choose to stay. And then with a final glance at him as if it too said its own goodbye, it seemed to collect its body, bowing low in his hands before spreading its wings in a graceful arc and taking to the sky.

It was gone! Lucas watched it disappear to a little dot, feathers dark against the vastness of the sky. He felt humbled by the enormity of what he had just witnessed and more than a little bereft.

"Are you okay honey?" his mother asked, wrapping an arm protectively around him. Lucas nodded, not trusting himself to speak. How could he tell her that he thought a part of him had disappeared with Brighteyes? That some vital bit of him was now missing. She tried to lead him back into the house but he was not ready for the emptiness of his bedroom just yet. "I think I will stay out here for a bit," he said.

She nodded sadly. "Martin will be back soon so we will head up to the school as soon as he arrives." Then to herself more than to him, "I guess I had better clear up the kitchen and throw the pie out."

"Could you save me a bit?" he asked.

"It's not fit for you to eat now Lucas!" his mother said, surprised.

"It's not for me," Lucas answered cryptically, hoping that she wouldn't press him for more information. For a moment it looked as if that was exactly what she would do, but then she turned away, without asking the question that had formed in her head.

Lucas was relieved; he wasn't entirely sure how she would have liked the idea that lodged in *his* head.

CHAPTER 23

The gym hall was packed. Tables and chairs lined the walls and the teachers all had name badges on. Parents clustered around the tables, weaving their way to and from them and between them, seeking out their next appointment. It seemed that everyone was talking at once, individual conversations blended with the overall thrum of the room so that it was impossible to distinguish one voice among the many. And yet when Lucas walked into the hall a sudden hush fell around the room. There was a crackle of feedback and the PA system leapt into life.

"Boys and girls, mums and dads: I hope you will join me in congratulating one of our own pupils for his quick-thinking, which resulted in him saving another of our pupils' life!"

As if he stood outside of his own body, Lucas saw himself freeze on the spot; saw his mother and Martin turn towards the Head Teacher who stood on the stage, microphone in her hand. Without looking, he knew that Mrs Macey was looking right at him. "I wonder what that's all about," Anna Pertwee muttered.

"Can we all give a big round of applause... to... Lucas Pertwee!" Mrs Macey exclaimed, sparking off a round of vigorous clapping by example.

The face that Lucas's mother turned towards him was confused and bewildered. "Lucas?" she asked.

"Perhaps we could ask Lucas to join us here on stage?" Mrs Macey seemed completely oblivious to the fact that he clearly hadn't told his mother what had happened.

"Lucas what's this about?" Anna sounded like a lost little girl.

"I'm sure Lucas will explain in a minute," Martin said, taking Anna by the hand as if afraid she might succumb to a panic attack at any moment. "He's being called up to the stage Anna, so just let him go for now."

Lucas shot Martin a grateful glance. He had had no idea that the Head was planning anything like this – if he had, he would have stayed home. But it was too late now, the cat was virtually out of the bag. He walked slowly towards the stage.

"Come up Lucas, come up!" Mrs Macey urged. Whilst Lucas climbed the few steps she carried on. "As most of you will be aware, Lucas saved one of our children's lives yesterday whilst at the park. Without his quick thinking little Kiera might have died, but Lucas acted swiftly

and decisively and for that we are all grateful."
She paused for breath. "So it is with our thanks
that we would like you to accept this," she waved
some sort of voucher aloft, "family ticket to a
theme park or adventure day of your choice. And
we all hope you have a fantastic time!" And then
to his everlasting shame, she hugged him.

"But there are others who want to say a more
personal thanks too Lucas…" she continued.
Lucas looked at his mother and Martin in the
crowd. Anna looked shocked and pale and Martin
looked no better. *I guess I should have told them*,
Lucas thought. He dragged his eyes away from
them and tried to focus on what was going on
around him. "…and Mrs King, parents of Kiera
would also like to offer their heartfelt thanks!"
Two people who were presumably Kiera and
Claudia's parents arrived on stage. Lucas felt the
whole room hold its breath to see the drama
unfold.

"We can never thank you enough for what
you did…" Kiera's mother was openly crying.
"And no gift could ever fully recognise the tragedy
you averted… but we would like you and your
family to enjoy a meal at Ricardo's on us." She
handed him a voucher that had the fancy emblem
of the restaurant emblazoned across it. Because
he didn't know what else to do, Lucas took both
of the proffered vouchers, said a polite thank
you to everyone and left the stage to thunderous

applause.

"You saved someone's life! And you never mentioned it?" Anna was clearly finding it a difficult situation to comprehend.

"It wasn't like that," Lucas protested.

"Well they certainly all seem to think it was!" Anna proclaimed.

"Look let's leave this for now. We will do what we came here to do and then Lucas can tell us in his own time. Okay, Lucas?" Martin said. Lucas nodded, grateful that Martin seemed intent on diffusing the situation. He couldn't see what it was that his mother was getting so worked up about.

They did the round of teachers, working their way through the subjects as they did every parent's evening. But unlike every similar event in the past, this time there was nothing but glowing comments about Lucas and his work. Everywhere they went, every teacher they spoke to said basically the same thing: Lucas was doing so much better than before, his grades were up, he was trying harder, working harder, focusing harder; every teacher was pleased and impressed.

But with each table they visited, Anna became visibly more and more withdrawn. As they left the presence of the last teacher on their schedule, Martin mentioned her reaction. "Aren't you glad he is doing so much better now?" he asked. Both his tone and his face indicated that he was frustrated; he really couldn't understand why Anna was behaving so strangely. And neither could Lucas. It wasn't that he had expected her to be jumping for joy but he thought she ought to have been at least a little pleased.

"It's like they are talking about someone else, not my Lucas." She replied to Martin but it was her son her gaze rested on.

"I'm still just me," Lucas said unsure how to answer her. But he also realised that there was a truth in what she had said. He *had* changed. Perhaps part of it was just normal growing up but more than a fair share of it was no doubt due to all that had happened in the last few months. Everything with Josh and his gran and Brighteyes and now this. And then of course there was the whole thing with finding out about his real dad.

"The boy has been through a lot," Martin said quietly.

Anna turned on the man, fire in her eyes and her words. "Do you really have the sheer audacity to try to tell me that Martin? About the boy I raised on my own whilst you were playing happy families with your WIFE?" Anna's voice had risen in temper as she rounded on Martin. Loud enough to cut across the polite teacher/parent conferences, it cut through the atmosphere like a hot knife through butter.

There was a deathly silence as all heads turned once more in their direction. "Come on let's get out of here," Martin urged, trying to steer Anna by her elbow.

"Get your hands off me!" Anna's tone could have curdled stone, Lucas thought and her eyes were icy cold but at least she had lowered her voice so that no one else could hear.

"Look Anna…"

"Don't you *look Anna* me!" she spat out. "I want you gone Martin. Out of my life and out of my son's!"

Martin was clearly bewildered. "I don't understand!" he said plaintively. "Lucas is doing well in school, we are all starting to get along…"

"Lucas is getting on in school but that's no reflection on you and as for getting along, well I actually think Lucas and I were getting along just fine before you arrived!"

"Look Anna if this is about the house…"

She cut him off. "No, Martin, it's not about the house. In fact I had a phone call this morning to say that the council have decided that we can stay in the house. That is *Lucas and I* can," she emphasised. "But when I took time to think about it… really think about how you had just barged into our lives and how you still had a wife living in your big house… well none of it seemed right at all. Not at all!" She didn't seem concerned that she had mentioned the thing about the house that she had previously been at pains to keep secret from Lucas. Either she thought that no longer mattered as it had been resolved, or it was just testament to how angry she really was.

Lucas thought about the pie she had bought and that Brighteyes had ruined. *Everything needs its own kind Lucas, that's just the way it is, wasn't that what she had said? Had she actually meant Martin? Had she meant that her and him were not the same kind of people at all?*

"I just don't understand…" Martin pleaded. Lucas thought he looked like a man who had just witnessed a horrific car crash.

"You don't need to understand anything other than that we are done!" she said, marching out of the hall with Lucas following forlornly behind. "Stay away tonight Martin. You can collect your things in the morning."

"But where will I sleep, where will I go?"

Anna shrugged. "That's not my problem, is it?"

Lucas was too shocked to speak. None of the events of the day had gone as he would have thought. It was as if someone had taken the day and its natural order and shook it up out of all recognition. But a memory from earlier played and replayed in his head – how she had encouraged him to release Brighteyes before Martin returned home. He had thought it was to give him some privacy for his feelings. *But had it been that?* Or had she just wanted to cut Martin out of their lives?

Lucas looked from one to the other of his parents. Was this really how it would end? His mother was crying but they were cold tears, squeezed from a face of stone; eyes and lips immoveable, heart and brain journeying on a set course.

"Lucas, I..." face blanched in shock and terror Martin didn't know how to make things better.

Lucas shook his head. Words were empty. It was actions which really mattered in the end. He thought about all the words that had been spoken since Martin arrived – words of anger, words of explanation, even words of love – but they were all as ethereal as motes of dust in a hurricane. Words were things of no substance, they could not change the course of fate...

He almost wanted to reach out a hand to Martin but he stifled the desire. His mother was right. She had been the one who had been there when he'd had measles, the one who had stayed up all night with him when he had been ill, the one who had always been there for him. What was Martin, but a guy who had turned up when all the hard work was done? He took a step closer to Anna and away from Martin.

Crushed, Martin still managed to hold his gaze for a moment. Reflected in the man's eyes Lucas saw the pain, the hurt, the betrayal. "I left my wife for you," Martin whispered but it wasn't immediately clear who the comment was directed at.

"No Martin," Anna said quietly. "You left your wife for *you*. If you had left for me, you would have left fourteen years ago!" She took hold of Lucas's arm. "Come on, we're going home!"

Being led briskly away, Lucas couldn't help but look back at Martin. He stood rigidly, watching them move further and further away, a sea of people surging around him like sharks around a drowning man. *If that is the last time I ever see him, that image will haunt me to my grave,* Lucas thought.

The walk home was grim. "Why didn't you tell me?" his mother asked.

"What about?" he said, even though he knew very well what she was referring to.

"That you had saved someone's life, for a start! And about how you were getting on so much better in school!"

Lucas hung his head. *Because you were otherwise occupied*, he wanted to say but those words were barbed. Hadn't she suffered enough already? "Because none of it seemed like a big deal." He tried to elaborate. "Well not compared with…" how could he finish so that she would understand?

"Compared with what was going on at home?" she ended for him. "Oh Lucas I never meant for you to be pushed out! I'm so sorry!" She stopped walking and turned to him, folding her arms around him like she used to when he was little.

Unashamedly they stood in the middle of the pavement in front of their house, both of them crying hot, scalding tears. Neither cathartic nor cleansing, the tears seemed to compound Lucas's miseries. So much had been found and lost in the space of a few short weeks: Brighteyes, Martin... perhaps now even his short-lived respect at school! Everything was just so temporary... love, relationships, even life itself!

"I'm so sorry you felt left out. It will never happen again," she promised.

Lucas tried to explain. "I didn't feel left out exactly, but it had always been just you and me and gran. And then suddenly everything was different." Like a runaway train his words speeded up – he had to get them out of him, had to halt the burning pain they caused that threatened to overwhelm him at any moment. "And it just kept on changing, like I never even knew who I was anymore, or where I was, or where I fitted in." He locked eyes with his mother, desperately willing her to understand. "Or even *if* I fitted in anymore!"

"Oh Lucas you and I will always fit together. Nothing and no one will change that." Her make-up had run as she cried and there were thick black streaks which marked the passage of her tears. Sensing his thoughts, she managed a shaky laugh. "I must look like a panda!"

He smiled a little back, grateful for the light reprieve in the conversation. "Do you know I really, really thought that Hugh Grant was my father," he said almost shyly. The idea seemed preposterous now.

Anna inserted the key into the door. "Me and Hugh Grant," she laughed, "now there's a thought!" She ushered them through the door and closed it behind them. "I need to get this make-up off, then I'll make us something to eat."

There were things Lucas needed to be getting on with too. In his hand he still held the restaurant and the day out tokens – family activities that were probably the norm for other boys, other families... what good were they to him now? He shoved them into a kitchen drawer and instead picked up the plastic bag containing some of the pie remains and carried it up to his bedroom.

Brighteyes's empty box nearly broke his heart and for a moment his mind played tricks on him, making him see what wasn't there, the little bobbing head, the iridescent sheen of feathers, the bright inquisitive eyes. His heart held on to the image, eager not to relinquish it to the reality of the empty room, his empty life...

He flung open the window. It was just starting to get dark outside although the hour was not late. No birds flew high in the sky or overhead but he sprinkled the contents of the bag across the outside of the ledge anyway. They would be there ready for the morning and that was for the best anyway. He ran a hand across the crumbs, evening them out and breaking the bigger chunks into more manageable bite sized pieces. Maybe the pie would attract all different types and sizes of birds, maybe only the braver ones would alight there. Time would tell. But he knew that as long as they were willing to come, he would be willing to feed them.

Then, closing the window once more, he gathered up all the bird's things. They would be cleaned and then stored in the shed. Perhaps they would come in handy some other time. He wasn't really sure if that was something he hoped for or against. To hope for it seemed almost a malicious thing, as it implied that a bird would be injured or harmed in some way and yet to not hope that something, somewhere would require his care, was equally heartrending.

He slid the bolt on the shed door across to open it. A little rusty and no longer completely aligned with its housing, it jammed a couple of times and he had to put all of his might behind it. Martin had said that he would fit a new catch but that clearly wouldn't happen now!

The door swung open on creaky hinges. Martin's bike stood propped up against one wall as if eager to be taken out one last time. Lucas placed the bird box and dishes on an empty shelf and turned towards the bike. Pulling it from where it rested he ran a hand appreciatively one last time over the frame. The bike would be gone soon, Martin would take it along with all the other things that belonged to him...

Except for me! The thought took Lucas by surprise, creeping silently into his consciousness, invading his heart and twisting it painfully. *Don't I belong to him as much as this bike? **More** than this bike?* What his mother had said was true and yet wasn't it also true that Martin belonged to Lucas as much as the other way around?

I miss you. Tomorrow and all the other tomorrows stretched out ahead and even though Martin had only recently come into his life, the thought of the future without him seemed bleak and desolate. *How did everything get so twisted? I didn't like him, didn't want him in my life... but now?* Lucas shrugged his shoulders in the empty shed. Now it was his mother who had turned against Martin and Lucas didn't see how the situation could possibly be made right.

He re-bolted the shed door and returned to the house. Someone was at the front door ringing the bell. The toilet flushed upstairs and Lucas rushed to the front door, opening it before Anna could get there and refuse to let Martin in. But when Lucas opened the door it wasn't Martin who was standing there. An older version of himself looked back at him, the stranger's features almost identical to his own.

The stranger looked once at Lucas, blinked then looked again. "Um," he swallowed hard and the lump of his Adam's apple jogged up and down in his throat. "Does Martin Smith live here? I am his son."

CHAPTER 24

Lucas must have said something but he couldn't for the life of him remember what that had been. All he knew was that words had come out of his mouth and that now the stranger sat at the kitchen table with him and his mother. Anna Pertwee rubbed a hand over eyes which were still red and swollen and threatened to overspill with tears at any second. She blinked them back valiantly. She would not embarrass Lucas in front of this other boy; this stranger who looked so like her only child.

"Are you sure Martin is your father?" It was the only question she had asked since she had come downstairs when Lucas called her, his voice tight with shock and unexpressed emotion. She bit her tongue as soon as she had finished the sentence, ensuring that she didn't tag anything else onto the end of it.

There was nothing guarded in Mark's expression, nothing to suggest that he was capable of lying. "I know he is because my mother said so," he said simply.

"Perhaps she was mistaken!" Anna clutched at straws, not meaning to cast aspersions on the character of the absent woman but simply to deny what her eyes already told her.

"Mum look at him!" Lucas said slowly. "He's like an older version of me…" It was true. Whilst Lucas and Mark had different mothers, there was little to doubt about the shared similarities between them and what it implied about the probability of some shared parentage.

"I'm sorry Mrs Smith but she wasn't mistaken…"

"Pertwee," Anna corrected. "I am Anna Pertwee… Mrs Smith… well…" she wasn't sure how to carry on. She didn't know how much Mark already knew or how much she wanted to rake up again in front of Lucas.

"Mum wasn't married to him," Lucas explained. "He was already married to someone else when they met." There was a deep silence for a moment as everyone thought about that comment. Anna flushed with shame at what the boy must surely be thinking. *And me, how do I really feel having to explain the circumstances of my conception?* Lucas wondered.

"Will he be back soon?" Mark asked nervously.

I didn't tell him that he wasn't coming back! That Mum threw him out! realised Lucas belatedly. He took a deep breath. "There was an argument tonight. Mum and Mar..." he hesitated. *Was it right to keep calling him Martin? When there was already someone else who wanted to lay claim to him as a father?* It wasn't that Lucas was jealous exactly, but there was a definite feeling of being first in line, first to lay claim to being his son, even if this boy was older by several years.

"My mum and our dad argued tonight. Mum told him not to come back." *Our dad*, how weird those two words felt coming from his mouth. The word 'dad' on its own was momentous enough but to be combined with the plural possessive pronoun 'our' as opposed to the singular one of 'my' almost caused Lucas to rupture an artery.

"Oh!" Mark pushed back his chair, causing the legs to scrape loudly on the floor tiles. "I should go then..." he half turned away from them, but Anna put a restraining hand on his arm.

"Not yet." She looked from her son to this other boy. "I know that you want to find your dad but there are things I need to ask you and I'm sure that there are things you would like to ask us too." It wasn't really a question but Mark nodded slowly, his eyes darting from Anna to Lucas and back again. "Sit down Mark." She stood up. "It's been a long day for Lucas and I and I'm sure it has for you too. We haven't eaten yet so if you don't mind holding on to your story for a few minutes I will make us some bacon sandwiches."

Mark and Lucas began to protest but Anna cut them both short. "Lucas I know you don't feel like eating but you'll feel a whole sight worse if you don't. And as for you Mark, well it seems like you have waited a long time to meet your father and find out things... will a few more minutes really make all that much difference now?" She moved as she spoke, getting out a heavy frying pan, plates and food.

The two boys watched her in silence as she moved around the kitchen, never settling in one place for longer than a few seconds, as if by being perpetually on the move she could force the situation to bend to her will. Finally when there was a huge pile of hot bacon sandwiches in the centre of the table, she laid out three plates and settled herself back into her seat. "Tell us what you already know," she told Mark.

Lucas bit into the sweet saltiness of the bacon, relishing the way the meat contrasted with the soft, buttered bread. It struck him as strange that he could even taste the food, let alone appreciate it under the circumstances. But if anything, the sandwich seemed more real to him, more concrete and tangible to him than the flesh and blood boy who sat next to him.

"I always thought that my dad *was* my dad," Mark began, not making much sense.

"I think maybe you need to start further back than that," Anna said. Lucas noticed that she had lifted her own sandwich towards her mouth as if preparing to take a bite but didn't do so. Instead she just held it there as if she was trying to work herself up to it, he thought.

"I was raised by my mum and dad... or at least the man I thought was my dad," Mark explained.

"How old are you Mark?" Anna asked, either trying just to establish some facts or trying to get him to tell the story in a more coherent way.

"Eighteen," he said.

"So we are going back over eighteen years ago," Anna said slowly as if she was explaining.

Lucas shot her a glance, "Was that when...?"

She shook her head. "No, that was years before I met Martin. In fact he wouldn't have been married then."

It was Mark's turn to shake his head. "No, he wasn't married then. My mum had been going out with him for over a year but she said they had started to drift apart. She finished the relationship and started going out with someone else. By the time she realised she was pregnant, she had been in a new relationship for a few months."

"Oh!" Anna looked intently at Mark. "Did she tell Martin?" Lucas wondered what she meant. *Did she tell him what?* Anna lowered her sandwich to her plate, still not having taken a bite. Lucas copied her.

Luckily Mark seemed to be following the flow of the conversation a little better than Lucas. "No. She told my dad, I mean the guy she was seeing and they decided to get married and raise the kid - me - as their own."

"So how did you find out?" Anna asked, confusing Lucas even more.

Mark laughed but it was mirthless. "Fate intervened. My dad got sick and they needed someone who was a genetic match to donate bone marrow to him. They tested me, his son and hey presto they found that I wasn't his son after all!"

The penny finally dropped into place with a huge clink in Lucas's brain. *His mother got pregnant to Martin, my dad,* **our** *dad... but she never said. Instead her and her new boyfriend acted like* **he** *was Mark's dad! And I always thought that I had it rough, never knowing who my father was... Mark's whole life was a lie, everything he believed! That had to hurt!* Lucas could only imagine the depth of pain which Mark must have felt when the truth came out.

"But him and your mother must have known that you wouldn't be a genetic match!" Anna said, eyes wide in amazement.

"I guess they just kind of hoped that somehow it either wouldn't come out or that miraculously the gene types would be close enough to be used anyway. But I guess genes are genes!" he shrugged. Neither Anna nor Lucas could think of anything to say.

"What a terrible way to find out," Lucas said finally. It occurred to him then that they might not already have heard the worst part of the story. "What happened to your dad? I mean the man who raised you?"

Mark smiled grimly. "Luckily his brother was a match and they managed to extract some useable marrow from him. My dad is getting better now, getting stronger every day." He looked at Lucas. "And he's still my dad." He spread his hands wide on the table. "Martin is my *father*, the man who I am genetically linked to but my *dad* will always be Bill Sanders and *I* will always be Mark Sanders, not Mark Smith."

Lucas nodded, he completely understood that sentiment.

"So Martin doesn't even know you exist!" Anna breathed. Some colour had come back into her face and Lucas thought that she looked pensive. He couldn't tell what she was thinking but something about the set of her eyes made him think that her mind was whirring at the implications of the situation.

"No, he doesn't," Mark agreed.

"I don't get it," Lucas said slowly. "You had a dad all your life and you still think of him as your dad… so why come looking for your *real* father?"

Temper flared a bright light in Mark's cheeks. "I didn't come looking for my *real* father…

Bill Sanders will always be that to me. I just ..." he took a calming breath. "I just wanted to meet the man whose genes I will carry on to my own children one day. I just wanted to see what he looked like, to hear how he sounded... wouldn't you have wanted that if you didn't know him?"

It was so exactly how Lucas had felt before Martin had entered his life that it took his breath away. "Yes, I understand," he said, comprehension dawning slowly. "I only met him recently and until then..." well until then he had almost managed to convince himself that Hugh Grant was his father, he reminded himself. And all because he had needed to have a face and a voice to cling to, something on which to hook his dreams.

It didn't take long for Anna and Lucas to explain their situation to Mark. All the while they spoke, Mark sat quietly, taking everything in. After they had finished, Anna had a final question to ask. "How did you trace Martin to this address?"

"My mum told me where he used to work and I made enquiries which led me to where he works now. I didn't want to turn up at his office so somehow I blagged the personnel lady to give me his address."

Anna nodded. "So because he was living here with us, you ended up here!"

"Except that now he's not here. So where *is*

he?" Mark asked. The three of them looked at one another.

Lucas cleared his throat. "Mark would you mind if I had a private word with my mum?" he asked, waiting until the other boy nodded before scraping back his chair and leading Anna into the lounge.

He sat down on the sofa, expecting her to do the same but she remained standing. "It's rude to leave him too long on his own," she said.

"Like you already said, he's waited this long to meet his father; he can wait a little longer," Lucas paraphrased.

Anna shrugged and perched on the arm of the sofa. "What is it then?"

"Why did you throw him out? I mean, the truth?" he asked softly.

Tears glimmered in her eyes once more but she blinked them back. "You already know why!"

"I know what you said, but I don't think that's the real reason…"

She tried to stare him out. Tried to hold back and hide her fears but he would not unlock her gaze from his own. "What is it you are so scared of Mum?"

The tears over spilled her eyes and she wiped them away angrily, smearing them across her face, wiping her hands together as if to rid herself of the emotion. "I was afraid of losing you. And of losing myself…" she said reluctantly, seeming to dredge the words up from her soul. "Martin was such a big part of my life back then, such a major force... and I loved him so much," her voice took on a wistfulness that twisted like a knife in Lucas's heart.

"You are young yet Lucas. But one day you will experience a love like that. It's not a normal love. It's one which takes over every fibre of your being. It's like an invasion by a virus," she ran her hands through her hair. "Maybe that's a silly way to explain it. But it's apt. A love like that only comes along once in your life I believe. And maybe that's for the best. Because when it comes, it consumes you. It *becomes* your life, your reason for breathing." She stopped suddenly, afraid to carry on.

Lucas was no less confused. "So you didn't love him like that this time?"

Anna laughed shakily. "Lucas that was the problem. I *still* loved him *exactly* like that!" One hand remained in her hair and he noticed how her finger tightened around the knot of hair, knuckles glowing whitely as if she was testing the tension in each strand. He stood up and placed his left hand on top of her right one, the one which was still tangled in her hair, forcing her to release the locks from her clenched fist.

The action seemed to prompt her into further explanation. "I got scared. Back there in the school it was like I didn't know you anymore.

Fourteen years ago you came out of my body Lucas, and I have loved you every day since." She took a deep shaky breath. "But you are growing up, changing, becoming your own man... and I was suddenly terrified that I was losing you, that the overwhelming love I felt for your father was somehow eroding what you and I had..." She pulled at the fabric of her short skirt. "I mean look at me... do I wear this sort of stuff?" she tried to laugh but it was a pathetic sound and Lucas hated how it rang emptily in the air between them.

"It doesn't matter what you wear, or how you look Mum. I just want you to be happy." He wished the window was open, that some breeze filled the room with fresh oxygen. "And you were happier when he was here than I have ever seen you before." He pulled her towards him for a cuddle, feeling her body shake with sobs. "I know how much you love me Mum. I always have. But I saw how much you loved him too." *And I loved him too. In the end*, he wanted to say but the words would not come.

Anna lifted her head and looked into Lucas's brightly shining eyes. "Do you think that you could learn to love him?" she asked. Lucas nodded, grateful that she didn't push the point. "So what do we do now?" Anna asked.

"Well I guess we have to get him back here!" Lucas said. Put like that it seemed a simple task but there were no guarantees in life, Lucas knew.

No guarantees at all!

CHAPTER 25

It hadn't taken long to explain things briefly to Mark and to convince him he should return the following day. After the other boy had left, Lucas and his mother sat alone at the kitchen table. "I could phone him," Lucas suggested.

"No it has to come from me," Anna smiled but her eyes remained worried.

"If you are sure," Lucas said slowly. "But will you tell him that I miss him too and that I want him to come back?"

Anna looked surprised. Lucas kissed her and made his way out of the kitchen. Just as his foot hit the second tread of the stairs he heard his mother say, "Hi, it's me!" followed by, "I know and I'm so sorry!" He didn't need to hear the rest of the conversation. If his dad couldn't see how all the emotions had been building up to this one volcanic crescendo, then he wasn't as bright as Lucas thought he was. His dad would see that both Lucas and his mum had been running scared but that that time was over now. And he would come back. Lucas just knew it.

The ledge outside his window was empty. No birds sheltered there from the encroaching darkness. Dimly he could see the large chunks of pie and the smaller crumbs scattered around them. They lay exactly as he had left them, completely undisturbed. He resisted the urge to open the window and smooth them over once more. What he had done would either be enough or it wouldn't. It was as simple as that. He got changed for bed and brushed his teeth. His mother was still downstairs, talking on the phone. He wondered whether she would tell his dad about Mark or leave it until they met. He figured that neither was an easy way of breaking the news. But he knew that however she chose to do it would be for the best.

He shut his eyes, thinking that the day had been so momentous that there was no way he would sleep, but when he opened them, night had somehow metamorphosed into morning and the bedside clock showed that it was already after ten! Almost against his wishes his eyes were drawn to the empty windowsill and the equally empty one outside, beyond the glass. *Where are you Brighteyes? Are you okay?*

What if a cat had caught the bird? Or it had flown into the path of an oncoming truck? Or if it hadn't been able to find the flock it was part of once more? What if it was cold and lonely and hungry? The thought made him sick to his stomach but there was absolutely nothing he could do about it.

He dragged himself down the stairs, still in the t-shirt and pants he had slept in. His mother was already in the kitchen, still in her dressing gown, standing in front of the kettle and spooning instant coffee into a mug, which stood in solitary confinement on the work surface. The dread that had curdled in his stomach when he thought of Brighteyes, now amplified so that his entire body was suffused with trepidation. "He's not coming back is he?" the words almost died in his throat.

Anna began to shake her head, then contradicted herself by nodding, before going back to shaking it as if she couldn't quite make up her mind. "He's coming over a little later, but he said he wants to speak to both of us before he makes any decisions."

"That's good, right?" He asked hopefully. Unable to meet his mother's eyes, to see what might be there, Lucas focused on fetching a bowl and the cereal box, making his way to the table without once looking up.

"I hope so." The catch in her voice indicated that she was not entirely sure. "But I think that it might not be enough to just hear it from me now..." Lucas poured milk into the bowl, concentrating fiercely on the task. "This thing with Mark, Lucas, how does it make you feel?"

Anna sat down next to her son. "I mean it was hard enough on you to discover that Martin was your father – now you have to contend with having an older brother too!"

Lucas shrugged. He nearly said that he didn't care but stopped himself before the words passed his lips. He *did* care. He cared very much. But the funny thing, the thing he couldn't quite get his head around was *how* he cared. For some reason Molly's face kept popping into his head when he thought of Mark.

The little girl had turned out to be a good friend. She was bright and funny and fun to be around, but more than any of those things, more than all of them combined perhaps, she had allowed him to develop a sense of who he was and where he fit in in the world. Maybe now he could pay that feeling forward, as it were. He could perhaps do for Mark what Molly had done for him! "It might be kind of cool to have a big brother," he said quietly. "I mean it's not like he's going to move in with us, or start bossing me around."

Anna startled him by coming around to his side of the table and giving him a hug. "You have taken all this so well, Lucas. Almost better than I have!" her voice threatened tears once more.

"Maybe because I had such low expectations to begin with," he tried to laugh it off as she sat back down on her own seat.

"Really? But you thought that Hugh Grant

was your dad!"

Lucas shrugged. "Yes but then I read that he had a few other children and suddenly he didn't seem much like the sort of father I wanted."

"And Martin?" she seemed to be holding her breath.

"Well he's not perfect." Lucas thought about how his dad had let him ride his brand new bike, about the spare tyre he had fitted on Lucas's own bike and about how he had looked at Lucas's mum every time she entered the room, how his eyes had seemed to light up. "But he's not bad. And maybe with practise, he will even improve." He slurped cereal into his mouth.

Anna tried to act as if what he had just said was not monumental. "Well its Saturday, so you know what you have to do – get dressed, change your bed and tidy your room. *Before* you do anything else." She picked up her mug and carried it up the stairs with her.

Lucas finished his cereal and dumped the empty bowl in the sink. Collecting clean bed linen from the cupboard, he took it up to his room. He dressed and began his morning tasks. He could hear his mother moving around the house, dusting, cleaning, vacuuming. The sounds were comforting in their normality.

The doorbell took him by surprise. Could it be his dad already? But if it was, why hadn't he used his key? Lucas moved to the top of the stairs.

"Hi." Martin's voice was subdued.

"Come in. Thanks for coming." How strangely formal his mother sounded. "Lucas," she called. "Your dad is here." The words which should have sounded so right to his ears came across as stilted as if Anna was unsure how they would be received.

"Look there is no need to push this 'dad' thing, well not now anyway," Lucas heard Martin say as he descended the stairs. Both of his parents stood in the hallway awkwardly, as if they were afraid that any movement might shatter the scene. Shoulders held too high and too rigid they looked like they were expecting an argument to kick-off at any moment, Lucas thought.

If he had thought about what he did next he probably wouldn't have done it so he chose not to think about it. Instead he went with his gut reaction and without a word approached his father, wrapping the man in a hug. He had never hugged anyone before apart from his mother; not even his gran when she had been alive had inspired such displays of affection from him.

At first Martin stood as if bewildered, unsure of exactly what was going on but after a moment he put his arms around his son. "Whatever happens, I will always be there for you when you need me, Lucas", he said gruffly as if he was trying hard to control his emotions.

Lucas pulled away. There was no need for

him to answer. He led the way into the kitchen and the adults followed, settling themselves around the table. "Where do we start this?" Anna asked shakily, looking at the two men she loved.

"Why don't we start with how Lucas feels first then we can take turns?" Martin suggested.

Lucas didn't want to speak first but he knew that unless he told Martin that he was finally okay with him being his dad, nothing else could move forward. "I missed you," he said. "Not just last night when you weren't around but even before that, for all the years I didn't know you." Anna hung her head at the accusation.

"I know Mum and Gran tried to protect me," he reached across to touch his mother's hand, "I really do. But I needed to know and because I didn't, I built up this fantasy in my head and then when the real you arrived, the fantasy and the reality just didn't match."

Martin held his gaze. "And now?" he asked.

"Well now I see what I should have seen all along, that you are a good man and that you do love Mum. And me." The last words were said quietly, infused with hope.

Martin nodded but the grim look was still set on his face. Lucas guess that Martin was afraid to hope that Anna would feel the same, that he was holding his own feelings in check just in case. "Anna?" he prompted.

Lucas's mum looked down at her hands for

a moment and when she looked up her eyes were once more filled with tears. "I got everything wrong Martin. I hid the truth from Lucas for so long and then when you turned up I just expected it all miraculously to work. I expected him to accept you and love you like I did. Without even knowing you!" She reached across the table and tried to take hold of Martin's hand but he kept it resolutely flat on the table top as if afraid that any contact with her would break his resolve. She pulled her hand back slowly and folded it in her lap.

"And now?" he asked the same question of her that he had already asked Lucas.

"And now I see that we are a family but a new one; one that will have to make up the rules as we go along because we haven't got all those years of being together behind us."

This time Martin reached across for her hand and she surrendered it willingly. "I will try not to bring up the past mistakes that we have both made. And I'll try to let go a little... to make room for you here," she said.

Martin astonished them both by shaking his head. "There's no need to make room for me."

Lucas thought he might throw up. Was this all for nothing? Would his dad refuse to come back? To accept the apology?

"This morning before I got here I went to the estate agents. I put my house up for sale and I told them I was looking for a new house. One where you and I and Lucas can live together." He looked at Lucas, "and I told him it needed to have a big garage for all the bikes and stuff we will want to put in there."

Anna pulled her hands free and cupped them around her nose and mouth as if she was in shock. Martin gestured around them. "I know the council have finally agreed that you can stay here Anna. But this was your mother's house... yours and hers. We need a place that is ours. I have arranged an appointment for us to see a few houses next week. They are all close by so that Lucas can stay in his school and you can still get to your job - that is if you want to keep working there. Is that okay?" he asked, suddenly sounding unsure.

Anna nodded, her eyes shining brightly but then the light in them dimmed as if she had just remembered something important. "Martin there is something else we have to tell you," she began but was cut off by the sound of the doorbell once more. She stood up, realising that she was probably out of time for explanations. Lucas felt a sudden change in the atmosphere in the room, happiness turning to apprehension in the flicker of an eye. He wasn't sure that Martin picked up on it but he knew for certain by the look on her face that his mother did.

"Leave it. Whoever it is will come back if

it's important. We have things to discuss," Martin said.

Anna shook her head. "This already *is* something important," she said cryptically, leaving him to stare at her empty chair as she went to answer the door. "Martin this is Mark," she said, leading the boy into the kitchen. "Mark is your son." She could not have said the words more kindly; her mouth smiled but her eyes were peppered with anxiety as she looked at the two young men and their father.

Mark swallowed nervously and held his hand out. "Hi."

Martin exploded off the chair and onto his feet. "I don't know what the hell kind of stunt you are trying to play here Anna but…" Lucas noticed that suddenly his dad had his car keys in his hand as if he was preparing to leave.

Anna too had noticed the keys. Her gaze fixed on them and was torn away to look Martin in the eye. "*Look* at him Martin. I mean *really* look," she held one hand over her mouth as if to steady a trembling there. Her eyes were wide and desperate looking, Lucas thought. This was not the way he had thought that things would go down. "Can't you see the resemblance between him and Lucas? For God's sake they are almost doubles!" her voice was raised, but not in anger. "He's eighteen Martin. Think back eighteen years. Before you and I met! Before you were even married!"

"Oh!" Martin grasped the back of the chair for support as Anna's words sank in. "Oh my God, it can't be... he can't be..." he stared at Mark as if unable to believe his own eyes.

"Mum didn't tell you because by the time she found out she was already in love with my dad," Mark used the word 'dad' sheepishly as if desperately trying not to offend. "They decided to raise me as his child and it wasn't until recently I found out the truth."

Lucas felt like he was watching the situation from afar. Even though they were all in one small room, he felt distanced from the others, separate and able to be objective. In a strange way Martin's reaction to this news was very similar to Lucas's reaction to him arriving on the doorstep and it occurred to him that somehow they had gone full circle now. It was as if all this had been planned by some celestial practical joker just to prove that what goes around really does come around. In time. Regardless of how long it takes.

The kitchen was filled with noise, words strung into sentences which Lucas let wash over him. The how, why and when's were not really that important, everything he needed to know he already knew. He watched Martin sit back down and Anna offer Mark her chair. It occurred to him that they could have gone into the lounge where there was more room but everyone seemed content to sit around the table whilst Anna stood, her back braced against the sink.

It was right that they were in the kitchen he thought. The lounge was for watching TV and entertaining visitors; the kitchen was the hub where the family met.

"Mum take my chair and I'll fetch the stool from my room," Lucas stood up, not waiting for her answer.

He was so intent on pulling the stool out from its resting place beside the wardrobe that at first he never noticed the movement outside the window. Only when he had the stool grasped firmly in both hands, did his eye get caught by something beyond the room.

A pigeon, feathers as pristine white as snow stared in at him. Ignoring the food either through genuine disinterest or nervous apprehension, the bird regarded him solemnly. Lucas felt a sad smile form at the corners of his mouth. This pigeon was lovely alright but she was not... Belatedly he realised the pigeon had a companion. He had been so focused on the gleaming whiteness of its plumage, he hadn't realised that at the other end of the sill, another bird, this one more self-assured, was pecking at the soft apple and little clumps of pastry he had scattered there.

Dream-like, hardly daring to hope what was in his heart, he turned his gaze and his full attention to the other pigeon. Brighteyes! It was Brighteyes. She had come back and she had brought someone with her!

Lucas wanted to jump up and down. He wanted to holler from the rooftops but he dared not move. Perhaps Brighteyes would not be scared away, but her companion most certainly would be. For a long moment he held Brighteyes gaze. People sometimes said that animals were telepathic. He wasn't sure if that was true but he was taking no chances!

Thank you for coming to visit Brighteyes! He thought at the bird. *I know you have to be free and I know you have to be with your own kind but please, please come and visit me, just so I know you are alright. And I will put out food every day for you, I promise.* And then a horrible thought entered his mind. They would be moving away, maybe only a few streets but it would be a different house and the bird would not know where to come.

And then an image filled his head. Just like that the solution appeared to him. He saw himself opening the window and taking Brighteyes into his hands once more. He would take her to the new house himself and place her on the windowsill of the room he wanted her to come back to. After an hour or so of looking out, she would be ready to fly away and he could release her once more, knowing that she would be able to find her way back to him.

It was then that something strange

happened. Brighteyes used the tip of her beak to rap sharply three times on the glass. Perhaps it was to indicate to the other bird that there was a barrier between them and the boy because almost immediately the white bird seemed reassured enough to eat.

But Lucas willed himself to believe something else. Brighteyes had sent him a message. She had rapped three times to let him know that she would be back. Aware that he still held the stool and that the others were still downstairs waiting, he shuffled over to the door. There would be days and weeks and years ahead to spend getting to know his feathered friends better, but for now his family needed him. Carefully he descended the stairs.

Just as he reached the bottom and before he could carry the stool into the kitchen, there was a light knock on the door. Lucas put the stool down and went to answer it, wondering who it could be this time.

Of all the faces and ideas which ran through his head, none of them could have prepared him for who actually stood there. Claudia King held a shoe box in front of her, which she thrust at Lucas as he opened the door. "My dad found this at the side of the road on his way to work this morning," she said by way of explanation. "Be careful how you open it," she cautioned.

Lucas looked at her. They had never really

spoken since she had thanked him for saving Kiera and now here she was, standing in all her glory on his front doorstep. "Your parents already gave me a reward for helping Kiera," he reminded her, wondering what the box contained.

"It's not a reward silly." Claudia laughed that melodious sound of hers. "It's a wounded pigeon! It would have died if he had just left it." She looked up into his face, her own big blue eyes serious and thoughtful. "To be honest I think in the past that's exactly what he would have done. But when Kiera told him about you the other day, how you had saved her and how you saved that pigeon before, I think it kind of made him think." She shrugged as if it was just a theory. "Anyway he picked it up and asked me to bring it to you."

"To bring it to me?" Lucas repeated stupidly as if he was the dumbest boy alive.

"Yes, you," she laughed again. "After all everyone knows that you are the boy who rescues pigeons." She smiled and turned away.

"Claudia... um would you like to come in?" he asked aware that it was a dumb question. Of course she wouldn't want to come in, why would she? Why would a girl like her ever be interested in a boy like him?

"Mum and Kiera are waiting for me back home. We are going shopping," she informed him, turning back towards his house. "Otherwise I would have." She seemed to be waiting for him to say something else.

"Oh okay," he said.

"But I'll be back later on. I could call round then? Check on the bird and stuff?"

Lucas was elated. He grinned. "That would be cool!" He watched her walk all the way to the bottom of the road before he shut the door and went into the kitchen with the stool, placing the shoe box carefully on the stairs.

He was apprehensive about explaining that another pigeon now needed his attention but to their credit neither Martin nor Anna raised any objections this time. Lucas promised to return as soon as he had settled the new pigeon into its temporary home in his room. Mark looked a little confused so Lucas left his mum and dad to explain.

He fetched the bird box and feed dishes from the shed and set about setting them up for the new resident. Gently he removed the lid from the box, feeling Brighteyes's watchful stare through the glass as if she was a little feathered guardian angel, sent to watch over her own kind.

This pigeon was a darker grey than Brighteyes and perhaps a little younger, he thought, from the smallness of it. It didn't have any obvious injuries other than to one wing but it was thin and very scruffy looking. *Time and love and attention will soon put you right*, Lucas thought.

For a moment he thought about how strange life had turned out to be. He had lost Josh and the friendship that he had thought could never be broken – until it turned out to be just a sham based on lies and deception.

He smiled at Brighteyes and her beautiful friend and then at this new, as yet unnamed pigeon and then he closed the bedroom door softly and went to join his family for a little while.

Maybe there were some things which couldn't be saved no matter how hard you tried. And maybe there were things too which couldn't ever be lost. And maybe, just maybe if you were extremely lucky, you found the things that neither time nor life could ever take from you. Lucas thought that perhaps he had done just that.

After all, wasn't he the boy who rescues pigeons?

BOOKS BY THIS AUTHOR

Jigsaw Girl

When fundamental pieces are missing, how do you put yourself together again?

"Do you think we'll get another dog?" he says.

I'm so shocked I stop in my tracks. "After Shadow?" Breath catches painfully in my chest and I have to force myself not to scream. "Is that what you would have done if I'd died, Charlie? Ask Mum and Dad to give you another sister?"

It's cruel and unfair, especially as the tone it's delivered in is acidic. None of this is Charlie's fault and he's only nine after all. But he can't be allowed to think that life – any life – is so easily replaceable. That like changing a lightbulb, the light of one life can ever replace the light of another, extinguished one. It doesn't work like that.

Not for me anyway.

But what if the end, wasn't the end at all? What if it was really only the beginning?

Because that's where my beginning started. At the end.

Future Imperfect

She's an Alpha. And she's not going to let anything stand in her way...

When a young Alpha's fiancé is injured and declassified to a Delta by ELSA, the dome's Enhanced Living System Autonomy, she has to set out across the ravaged world to bring him safely back. Luckily Fortitude Smith isn't just any ordinary Alpha. Unfortunately ELSA isn't what it appears to be either.

In this dystopian future, people live according to their birth classes. Beta and lower live in the supposed ravaged outside world, whilst Alphas are protected in the dome, watched over by ELSA - the dome's AI. But ELSA has more than one secret...

Split Descision

Two boys. One chance.

How was Natalie to know that the decision she was about to make between two potential dates, would forever be a pivotal point in her life? That it would mark the time where childhood innocence ended? How could she even imagine that the wrong decision would send her life spiralling into the stuff of nightmares from where she might not come out alive?

Life takes a cruel twist of fate when Natalie, a completely average [almost] 16 year old, is forced to make a split-second decision...a decision that will change her future and forever alter her perception of trust, love and the realities of life. A contemporary coming of age thriller.

Printed in Great Britain
by Amazon

23760651R00195